What Child Is This?

An Ellie Kent Mystery

by

Alice K. Boatwright

For information, email **Cozy Cat Press**, cozycatpress@aol.com or visit our website at: www.cozycatpress.com

ISBN: 978-1-946063-40-3

Printed in the United States of America

Cover design by Keri Knutson
https://www.alchemybookcovers.com/

1 2 3 4 5 6 7 8 9 10

For my parents, Helen and Howard Boatwright,
who loved Christmas

Tuesday, December 22
Winter Solstice

Chapter 1

All we want for Christmas is our Anthea. The MISSING posters were tacked to every telephone pole on the high street of Little Beecham. The message in bold red type created a plaintive contrast to the evergreen swags and fairy lights that decorated the honey-colored limestone cottages and shops of the Cotswold village.

Ellie Kent could only imagine the need that had driven someone to hang them on a day like this when the temperature had been dropping steadily from raw to bitter cold. And now it was snowing. The swirling flakes that made the village look like an enchanted snow globe were quickly puckering the signs. There were more shoppers about than usual, but they hurried past without a glance, heads bent against the storm, eager to be home for their tea. It was only three o'clock, but the turn toward dusk had begun.

Ellie tightened her grip on her own packages and leaned in for a closer look at the photo of a slim, dark-haired young woman. It showed her laughing, with her arms spread wide as if to embrace the world and her future. A student at Oxford, the poster said.

Name: Anthea Davies
Age: 20
Last seen: 1st October in Oxford

She studied the face and felt an uncomfortable twinge of recognition. Anthea Davies looked a lot like she had at that age.

All we want for Christmas is our Anthea. Please help.

The number was local.

But there was really nothing she could do to help, Ellie told herself, as she walked quickly away. She had only moved to Little Beecham from San Francisco in the autumn and still had trouble navigating the winding lanes from there to anywhere. She was more likely to get lost herself than to find a missing person.

Still. She couldn't help wondering what had happened to Anthea, whose joyful confidence had taken her down some wrong road. That was another thing Ellie recognized.

As she approached The Vicarage, a rambling brick Georgian house that stood at the end of the high street next to the church, she turned her focus back to the challenge she had already taken on: what she had come to think of as the 40 days of Christmas.

When she was younger, she had always enjoyed Christmas, but, since the end of her first marriage (admittedly, a major wrong road), she had limited her holiday celebrations to the obligatory party for the English Department at the university where she taught, Chinese food with friends on Christmas Eve, and Christmas Day with her parents where they ate turkey and exchanged books.

She had fantasized about someday spending this time of year in the place she'd studied for so long, imagining an idyllic season of frosty winds and candlelit Christmas trees, roasting chestnuts and pink-cheeked carolers, flaming puddings and the appearance of a ghost or three. Now she was here—and it was even snowing—but she was not on a vacation. Four months ago she had married Graham Kent, the vicar of Little Beecham's Church of St. Michael and All Angels, and that meant she was in for what she jokingly called "the full English" when it came to Christmas. Today was day 25, starting from the church's annual Christmas coffee morning, with 15 days to go until the three kings would arrive in Bethlehem, and the season would be over.

Today at least she could cross off one big item on her to-do list. She had settled on her family gifts, which she purchased after endless rumination at the village antique shop, The Chestnut Tree. Her friend Michael-John Parker owned the shop, and he had congratulated her roundly on her final choices: an antique rosewood fife with brass fittings for Graham and delicate gold Victorian earrings for his daughter—her new stepdaughter—Isabelle.

"Now I hope you'll begin to relax and enjoy yourself," said Michael-John, as he handed her a gift bag embossed with a spreading chestnut tree. "You should be excited. I'm sure the Kent family Christmas will be just like one of those Leech illustrations of Dickens that we all love so much."

"I am excited," said Ellie. "I'm just having trouble seeing myself as part of the picture, instead of looking at it."

"Put on your paper crown, say 'Please pass the bread sauce', and you'll fit in perfectly."

"Bread sauce?" said Ellie. "Isn't that an oxymoron?"

He laughed. "Oh, you do have a lot to learn," he said, and wished her luck.

She thanked him for his help and for the luck, both of which she surely needed. Even Graham, who appeared to love Christmas unreservedly, had looked tired that morning, hunched over his typewriter, banging out yet another sermon conveying the world-changing importance of one long-ago birth to people addled with more immediate expectations—both good and bad.

All we want for Christmas is our Anthea. Please help.

The electric candles in The Vicarage windows were already lit, a welcome sight twinkling through the blue dusk and falling snow. Ellie crossed the snowy yard to the back door, as always a little amazed that this 18th century Georgian house was where she now lived.

The kitchen was so toasty from the day's baking that Hector, their rough-coated Jack Russell, barely opened his eyes to greet her then promptly went back to sleep in his basket by the Aga. Mrs. Finch, The Vicarage's longtime housekeeper, had left for the day, but on the farmhouse table that doubled as a worktop, a new batch of her mini mince pies was cooling on racks. Ellie had begun the season eating these traditional pastries with gusto, but by now the smell alone gave her heartburn. She stowed her gifts at the back of the china cupboard and went to find Graham.

When they'd met at her parents' home in Berkeley nearly a year ago, Ellie hadn't known Graham was a vicar. She had dropped by to see how her mother was faring after some minor surgery and found her on the patio drinking iced tea and carrying on a lively discussion about the subject–object dichotomy with Ellie's philosophy professor father and an attractive Englishman. A widower, it turned out, a few years older than Ellie, but with a lanky body, gingery hair, and lively blue eyes that gave him an aura of boyishness.

Of course she joined in the discussion of whether the subjective realm of perception and belief is separate from the world of events and objects—and ended up staying for dinner. Of course she rode back to San

Francisco on the BART train with the Englishman, who happened to be renting a room not far from where she lived while he was in the Bay Area on sabbatical. Of course, she saw him again, the very next day. She had been certain from the first moment that this was not a wrong road taken, but who ever knew where a new road would lead?

The door to the study where Graham worked and conducted parish business was closed, but she could hear the clatter of typewriter keys, which meant he was alone. Ellie went back to the kitchen and put together a tray for tea then returned, saying, "Room service," as she opened the door.

He pulled a piece of paper out of the typewriter with a flourish, turned to her, and smiled. Dressed in old corduroys, denim shirt, and a sweater with patched elbows, he was what she thought of as "her Graham," not the priest in Holy Orders whose closest ties were beyond her comprehension.

"Just what I need," he said, helping himself to a McVitie's digestive biscuit coated with dark chocolate.

"Biscuits, tea, or me?" asked Ellie, as she handed him a mug and settled into the chair beside his desk.

"You, of course. But the tea and biscuits are brilliant too."

A mountain of crumpled paper had been consigned to the wastebasket, and three neat piles of pages were lined up on the desk. How he could write on a typewriter was beyond her comprehension too.

He yawned, stretched his full length, and took off his tortoiseshell glasses. "I'm always amazed when I finish. Until I get there, it seems like I never will," he said, coming back to upright.

"I know what you mean. So what did you decide to say about the virgin mother and her little babe?"

"I can't tell you," he said, with a twinkle in his eyes. "It would spoil the surprise."

"You mean I'll have to come to church to find out?"

He nodded. "All three times."

"It's the magic number," she said and leaned over to give him a kiss.

The snow was still falling at five o'clock when Graham set off to meet the members of Beecham Morris, the Morris dance side he belonged to. As part of a longstanding tradition, they were performing a medieval mummers' play at several pubs in the area that evening. This was called a Christmas play, but it was really about the Winter Solstice: the death of the old year and the birth of the new.

Ellie had never given much thought to the Solstice before, but in a place where the shortest day offered only seven hours, 49 minutes, and 45 seconds of light, she could see why you'd want to celebrate the fact that the next day would be one second longer. According to Graham, the date of Christmas had been arbitrarily set in December to piggyback on the hope generated by this seasonal change.

He was playing Saint George this year and, before he left, he put on his costume with its tin knight's helmet and demonstrated his sword-fighting moves for Ellie and Hector, swinging and thrusting at an imaginary dragon. Ellie was impressed—she hadn't known he was on the fencing team when he was at Oxford—but Hector was beside himself, barking and leaping until he collapsed, exhausted with pleasure.

When she was alone, she tidied up the kitchen and then sat idly watching the snow beat against the window and transform the landscape of church, churchyard, and the woods beyond. She had been warned not to expect a white Christmas. The "snow on snow, snow on snow" described in one of her favorite carols was hardly more true for Oxfordshire than it was for Bethlehem, and a cold, dismal rain was far more likely. Still, this storm showed no signs of stopping, so maybe she was going to be lucky. Her first English Christmas would include all the special effects.

As she drank a cup of chamomile tea, her thoughts drifted and eddied from memories of Christmases past to the face of Anthea Davies, who might or might not fulfill her parents' wish by turning up for the holiday. Who might or might not turn up anywhere ever again.

Ellie had run away once, when she was 16—even younger than Anthea. At the time she'd thought of it as a highly romantic adventure—a lark—and a chance to show she was not a child any longer. She had never even considered the impact on her parents until she saw the look on her father's face when he found her three days later in a motel with the boy she loved. It was years before he could say out loud how terrified he'd been that he would never see her again, and 20 years on, Ellie knew her mother hadn't entirely forgiven her for not being the girl she thought she was.

Three months was a lot longer than three days though. She checked the clock and decided she had time to see what was online about Anthea Davies' disappearance before she had to get to the pub for the mummers' play. She went up to her study on the third floor, which was her little bit of home filled with the things she had brought from California. Moving aside a pile of books on Jane Austen that she had been using to research a book idea, she set down her mug of tea, opened her laptop, and entered the words: Anthea Davies Oxford.

There had been a flurry of coverage in the Oxford and local papers with stories illustrated by the same photo as appeared on the poster. This had apparently been taken in Oxford, and Anthea had emailed it to her parents on the first of October with a brief message saying she would see them soon, but that was the last time they heard from her.

She had spent the summer in London, working as an intern at the Joffrey Museum of British History, and had left her job and lodging there as scheduled at the end of September. Her parents expected her to visit before the start of the Michelmas term and then join the other students, with whom she shared a flat in Oxford, but she had never arrived at either place.

Arthur and Frances Davies of Pidlington reported her missing on October 7th, and the police had launched an investigation. Although there was evidence, in addition to the photo, that confirmed she was in Oxford on the first of the month, no trace of her had been found since. Detective Inspector Derek Mullane of the Thames Valley Constabulary said the police were doing everything they could to locate Miss Davies, and members of the public were urged to call if they had any information. But the story petered out fairly quickly. You could only report that there was no new information so often. No wonder her parents were desperate.

Ellie checked the places she knew students went online, but Anthea Davies was apparently not a fan of social media. The only thing she found was a Facebook page that offered the minimum of public information and a photo that appeared to be Anthea with her back to the camera and only a suggestion of her face looking over her shoulder. On October 18th, a Melanie Thomas had posted: "PM me," but if there had been a reply, it was not visible. Ellie looked at Melanie's page and learned that she was also an undergraduate at Oxford but all of her other information was private.

The village of Pidlington, where the Davies family lived, was about 10 miles southwest of Little Beecham. So why had posters about Anthea's disappearance been put up in their village? Did she have connections here? And why were they put up now, so long after she had last been heard from?

Perhaps her parents were blanketing the area, hoping to stir up some fresh information. Losing a daughter was not, after all, something you could easily come to accept and choose to move on. Also it was Christmas: the season when your happiness and all of your relationships come under a microscope that defines your life. How well it is—or isn't—going.

All we want for Christmas is our Anthea. Please help.

She put her computer on sleep and then pawed through a Plexiglas box that held business cards and other scraps of paper until she found the one she wanted. On the front it said Detective Inspector Derek Mullane with the seal of the Thames Valley Constabulary. On the back, his mobile phone number was written in his awkward sloping hand.

The snow was still coming down quickly when Ellie walked to The Three Lambs on the high street. There were few streetlights in the village, but the golden squares of the lamp-lit windows illuminated the way and reminded her of the old-fashioned Advent calendar Graham had put on the mantel in the sitting room. Her boots squeaked, and she tipped her face to feel the icy flakes kiss her cheeks. There was something wonderful about snow that made it seem like all should be right in the world, even though you knew it wasn't.

The Lambs was surprisingly crowded for a Tuesday night. Dark and low-ceilinged, Little Beecham's only pub prided itself on not giving in to new marketing ploys, such as white tablecloths and posh food, and mainly catered to the locals as a place for a quiet pint, a bag of crisps, and a good gossip. Ellie recognized a few faces—Mrs. Wiggins from the village shop and Mrs. Tiddington, the butcher's wife—but she also received looks that made it clear that she was recognized as an incomer, despite wearing an ancient Barbour parka she'd found in the coat closet, jeans, and wellingtons.

She was standing uncertainly with her pint of Hooky Bitter, looking for a place to sit, when a familiar voice called "Over here, Guv!" and she saw her friend Morag MacDonald's son Seamus waving to her. Relieved, she waved back and made her way through the jostling crowd to where he and his mother were sitting.

Like herself a former teacher, Morag was the first friend Ellie had made in the village, and 14-year-old Seamus had become a good friend too. With their dark curly hair, fair skin, and pink cheeks, the two were as unmistakably related as a pair of twins.

"Wow," she said, as she slid into a chair at their small corner table. "I had no idea a mummers' play would draw a standing-room-only crowd in Little Beecham."

Morag laughed and patted her hand. "I hate to disillusion you, but I expect the weather has more to do with it than the mummers. We wanted to go to the cinema, but the roads were so rubbish, we turned back."

"I think it was fate that we've met. The game is afoot, you know," Seamus said, taking a damp copy of the MISSING poster out of his pocket. "Have you seen this?"

"I have," said Ellie, not quite liking the eager look on Seamus's face. His ambition was to be a private detective, and he thought there was no reason to wait until he grew up to pursue this career.

"Don't you think we should help? I mean, they're asking everyone, aren't they?"

"Seamus, what are you talking about—the game is afoot?" said Morag, taking the flyer. She frowned. "This does not look like a game to me. And since when do you call Ellie 'Guv'? Have you both joined the police force?"

Seamus glared at his mother. "We did solve a murder together, you know. Better than the police," he claimed, and this was more or less true. Soon after she arrived in Little Beecham, Ellie had found a dead man in the churchyard and had ended up trying to discover what happened if only to fend off the suggestion that she was responsible for the death herself. Seamus and his network of friends had proved a valuable asset in finding the truth.

"But, Seamus, that was different. I was forced to become involved by the circumstances. I had to clear my name. This really isn't any of my business."

"So you don't want to help?" he asked, and Ellie was glad that Morag did not give her time to answer.

"Whether *you* want to help or not, you are not going off looking for missing girls," she said. "I am taking you to your dad's parents tomorrow so you can celebrate Christmas with them. Remember?"

The boy scowled and shrank back in his chair with his arms crossed. "And you'll spend all the time I'm gone with Crispix, I suppose."

"Crispix?" asked Ellie, pleased to find the subject changing.

"He's not a cereal. His name is Crispin," said Morag. For Ellie, she added, "He's a former colleague from Shepherd's Hill School, and I've been seeing him a bit."

This was news. In the past Morag had claimed she was off men forever since her divorce from Seamus's father.

"You mean Crispin—like in *Henry the Fifth*? St. Crispin's Crispian?" Ellie asked.

"Yes. And he's really a very nice man, even though Seamus can't abide him."

"I just hope I won't have to abide with him, that's all. You hardly know him, and he already acts like he's moved in with us."

"Seamus, you sound jealous," said Ellie, teasing, and the boy's face flared pink.

"I am not. I'd just sooner be here doing something useful than off at my gran's playing darts with my cousins. I already launched my inquiries this afternoon."

"Meaning what?" asked Ellie, but before he could reply, the pub lights flashed twice and, across the crowded room, chattering voices died down.

Then John Tiddington, local butcher and leader of Beecham Morris, strode through the front door dressed as Father Christmas with a dramatic flourish of blowing snow. "Here come I, old Father Christmas!" he bellowed, "Welcome or welcome not, I hope old Father Christmas will ne'er be forgot!"

A few girls giggled, and someone shouted, "Welcome not!" But he was quickly drowned out by a chorus of "Welcome!" and the crowd tightened up to make room for the mummers who danced in dressed as Saint George, the Turkish Knight, Princess Sabra, the Doctor, the Fool, and the Dragon. A musician playing a pipe and tabor brought up the rear.

A few people turned away to watch sports on a silent TV hanging behind the bar, but most were prepared to ooh-and-ah in exchange for the novelty of having a green dragon and a lot of sword fighting enliven an evening at the pub.

The story, with its mish-mash of characters from the Crusades to mythology, didn't make much sense to Ellie. Nonetheless, the singsong speeches and cheerful music, the worn felt costumes, and slapstick action charmed her completely.

Graham threw himself into his role as Saint George, getting loud cheers as he rescued the Princess, killed the Knight, and slayed the Dragon, though at the cost of his own life. There was a hush when they all lay still on the floor, until the Doctor's silly incantations brought them back from the dead. Then the audience clapped and stamped their feet as the mummers, with clashing swords and jingling bells, came together for the closing sword dance.

Did the crowd gathered at The Three Lambs know—or care—that for centuries this story had represented the return of light and life? The triumph of faith over fear? Probably not. But when Father Christmas circulated among them, saying, "Come throw in your money and think it no wrong," they dug into their pockets to give to the poor anyway.

Ellie put a five-pound note in the basket, thinking how perverse it was that every person who wished her "Happy Christmas" reminded her sharply that she was in a foreign country, while this medieval play made her feel that she had at last found her way to where she belonged in the world. How did that work? Which was the true truth? She had no idea.

Nevertheless, when it was all over, and her grimy, sweaty Saint George came through the crowd to claim her, she felt proud and happy. They had a pint with the other mummers and their friends, then there was a rush of good nights and good wishes.

"I'll let you know what I find out," said Seamus, as Morag urged him toward the door with a goodbye wave to Ellie and Graham.

"Find out about what?" asked Graham, when he and Ellie had stepped out into the snow. It glittered in the lights from the pub, and the fresh, cold air was a relief after the stifling atmosphere inside.

"He's all gung-ho to help to find that missing girl."

"What missing girl?" asked Graham.

"Never mind about that now," said Ellie, putting her arm through his. "Let's take a walk in the snow before bed," and they did. But later, she found it hard not to mind and lay awake for a long time thinking of that plea:

All we want for Christmas is our Anthea. Please help.

Wednesday, December 23
Chapter 2

Snow was festive and lovely while it was falling, but once the storm was over, it became just something heavy, wet, and cold to be dealt with. By the next afternoon, when they had to pick up Isabelle at the train in Kingbrook, Ellie was both sweaty and frozen from helping Graham and the sexton, Mr. Finch, shovel paths and set up a half dozen Norway Spruces in the church and The Vicarage.

There were no snowplows to serve the villages, so rock salt had been sprinkled on the roads, which did not help much. The trip through the countryside was made dazzling by the sun on the snow, but slowed by fearful drivers who crawled along the lanes and over-optimistic ones who slid into the ditches.

The Kingbrook train station was little more than a hut where passengers could buy tickets and stay out of the weather, but today it was crowded with people, heading off or arriving with suitcases and armloads of gaily-wrapped packages. As Ellie stamped her cold feet and watched for the London train, she saw a gaunt woman with thin, dark hair and circles under her eyes handing out flyers to anyone who would take one. At first she assumed they were sale announcements, something like two-for-one dinners at a local fish-and-chip shop. Then she noticed one trampled on the platform, already ground into the snow and dirt, and recognized the slash of red type: *All we want. . .help.*

This must be the mother, she thought, seeing in her face a shattered memory of her daughter's beauty. Ellie wondered again what she hoped to learn from all these coming-and-going people with their minds on their own families and friends. The pity on their faces as they shoved the flyers carelessly into their pockets had to be lacerating, but she supposed if the alternative was to sit at home and wait, it was better to be here in the shivering cold.

She had made up her mind to try to speak to the woman, when the blaring horn of an approaching train caused the greeters and passengers to surge forward, and the missing girl's mother was lost to sight. Instead, the flesh-and-blood daughter Isabelle bounded off the train into her father's arms, and the whirlwind of her arrival swept them away.

It was a bit of a shock how one teenager could suddenly make the house feel so much more full, even crowded. All legs and long blonde hair, at 19, Isabelle Kent was a gamine version of her pretty English mother with Graham's sparkling, intelligent blue eyes. Ellie tried to take in stride his obvious happiness at seeing his daughter—how they clung to each other and how his gaze followed her wherever she went. Ellie hoped she did not have the expression on her face that she had sometimes noticed on her mother's: a kind of stiff pleasure and approval of the closeness between father and daughter tinged with disappointment at being outside that magic circle.

In this case, Isabelle did not have to do or say a thing to remind Ellie that she was an outsider. Despite their official—historically dubious—roles as stepdaughter and stepmother, they were still little more than strangers, given the amount of time they had spent together so far.

Every detail from the casual way Isabelle dropped her bags in the hall to her easy banter with Mrs. Finch spoke of a lifetime of living in this place with these people. The gap created by a few months away was filled in minutes.

After serving them a steak and kidney pie—Isabelle's favorite—Mrs. Finch took off her apron, sat down at the table, and put on her wire spectacles to walk Ellie and Isabelle through her instructions for cooking Christmas lunch while she was away at her sister's. From time to time she looked up from her handwritten recipes and cookbooks with such an anxious expression that Isabelle finally laughed. "Now, Mrs. Finch, you mustn't worry. Haven't I helped you make Christmas lunch ever since Mum died? You know you've trained me very well."

Poring over recipes for mysteries, such as the apparently famous bread sauce, Ellie was glad Isabelle felt so confident. Her idea of cooking was to make a quick stir-fry, and the big red enameled Aga stove, with its four ovens, intimidated her. "In that case, I'll be your *sous-chef*, Isabelle, and do whatever you tell me," she said, at which Mrs. Finch frowned disapprovingly, but Isabelle looked pleased.

At four o'clock, Ellie left Graham and Isabelle still sitting at the kitchen table, surrounded by cold cups of tea, having segued from a discussion of Brexit, which did interest her, to the upcoming cricket season, which did not. She was glad to have an excuse to get out of the house for a while before the main event, that *pièce de résistance* of the family Christmas: the trimming of the tree.

It was already dusk when she set off across the churchyard that lay between The Vicarage and St. Michael's, and the lights in the church made the stained-glass windows glow in the gathering darkness. A new storm had begun with fine, light snow rapidly covering every surface they had cleared that morning with a fresh coat of white.

She was to meet Sarah Henning, one of the girls from the village, for a rehearsal of their contribution to the Christmas Eve service. However, the choir was still practicing when she arrived, so she slipped into a back pew and sat down.

The 13th-century Norman church looked especially lovely decked out for the Christmas season. Ellie and several women from the parish had decorated the ends of the pews with evergreens and arranged branches of holly and candles on the windowsills. Two of the Norway Spruces now stood like sentinels on either side of the altar, and three more framed the large crèche where Mary, Joseph, and the animals awaited the arrival of the rest of the cast.

A dozen or so people were huddled around the Victorian pipe organ bundled in their coats because the heat had not been turned on that day. They were volunteers who came together to sing for special services, and the retired music teacher Mr. Dunn, who served as organist, was valiantly leading them through the Bach chorale "Break Forth, O Beauteous Heavenly Light". This was one of Ellie's favorites, but at the moment it sounded rather more like a dirge than a joyful exhortation. Presumably they would pick up the tempo by tomorrow. In any case, she was glad to have a few minutes to herself to listen to the music and breathe in the scents of centuries-old stone and fresh-cut evergreens.

The last of the choir members were still drifting out when Sarah rushed in, coat askew, red hair streaming, as if she had run all the way from home. "Sorry to be late, Mrs. Kent, but my dad is back, and it was a bit tricky to get away."

"You're not late, the choir has just finished," said Ellie, who knew that Sarah's father worked on an oilrig and used his time at home to drink and berate his family for enjoying his absences. This already difficult situation had been exacerbated by the death of Sarah's older brother Jackie in November.

Ellie had been helping the family wherever she could, and, when Sarah confided her ambition to become an actor, she had suggested the girl could begin by participating in the Christmas Eve service. Sarah had no doubt been imagining herself in a part more along the lines of Katniss in *The Hunger Games* than the Virgin Mary, but she proved to be willing. In fact, more than willing when Ellie pointed out that Mary was a young teenager like herself when she spoke the words of the *Magnificat*, a radical manifesto throwing down the gauntlet before the Romans and other powerful elites.

Unfortunately, this inspired Sarah to ask a lot of questions, such as why grown-ups who accepted that Father Christmas didn't exist still believed in virgin birth and why God would pick such a young girl to be the mother of his son. Fortunately, her years as a professor had made Ellie skillful at seeming to answer such unanswerable questions.

Today was supposed to be the final practice, but Sarah slumped down next to Ellie in the pew and showed no sign of wanting to begin. The tips of her ears sticking through her shaggy hair were still red with cold, and she hugged herself tightly.

"Has something happened, Sarah? Is it your dad?"

The girl lifted her shoulders in a shrug, but a tear leaked down her cheek. "Always. That's nothing new. But today I upset Mum, and I never meant to."

"Do you want to talk about it?" asked Ellie.

She shrugged again. "It's all because of that bloody Anthea Davies," she said, much to Ellie's surprise. "This morning Mum went to the shop and saw the posters about her being missing, so she got all upset and came home crying about when Jackie went missing and was found dead. It took forever to calm her down. Then Dad came back from the pub when I was trying to leave, and he started going on about how everyone knew Anthea ran away because she was pregnant, and if Lucy or I ever got up the spout we needn't bother coming home either."

Sarah shook her head as if to get rid of the memory. "I don't care what rubbish he says to me, but Lucy heard, and I was so mad I said not to worry, home was the last place I'd ever look for help, and that got Mum going all over again."

"Oh shit," said Ellie, forgetting this was probably not the right thing for a vicar's wife to say.

Sarah nodded, her face stiff with misery. "I know I can make it up with Mum, but I already can't wait for Dad to leave. That feels like shite, and all I can say is the Virgin Mary's life would've turned out a lot different if she'd had a dad like mine."

Ellie smiled and put her arm around the girl's shoulders. "You're right. She was lucky."

"Not that it matters. I know this is make believe—her telling off the world with her mysterious babe in her arms."

Then she gave a big sigh, stood up resolutely, and clumped to the front of the church in boots that looked impossibly heavy for her slender legs. There she squared her shoulders, lifted her chin, looked straight ahead, and paused, the way Ellie had taught her.

In the silence of the church, Ellie waited. Then, real or make believe, she witnessed the transformation of that teary 14-year-old when she opened her mouth and hurled out Mary's proclamation that God would scatter the proud, put down the mighty, exalt the humble and meek, fill the hungry with good things, and send the rich empty away.

She sounded more like the Celtic rebel queen Boadicea or Joan of Arc than an awestruck virgin mother. When she finished, Ellie jumped up, applauding, which made Sarah's face turn as red as her hair, but there was also a pride in her eyes that spoke well for her future. Actor or not.

Ellie set off for home thinking how listening to Sarah reminded her of the best part of teaching—when a student caught fire over an idea or a project and grew so fast you could practically stand back and watch it happen. The idea that she could still have that experience in this new life, but without grades, committee meetings, or departmental politics, was gratifying. Of course, Sarah was raw, hungry, parentless in a way, and open to help. The girl she most needed to connect with—the vicar's daughter—presented a very different kind of challenge, and she hoped she could meet it.

Now as she followed the rapidly refilling path through the churchyard, she caught sight of Louise Kent's grave. A wreath of holly decorated the stone, and she could see from a trail of slender boot prints that someone had stood there not long ago. Ellie paused in front of it to reflect, as she often did, on the fact that she was there because of the tragedy that had befallen this other woman.

At first she had felt an uneasy jealousy of Graham and Isabelle's devotion to Louise, but now she saw her as part of the family, a sort of friend. She even talked to her at times, and today she stopped to wish her Merry

Christmas and ask her help in getting to know her daughter. Snow had gathered on her shoulders before she carried on toward the lighted windows of The Vicarage.

Graham and Isabelle had moved into the sitting room, where they sat cozily on the sofa as a fire crackled in the fireplace, and the Norway Spruce filled the space with its wild, woodsy scent. The topic of discussion was whether Cambridge or Oxford had a better faculty in philosophy and did Graham regret going to Oxford.

"No," he said smiling, as Ellie came in with her mug of tea. "For one thing, if I hadn't gone to Oxford I would never have met Ellie, and we wouldn't all be here today."

"But that was like twenty-five years ago," said Isabelle, pulling Hector onto her lap for a hug.

"It's a cautionary tale," said Ellie, sitting down in Graham's leather armchair. "You can never know the future meaning of what you do today."

"That's even weirder."

"But true," said Graham. "If I had got a place at Cambridge as I wanted. . . and if Ellie's father had not come to lecture at Oxford. . . this event would not be happening."

Isabelle pretended to shiver. "It reminds me of *A Christmas Carol*. That thing with the ghosts."

"Precisely," said Graham, going to the CD player and putting on some music: the sweet caroling of a boys' choir. "So now that we are all assembled, let's get on with Christmas Present."

He rummaged in one of the boxes of ornaments that Mrs. Finch had brought down from the attic. "Here we are," he said, pulling out a star made of yellow yarn wrapped around sticks. "Izzy, this one goes on first, I believe?"

Isabelle gave a little frowning smile. “Yes, Dad, but please don’t call me Izzy. It makes me feel five years old.” She set Hector down and went to take the ornament.

“Isabelle made that in infant school, and, by tradition, it must always go on first,” he told Ellie, handing her a tiny papier-mâché crèche. “You’re next. We got that on our one-and-only family trip abroad to Portugal, didn’t we, Is? After you, I have a go. Then it’s a free-for-all, or we’ll be here all night.”

Ellie hung the colorful little crèche, while Graham chose a Father Christmas made of felt. Then, one by one, they emptied the old cardboard boxes and covered the tree with ornaments. Ellie had always liked Christmas trees that told the story of the people who decorated them, and this one carried on its fragrant branches the history of the Kent family from handed-down crystal icicles and baby photos preserved in plastic to ceramic ornaments made each year by Louise, the last one dated four years ago. There were moments when she saw the shadows of nostalgia and sadness cross Isabelle’s face, and Ellie was aware of the person she was not, but Graham kept up a cheerful patter of stories that made them all laugh too.

When the last box had been emptied, Ellie said: “My mother sent some of our family ornaments,” and brought out her own small box.

“That was thoughtful of her,” said Graham, unaware that as she lifted off the layer of packing material Ellie could feel her own memories wafting into the room.

“What are these?” asked Isabelle, holding up a matched pair of glass balls with “Ellie” and “Tom” written on them in glitter.

“Oh, my God. I can’t believe she sent those,” said Ellie, blushing. “I haven’t seen them for years!”

"Who was Tom?" asked Graham. "I've never heard you mention him."

"He was a cousin who lived with my family for a while."

"Long enough to have his own Christmas ornament," remarked Isabelle.

Sensing a story, they both looked at her curiously, but all Ellie would add was, "Yes, but we've been out of touch forever."

"Shall we just hang the one then?" said Isabelle.

"Sure," said Ellie and watched as the girl placed the ball with her name on it right in the center of the tree.

Then they turned off the lamps and sat down on the sofa to admire their work. Graham put an arm around each of them and held them close in the fairy-lit darkness. With snowflakes lacing the windowpanes, the lighted tree, the glowing embers of the fire, the man, the girl, and the dog, this was a scene straight from Ellie's perfect English Christmas fantasy. She had the urge to hold her breath so it would last, but, of course, it didn't.

The CD came to an end, and, in the sudden silence, Graham said, "We're very lucky to be together, you know. Ellie, do you remember that last night you mentioned a missing girl?"

"Yes," said Ellie, who felt her thoughts dance unpleasantly away from sugarplums.

"Her father called me this afternoon."

"Anthea Davies' father called you?"

"Yes, that's the one. His wife is a cousin of John Tiddington's wife, and John suggested I might be able to help them. Actually, what Mr. Davies said was that he hoped *we* might be able to help them."

"We?"

"I think he probably really means *you* we," Isabelle said to Ellie, sighing dramatically. She got up and began switching the lamps back on. "Here I thought we were going to have a nice quiet Christmas. No guests. No fuss."

"We are," said Graham stoutly. "But we can't not help people who need our help."

"I suppose, but whatever happened to all those dreary divorcees and middle-aged men in spiritual crisis who used to show up on our doorstep. How come now the people who need your help always seem to be mixed up with the police?"

"If you could pick and choose who you were going to help it wouldn't be quite the same, Is. These people are at their wits' end. They've never dealt with the police and we have."

"What kind of help do they want?" asked Ellie.

"I'm not sure. They haven't heard a word from their daughter in nearly three months, and the police investigation has drawn a blank. Apparently his wife thought putting up posters would bring them some news, but instead they've been besieged by crank callers and reporters."

"I don't see what you can do to help. They should hire a proper detective," said Isabelle.

"At the very least we can talk to them. Listen to them," said Graham.

"True. New information sometimes comes out that way," said Ellie. "I read that the police are stumped and, since Anthea isn't a minor, she is entitled to disappear if that's what she wants to do."

"You've already read up on this?" said Graham, surprised.

Ellie blushed. "I saw the posters. I mean, everyone in the village has noticed those posters except you, dear."

"I've been very busy," said Graham.

"Of course you have," said Ellie.

"I suppose the good news is that at least this time no one can blame you," said Isabelle, going to a side table that held bottles of sherry and whisky and pouring a sherry for each of them. "It's not like you kidnapped the girl."

"What a good point, Isabelle. It's always nice to have someone around with a handle on the bright side," said Ellie, taking the proffered drink.

"Then I think it must be time for us to raise a glass to a Happy Christmas," said Graham, and Hector began to bark, sure that a treat must be in the offing.

Thursday, December 24
Christmas Eve
Chapter 3

Over breakfast the next morning, they talked about the day ahead with its two important church services, but the subject of Anthea Davies kept creeping into the conversation. Mr. Davies had already called again, and Graham had told him he could come over with his wife for a meeting at two p.m. When she heard this, Isabelle looked askance from Ellie to Graham and announced that she would devote herself to the preparation of Christmas lunch.

"Super," said Ellie, who would rather be outdoors than cooking, even if it meant shoveling snow; and they left her trimming what looked like a lifetime supply of Brussels sprouts as she sang along to Handel's *Messiah* on the radio.

It wasn't snowing, but the sky was heavy with blue-gray clouds that rippled and bulged, folding against each other. The wind had dropped, silencing the rustle of the trees, and the winter birds twittered softly, as if they were whispering secrets. The temperature was below freezing, and Ellie wore one of Graham's thick sweaters under the Barbour parka; her California sweaters were just not up to the job.

It was the 27th day of Christmas, by her personal count, and the events they had been anticipating for a month were at last upon them. She was excited about that—but first would come the meeting where she would learn more about Anthea Davies. She had to admit she was excited about that too.

"Do you think we should call Derek Mullane?" she asked Graham, as she scraped her shovel along the walk leading from the lych gate to the front of St. Michael's.

"Mullane?" said Graham, who was wearing a deerstalker with the flaps down and a red muffler wound around his neck. He chucked a shovelful of snow onto the verge of the path. "Is he involved with the disappearance of the Davies girl?" Detective Inspector Mullane had been in charge of solving the murder of the dead man found in their churchyard.

"He was quoted in one of the newspaper stories I read."

"Oh. Well. Do you think he'd tell us anything that the family doesn't already know?"

"I suppose not," said Ellie, stopping to adjust her own scarf. The cold had a way of fingering into the tiniest of gaps. "But there must be something more we can do than simply listen."

"In my job, that's what I do. I advise, I don't solve," said Graham.

"Really?"

"Really."

"Hmm," said Ellie, as she stabbed her shovel into the snow and began a fresh pass.

When the walks were all cleared, they went back to The Vicarage, where they unpeeled their wet garments and boots in the entryway off the kitchen. Isabelle was now cutting up potatoes, with her head crooked to her shoulder, while she talked on the phone. A strainer full of freshly steamed Brussels sprouts stood in the sink, and the room was fragrant with the smell of baking butternut squash.

"Gotta run," she said, "Dad and Ellie are back." She set down the phone, looking pleased with herself. "That was Jillian Wickesworth. A girl I used to go riding with," she added for Ellie's benefit.

"That Jillian? You haven't spoken to her for years, have you?" said Graham.

"I know. It seemed a good time to check in and say Happy Christmas. Also I thought she might have known Anthea Davies since she lives in Pidlington, and she did. She hadn't heard she was missing though. She was really shocked by that."

"Isabelle, I hope you aren't getting involved in this too," said Graham sharply.

"I'm not, promise, but I did ask her what she was like. I mean you don't imagine you're going to learn what happened by talking to her parents, do you? They're the least likely to know."

Graham frowned, but Ellie thought she was right.

"Do you want to hear what she said or not?"

He nodded, albeit reluctantly.

"She said Anthea was too smart to be liked in primary school, and the village kids resented it when she won a place at Kingbrook Grammar. That's like a public school, you know," she told Ellie. "Very high standards and competitive, but free. The most surprising thing she remembered though was that Anthea was a cracking good liar."

"Really," said Ellie. "That's interesting. Did she give you an example?"

"She did. When she was about ten, she claimed she was a direct descendant of Shakespeare and could rattle off all the generations for the past four hundred years. She also claimed there was a special scholarship at Oxford just for her because of this. Everyone believed her. Even the teachers."

"And it wasn't true?"

Isabelle laughed. "Not a bit of it, but she would never admit it. Are you hungry? I made some sandwiches."

"Thank you, Is," said Graham, sitting down at the table. He seemed pleased that the subject of Anthea might now be dropped.

Ellie was pleased too, but for a different reason. It seemed to her that however annoyed Isabelle had been yesterday about the Davies family's intrusion into their holiday, she had gotten over it now. It might have even brought them all a notch closer, because the talk flowed easily as they ate sandwiches made from sharp cheddar and Branston's Pickle on Mrs. Finch's sturdy whole meal bread.

When they had cleaned up and duly admired the progress toward tomorrow's lunch, Graham and Ellie went off to their separate studies. Ellie needed to wrap her gifts, but she decided to check her email first.

As good as his word, Seamus had sent her a report on his inquiries:

Dear Guv,

Here's what I've learned about our case so far: There's a rumour that Anthea Davies disappeared because she'd been knocked up. No one I've talked to believes that. My friend Jack Villiers' brother Gerald was in love with her, but she wouldn't give the time of day to him or any other blokes at Kingbrook and never had a boyfriend the whole time she was there. They thought she was a stuck-up swot and probably gay. A few people still haven't got back to me. Will keep you posted.

Happy Christmas,

Seamus

Captain, High Street Irregulars

Ellie laughed at his signature. Seamus might like to compare himself to Sherlock Holmes' boy assistants, the Baker Street Irregulars, but she did not see herself in the role of Sherlock. She knew she was being pulled into this new mystery, but she had no expectation that she was going to be able to solve it when the police had failed—and she hoped no one else did either.

She also had a message from her father saying he hoped she was enjoying the snow since the weather in Berkeley was warm and sunny. She sent a reply, thanking both parents for their package, and attached photos of their Christmas tree and The Vicarage in the snow. She didn't make any comment on the selection of ornaments, even though she doubted her mother had sent the one with Tom's name on it by mistake. More likely it was her way of reminding Ellie that moving 6,000 miles away did not erase her history even if she was now doing her best to be a good English vicar's wife.

A sigh escaped her, as she turned her attention to wrapping her gifts for Graham and Isabelle. For as long as she could remember, she'd been seesawing between efforts to please her mother and rebellion against her failure to do so. With two quick pulls across the blade of her scissors, she curled the ribbons on Isabelle's gift. No matter what kind of stepmother she turned out to be, she vowed not to corrode their relationship with acid drips of disappointment and disapproval.

She wondered what sort of relationship Anthea Davies, another only child, had with her parents. Of all the things she'd heard so far, the most important seemed to be that she liked to lie about herself. This was consistent with what Seamus learned—that she kept her attachments secret—whatever they were. Ellie thought it also suggested that her disappearance might have been carefully planned, even though it took both her family and friends by surprise. Hopefully that meant she was not someone who'd been snatched in the dark and carried off, never to be seen again.

At one-thirty p.m., she dressed for the evening's services, putting on a cream cashmere turtleneck and silk scarf, wine-colored wool jacket, and black wool slacks. She tousled her hair until it framed her face in unruly dark waves and splashed out on a touch of mascara and lipstick. Just because she lived in a village now, there was no need to become a frump.

When she came downstairs, she found Graham already in the front hall greeting the woman she'd seen at the Kingbrook train station. She was accompanied by a thin, careworn man, who was probably only in his late forties, but looked much older. Mr. and Mrs. Davies. It was hard to picture them ever having the vitality to produce a spirited-looking daughter like Anthea, but the stress of her disappearance had undoubtedly been debilitating.

As Graham introduced them, Ellie could feel Mrs. Davies' dark eyes absorbing every detail of her. "Mrs. Kent," she said, holding her hand a little too tight and too long. "I believe I've read about you and your activities."

Ellie didn't know how to respond—it wasn't a compliment—so all she said was, "I was very sorry to hear about your situation."

Once they were settled in Graham's study with the obligatory tea and biscuits, Mr. Davies said: "We're very grateful that you're giving us your time today—losing touch with Anthea has been shattering, and Christmas has made it worse, especially for Frances." He put his hand protectively on his wife's shoulder.

She held a white handkerchief childishly embroidered with the word 'Mum' that she folded into smaller and smaller squares then started again. "That's true," she said, "because now, you see, it's impossible to believe that we would not hear from her if she could be in touch. So if she isn't, it can only mean one thing. Don't you agree?"

No one wanted to answer that question, much less address the unspoken possibilities of the "one thing" that might have happened.

Graham cleared his throat, sipped his tea then said in his most soothing tones, "Forgive me for asking painful questions, but it would be helpful for us to have some background. For example, could you tell us about the last time you had contact with Anthea?"

Mrs. Davies looked to her husband to answer him.

"She was meant to come home after London for a visit before the new term began," he said. "We offered to help her move house, but she said no, a friend was helping her. And, no, she did not give us the name, and we've never been able to find out who that was. The police tried, but no one seemed to notice or remember anything.

"At first, we expected to hear from her any day, but we didn't. Whenever we called, her mobile was turned off. That in itself was not terribly unusual—Anthea often turns off her phone when she's working on something. She's doesn't like to be disturbed, and we've, well, we've tried to learn not to hover, since it just upsets her.

"After a week, we called her flat mates in Oxford, but they had assumed she was with us. They hadn't heard from her either. Then I contacted the place where she stayed and the museum where she'd worked in London, and they said she had left, and there had been nothing out of the ordinary about her departure, so no one remembered any details.

"Of course, by then, we were frantic and called the police to report her missing. They launched an investigation, but at first they were suspicious of us because we hadn't reported her sooner." Both parents looked ashen as he said this, and Ellie could only imagine their regret.

"Don't forget the bank and the photo," Mrs. Davies said, as if she couldn't wait for her husband to go on.

Graham nodded encouragingly, while Ellie sat quietly listening to the story unfold.

"On the first of October, we received a brief email from her along with a photo taken in Oxford, so we understood that she had safely arrived. But from that time on, the only trace of her was that she withdrew money from her account that day, and there have been no sightings and no activity on her bank account, credit cards, phone, or email since," Mr. Davies told them.

"The withdrawal and photo were both from Oxford?" asked Ellie.

"Yes," interrupted Mrs. Davies again. "The police let us see the CCTV tape from the bank, and she looked perfectly all right then. But that was the last sign of her."

"So it sounds like something happened in Oxford that caused her willingly or unwillingly to change her plans," said Ellie.

"The police have drawn a blank even with repeated appeals to the public and Arthur going on TV. The case is still open, but they told us frankly that most people who go missing return within forty-eight hours. With every passing day, it becomes harder to trace them.

"At first they questioned us repeatedly about why we didn't call them in sooner. They wanted to know if we had had a disagreement and even hinted that we might be involved in her disappearance ourselves," said Mrs. Davies, in a shocked voice. "Finally one young sergeant said that Anthea was twenty years old and could go where she liked. She didn't have to tell us anything."

"I suppose the police become accustomed to people lying and therefore come to expect it," said Graham drily. "Unfortunately we know exactly what it's like when they disbelieve everything you say down to the most insignificant detail."

The expressions on their visitors' faces showed the news that they had not been singled out in receiving this treatment was like a lifeline thrown into a dark sea.

"I suppose you must have tried to imagine where she might have gone, assuming she went willingly. What she might have wanted to do other than return to university," Graham said, trying to lead them forward.

"Yes," Mrs. Davies said, hesitantly, "but we really have no idea. All she ever wanted was to go to Oxford." Tears ran down her cheeks, and she clutched her hands together, crushing the hanky.

"Over the summer, had she expressed any symptoms of restlessness? Or last term, perhaps, was she unhappy about something related to her studies?"

"That's what the police kept on at us about, but we couldn't think of anything," said Mr. Davies.

"I've gone over and over everything she said, and it seems so little," said his wife. "It's terrible to say, but I hardly remember what we talked about—and to think those could have been our last words. . . ."

"It was our vicar, Reverend Stiller at St. Stephen's in Pidlington, who advised us to prepare for Christmas as usual," Mr. Davies continued in a hard voice. "He said it would be an act of faith to show we believed she would come home safely. The worst rubbish I've ever heard if you want my opinion."

"I thought it might help, but I couldn't bear sitting home by the tree, waiting," said Mrs. Davies. "That's why I had the posters made. In the ones the police make, everyone looks alike."

"And then the fun started all over again. Just like in October," said Mr. Davies. "Crank callers saying the most horrible things about us. Swine claiming to know where Anthea is and they would tell us for money. Reporters looking for updates we don't have. But we have to answer the phone. What if it's her? We don't know what number she might be calling from. Where she might be."

With that question hanging in the air, they fell silent again.

"If there had been a breach with you—one significant enough for her to break off relations—I am sure you would remember it," said Ellie. "So the next question is, I think, are there other people in her life who are important enough to push her into making such a decision? Either to run away with them or run away from them?"

The parents glanced at each other and then turned blank faces to Ellie and Graham. "No," said her mother first. "She didn't have a boyfriend, if that's what you mean."

"That you know of. She might have met someone in London. Or at Oxford."

"But she would've said! We would have been so pleased!"

"Of course. Although young people don't always share this type of information," said Ellie gently, and she could tell it had not occurred to them that their daughter might have a life they didn't know about, one in which her disappearance was a logical outcome of other events. Was this true of all parents? It had certainly been the case with hers.

Mrs. Davies drew in her breath sharply. "Some people have been saying she's gone off with a man. Even that she is going to have a baby and doesn't want us to know."

Mr. Davies' face became tight and bitter. "I'm sure that's not—"

"But that's just it. We can't be sure of anything," his wife cut in.

"She would never—" he said, and she simply glared at him.

"I know you would both be very disappointed if Anthea did not finish her degree right now, but do you think she would feel that she had to hide a pregnancy from you?" asked Ellie.

The two parents stared at the floor with stony expressions, and Ellie felt a twinge of annoyance. She turned to Graham hoping he would know what to say next.

But it was Mrs. Davies who pulled herself together to speak first. "Of course we would be upset. We have worked hard and sacrificed to give her the education she wanted and deserved, but now, it's been so long, I just want to know she's alive. You can't imagine what it's like to have your child vanish into thin air from one moment to the next."

Ellie felt her eyes on her again with that desperate need. "I can't," she said, but stopped, glanced at Graham, and then went on. "I can't promise anything, of course, but I could go over the circumstances with you again and talk to people for you. I'm sure the police have done a thorough job, but maybe, between us, we can turn up something new." She wanted to add that this might also revive interest in the case, but she didn't. There would be time enough to go into that later. "How would it be if I come over on Boxing Day to talk further? In the afternoon?" asked Ellie, and they nodded eagerly.

Graham looked relieved, which surprised her, but maybe her offer fell into his categories of helping people and giving advice, not solving mysteries.

"Of course, in the meantime, if you do hear anything, please let us know," he said, standing up and holding out his hand. "Your vicar was right about one thing. None of us knows the future."

Ellie had never been to a Crib Service before, so she had no way to judge, but she thought the St. Michael's committee had planned an extremely ambitious agenda for this family service. In addition to giving out Christingles—decorated oranges symbolizing the Earth stuck with candles representing the light of Christ—they had invited the children to dress up as the figures in the story and bring their stuffed animals to join the manger scene. One of the older girls had been deputized to carry the figure of the baby Jesus and lay him in the crèche, and they would close with all the children singing "Away in a Manger" by candlelight.

They had barely finished setting up for the service, when over-excited shepherds and angels, Marys and Josephs, kings and sheep began to pour in with their exhausted parents in tow. For the next hour, Ellie sat rigid on the edge of her pew, but all went well despite crying babies, wandering toddlers, and a small but fierce disagreement over whose brown bunny was whose at the end.

"I'm amazed the church hasn't burnt to the ground long before this," said Ellie, as she stretched out on the sitting room sofa afterward, nursing a glass of sherry. The lighted tree and crackling fire created a cozy atmosphere in which to rest up for the late service.

"I know," said Graham, "but everyone loves it, and we've never had an accident."

"I have to admit, the children singing around the crèche with their candles was enchanting. And your sermon about how the story of Mary and Jesus reminds us that all children are born with unknown potential, no matter what their circumstances, was perfect."

"Hmm, thanks. You were probably the only person listening," said Graham, who was re-reading his next sermon with a red pen in his hand.

Ellie watched him affectionately, wondering if he planned to keep changing it until it was time to leave.

"You know what I was doing a year ago?" she said, sitting up. "Eating Peking duck in Chinatown. Four of us ate two whole ducks."

"I'll bet it was good," said Graham, continuing to make changes in his text.

"It was. Delicious. But afterward I went home with a terrible stomach ache and lay awake most of the night wondering where my life was headed."

"Little did you know," he said, looking up. "I was right here watching the logs change from wood to ash."

"And editing your sermon for the one-hundredth time?"

"Undoubtedly." He smiled. "What time did Isabelle say she would get back from that party?"

"She's going to meet me at the church."

"Well then," he said, putting his work aside, "maybe we should celebrate the change in our affairs in a way we could only have daydreamed about a year ago."

Later, as the first round of bells began to ring, they headed back to the church through lightly falling snow. These were big flakes whose delicate patterns you could see on your coat for an instant before they vanished. Ellie took in everything to remember as another moment of Christmas magic: the frosty plumes of their breath, Graham's hand in hers, and the sight of people with flashlights and lanterns coming through the snow from all directions for this holy celebration.

Graham left Ellie to go around to the vestry door, while she went to find Sarah Henning. Apparently her family was not coming, because she stood alone at the front door, shivering in the short navy dress and tights that she and Ellie had chosen as her costume.

On most Sundays, the congregation consisted of a scattering of stalwart members of the parish, but tonight the whole village—except the Hennings—seemed to have turned out, and in the flickering candlelight, the atmosphere hummed with expectation. As they made their way through the church, Ellie greeted her neighbors, pleased to note how many she now knew. The older members of the Worthy clan were there, the youngers having come to the early service. She spotted Michael-John Parker wearing a red vest under his usual impeccable black Armani suit, and Morag MacDonald was tucked in a corner at the back, looking flushed, as she whispered happily to the handsome stranger at her side. Crispin, Ellie guessed, and was not surprised that Seamus felt displaced.

Up by the altar, the warden Charles Bell and John Tiddington were trying to straighten one of the Norway Spruces, which had begun to list. The members of the choir sat together near the organ holding their music, and, from the bell loft, she heard the leader give the order to begin the second peal.

Ellie had reserved seats for herself, Isabelle, and Sarah in the front pew near the crèche. Sarah sat down, clutching her program open to the page where her name appeared in print. Ellie craned her neck to catch sight of Isabelle, who slipped into her seat just as the bells finished cling-clanging the news that it was time for the service to begin.

There was a moment's hush, a last chance for people to settle themselves and whisper "Happy Christmas" to their neighbors. Then the organ prelude began and Mr.

Dunn gave it his all with hands and feet flying. He continued without pause into the processional hymn, so it was not until the congregation sat down and the reverberations of "O Come, All Ye Faithful" died away that Ellie first heard the sound like a mewing kitten. It registered as out of place, but then Graham stepped forward to speak, resplendent in his white vestments, and she was caught up in the familiar drama of the nativity.

She heard the soft mewing again as Mary Bell, the warden's wife, stepped up to the lectern wearing a winter white suit with a holly corsage to read the Lesson. Ellie looked around to see if her companions had noticed anything, but Sarah was reciting to herself with her eyes closed, while Isabelle watched Mrs. Bell with an expression that managed to be both attentive and absent. The English really had cornered the market on sounding pompous, Ellie thought, as Mrs. Bell intoned the words of her reading in her best upper-crust accent.

Could some child have brought a kitten for the manger and then left it? The menagerie of stuffed animals had been removed from the crèche, leaving the plaster figures in a motionless tableau. Ellie continued to scan the area for the source of that mewing sound, but, as far as she could see, there was no kitten.

Something was different than it had been a few hours before when the children gathered around with their Christingles—but it took a moment for her to realize what it was. The baby Jesus had changed his clothes.

At five o'clock, he had been a blond rosy-cheeked babe in blue swaddling clothes with his plaster arms upraised in a blessing. Now he was tightly wrapped in a gray blanket with only his small face peeking out.

From afar she heard Mrs. Bell speaking, but her attention was now riveted on the still, small figure. When he opened his mouth and made that mewing sound again, she slipped past Sarah, and, with a pounding heart, knelt down by the crèche. This new Jesus had a wisp of dark hair and tiny lashes lying against flushed cheeks that seemed way too hot to her touch. When Mrs. Bell announced with self-important dignity, "Here endeth the Lesson," Ellie scooped the gray bundle out of the manger and stood up.

The people nearest to her were attracted by the movement and turned to look, and the news that something unusual was happening rippled across the congregation so that in no time, attention had shifted to Ellie, standing in the side aisle with the baby Jesus—or something—in her arms.

"Call an ambulance," she whispered urgently to Sarah, but Isabelle grasped the situation quicker and said, "I'll get the car instead."

Graham had just begun to read, "For unto you is born this day in the city of David," when Isabelle went rushing down the side aisle to the front door, and he looked up.

All pretense of continuing the service ended when he realized Sarah was helping Ellie with her coat, and he hurried toward them to find out what was going on. By now the bell ringers were craning over the rail of the bell loft, and the entire congregation was on their feet.

"Someone put a real baby in the manger," Ellie whispered, showing him the tiny infant wrapped in a blanket. "It must have been left here between the services."

Graham looked from the bundle to the empty manger and back, his face registering surprise for only a moment. Then taking Ellie by the elbow, he quickly escorted her to the front door, just as Isabelle pulled up in the Mini Cooper to drive them to the Kingbrook Regional Hospital.

By the time Ellie and Isabelle made it back to Little Beecham, it was late. The church was dark, the service long over. Graham was in his pajamas and robe, dozing by the sitting room fire with Hector at his feet. "What happened?" he asked rousing himself. "Is he all right?"

"He is not a he, Dad. He is a girl," said Isabelle, pulling off her coat and flopping down on the sofa.

"They admitted her to the hospital. Finally," said Ellie. "I don't know what I expected, but showing up at a hospital with a newborn that you say is not yours, has no name, address, or National Health number sets off a lot of alarm bells. It was a good thing Isabelle was on hand to help me navigate the rough waters of NHS bureaucracy. I put us down as her contacts, so I hope you don't mind, but, at least for the moment, our family has a new member."

"I'm sure I'm delighted. What an unexpected Christmas present."

Isabelle laughed. "I need a drink," she said, and Graham got up to pour them each a whisky.

"So how is she? The baby."

"I don't know. They took her away, and that was that. If she had been my child, I would have been furious. As it is, my head is spinning. How did the service turn out?"

"It was fine. After the excitement of your departure, we all outdid ourselves to live up to the special occasion. I must say a lot of people seemed to be texting and sneaking photos of the empty manger though."

"Oh, my God, the empty manger. What a horrible symbol."

"Yes. But Sarah Henning saved the day. She spotted our Jesus under the hay and dug him out before she came forward to say the *Magnificat*."

"Really? That girl does have a flair for the dramatic. How did she do?"

"She was brilliant. I've never heard that text sound so much like a declaration of war. It reminded me of why it never used to be read in English, only Latin."

They all laughed.

"How was your sermon?" asked Ellie.

"I'm afraid you and Sarah put paid to anyone remembering that."

"You can always give it again next Christmas like other vicars do," said Isabelle. "Meanwhile, it's time for this old family member to be asleep in the hay. Or should I say it's time I hit the hay? Isn't that the expression in America, Ellie? I'm knackered."

Graham stood up to give her a kiss. "Good night then, Is. Happy Christmas."

The girl bent over and kissed Ellie good night too.

"Happy Christmas, Isabelle. And thanks so much for coming with me."

"No problem. It was a real adventure."

"Is that good?" asked Ellie, and Isabelle smiled.

Friday, December 25
Christmas Day
Chapter 4

Once Isabelle had gone to bed, Graham stoked the fire, refreshed their drinks, and said, "So, have you had time to develop a theory about how that baby ended up in our crèche?" He swirled his whisky as if the answer might float up from its fumes.

"You mean while we were waiting in the emergency room, surrounded by the sick, the lost, the bleeding, and the hysterical?"

"I mean I'm sure you had the same thought I had the moment you saw her—that it was strange we'd just been discussing a runaway rumored to be pregnant and suddenly an infant materializes on our doorstep."

"True. You think she could be Anthea Davies' child then?"

"It's possible, isn't it?"

Ellie shrugged. "Possible covers a very wide range of events."

"Mrs. Bigelow claims she saw a young dark-haired woman with a bundle in her arms go into the church just after the Crib Service. She thought it was one of the mothers going back to retrieve something she'd left behind."

Ellie laughed. "We both know how much weight to give that report." Geraldine Bigelow was a widow who claimed to have had a successful career as an opera singer in Europe. Now she lived in a cottage across from St. Michael's and The Vicarage and devoted her time to watching the comings and goings of everyone at that end of the village.

"The doctor did say the baby was only a few hours old. That means if she were Anthea's, she must have been nearby, giving birth, while we were talking to her parents. That seems very, very unlikely."

Graham looked chagrined. "You're right. I'm just dreaming up ways to solve the whole problem of the Davies family by breakfast."

Ellie got up and gave him a hug. "I don't think that's going to happen, but the baby, whomever she is, is safe. At least, I hope so. Maybe I should call and check up on her."

The nurse who answered the phone sounded tired, but her voice brightened when Ellie explained why she was calling. "Yes, we have her here," she said. "She's been admitted to the Special Care Baby Unit. I'm afraid that's all I am allowed to say. We only give information to family members."

"But this patient doesn't have any family members. I'm the one who brought her in."

"Oh yes, I see," said the nurse, uncertainly, and Ellie suddenly couldn't bear the thought of that tiny baby alone in the hospital on the first night of her life.

"Good," she said, as if the nurse had agreed that Ellie was family. "Can I visit her then? Now?" she heard herself say, despite the late hour.

There was a pause then the nurse said, "Family members may visit the babies on that Unit at any time. I suppose, under the circumstances, that includes you."

"I'm on my way," said Ellie and hung up before either of them could have second thoughts.

In the sitting room, Graham had dozed off again in his leather chair, but he woke up right away. "She's all right?" he asked. There were circles of fatigue under his eyes.

"They wouldn't really say. She's in something called the Special Care Baby Unit."

"It's probably just routine until they can check her out thoroughly." He stood up, yawning.

"Maybe, but I want to go see for myself. Now. I mean I hardly got a chance to see her before they took her, and I'm much too wound up to sleep. I'd like to sit with her for a while."

"Would you like me to come too?"

"No, that's okay. You need to sleep. I promise to drive carefully, and I won't stay long."

"What's going on? I thought you were coming to bed," said Isabelle, reappearing in her nightgown. Her blonde hair hung over her shoulders in two long braids, and she looked about eight years old.

"Ellie's going to pop over to the hospital and check on the baby."

"Oh, good idea," said Isabelle, sitting down on the sofa as if she had never said she was exhausted. "I've been lying awake thinking about hot chocolate."

"That sounds great," said Ellie, and she felt a slight pang of regret as she left them heating milk in the kitchen, while she bundled up to brave the winter night.

The cottages in the village were almost all dark now; only one or two still showed a light. Someone wrapping presents. Someone lonely and wakeful. It was strange to be going out again, but she knew it was the right thing to do, and not only for herself and the baby. Graham and Isabelle should have some time alone tonight, some space to be together without her, but she did not want to feel "surplus to requirements," as the English would say. The best way to avoid that was to be useful to someone else.

The snow had stopped, and from behind the scudding clouds, the moon lit the landscape with a shimmering silver light. She sang as she cruised along the empty roads: "Yet in thy dark streets shineth the everlasting light, the hopes and fears of all the years are met in thee tonight."

But what exactly did that bit about hopes and fears mean? Ellie wondered, as she pulled into the nearly deserted parking lot of the Victorian pile that had become Kingbrook Regional Hospital.

She hurried inside, took the elevator to the fourth floor, and found her way to the Special Care Baby Unit. This turned out to be a quiet, dimly lit room serving eight babies and a lot of equipment. The nurse in charge showed Ellie to the infant she now referred to as "your baby", who was asleep in a clear plastic bassinet with IV antibiotics in one arm, a nasal cannula for oxygen and a feeding tube in her nose. All around her, monitors tracking her vital signs flashed and beeped. If Ellie hadn't been assured that all this was necessary, she would have thought the baby looked better in the manger. She was terribly small: a scrap of human being with wisps of dark hair sticking out from the little cap they had put on her head and the tiniest of fists raised above her blanket. That fist made her think of herself.

It made her think of Anthea too. She studied the little face but there was no way she could see a resemblance to the young woman she knew only from a photograph. She was just a newborn baby.

"How is she? Is she sick?" Ellie asked a plump young nurse, who was making rounds checking all the babies' monitors.

"She has a fever, so there's a risk of pneumonia, but she's survived one close call already, hasn't she? I heard you're the one who found her."

"Yes, I am. But, you know, there was nothing heroic about it. If I hadn't noticed her, someone else would have. The church was full of people."

"Well, lucky for her she didn't have to wait too long. If you'd like a cup of tea, let me know."

Finally the nurse finished her rounds, and Ellie was alone, seated by the bassinet, watching the baby breathe. "Who are you?" she wanted to ask, and it was strange to think that, complete as the baby was, with complex systems already humming along, she might never know that basic information about herself.

Ellie stroked her velvety little arm with one finger. She'd never been much of a baby person: she hadn't cared for dolls and didn't want to play mommy or babysit for the neighbors. She had supposed this was part of being an only child—that she always viewed herself as one of the adults. Smaller, but same as.

Tonight, though, she wanted to be the mother this baby should have had at her side. Since she didn't know any lullabies, she sang Christmas carols in a voice no louder than a whisper and held the tiny hand that opened and clutched her finger.

She woke with a start, when the plump nurse came back on rounds again. Suddenly the oddness of her being there—on Christmas morning no less—made her blush. She rose, touched the baby's cheek gently, then pulled on her coat and said good night.

At home Hector looked up from his basket and woofed in greeting. From the state of the kitchen, she could tell Graham and Isabelle had advanced from hot chocolate to sandwiches—and had left a sandwich for her with a goodnight note they had both signed. The note, which she tucked into her pocket, made her very happy, and she ate the sandwich quickly, looking out the window at the starry night.

It was after three a.m. when she finally slid under the duvet warmed by Graham's body. As she settled herself, she thought of the baby alone in her bassinet surrounded by machines and wondered what would become of her. The familiar words of the chorale that she had heard the choir rehearsing the day before came back to her: "This child now weak in infancy, our confidence and joy shall be." From generation to generation, this was surely the hope of every parent, but how often did things turn out that way?

All we want for Christmas is our Anthea. Please help.

It was Morag who alerted Ellie that the story of the abandoned baby was trending on social media. She had been still half-asleep, trying to get down a cup of tea before church, when her phone beeped, alerting her that she had a text.

"You're big news today. See Twitter," she read and closed the phone immediately, glancing up at Graham and Isabelle. Whatever people were saying online, they were unaware of it. He was eating a mini mince pie with his coat on, his cheeks still pink from an early round of shoveling snow and a hot bath. Isabelle was in her nightgown, absorbed in studying a cookbook, with her feet up on a chair. Ellie decided not to look at what was being posted or say anything to them.

Graham had told her this service was usually a quiet one. Most people had come the day before so this morning they stayed home to open gifts, cook Christmas lunch, or entertain guests. But this year proved to be an exception.

There was a crowd in front of the church and a gaggle of photographers and reporters milling around. As the church warden, Charles Bell took his responsibility for the property seriously and stood on the front steps, red-faced and angry, trying to prevent any media interlopers from disrupting the Christmas service. He looked relieved at the sight of Graham, but had only a scowl for Ellie as if she had contacted the journalists herself. Never before her arrival in Little Beecham had St. Michael's generated interest from even the local media, much less anyone else. She was sorry now that she hadn't passed on Morag's warning to Graham.

"Tell us what happened," demanded one reporter who shoved a tablet at them showing the online headline: "Jesus Has Left the Building!" A dimly lit photo of Graham escorting Ellie and the baby out of the church accompanied the story.

"No Room at the Inn, Baby Is Abandoned," shouted the headline to a story that focused on how hard life is for poor mothers in the UK and how often they ended up homeless.

"Live Baby in Manger! Church of England Sinks to New Low to Attract Congregations," declared another that decried the decline of the state religion.

"Crimestoppers Seek Missing Mother! Call This Number Now!" appeared in bold at the end of every story.

Neither Graham nor Ellie had time to react before a police car pulled up in front of the church. A young constable stepped out, looking grumpy, as if he had been called away from his Christmas celebration for no good reason. But Mr. Bell, who must have rung for help, rushed to his side with relief, and he did manage to clear a path for Ellie and Graham to enter the church without being interviewed.

Mrs. Bell, dressed today in an emerald green suit, hovered anxiously inside the doors and tried to persuade Ellie that she should join her and her husband in the warden's pew as if she needed the Bells for protection. As politely as possible, Ellie declined her offer, but she did choose a seat where she could not be photographed with the crèche in the background. As people poured in, many went to gawk at the crèche even though there was nothing to see except the usual plaster figure in the manger.

The vigorous work of the bellringers dampened conversation and then Mr. Dunn began to play the organ with all the stops out. This eventually conveyed to most people that a service was about to begin. Nonetheless she could see them documenting everything Graham said and did while he assiduously ignored them. They exchanged knowing looks over the choice of the carol “What Child Is This?” and closed with a lusty performance of “Joy to the World” in case anyone was recording the moment for broadcast or posterity.

Ellie was annoyed. She wasn’t used to the role of defending the sacred nature of religious holidays, but if any part of Christmas ought still to be held apart from the circus of modern life, she thought this was it. Not that anyone cared about her opinion.

During tea after the service, she confined her remarks to “Happy Christmas.” She’d brought over the last of Mrs. Finch’s supply of mini mince pies, and the hungry mob decimated them, leaving behind only crumbs and teetering stacks of dirty cups.

Some of the villagers were more obliging about discussing the discovery of the baby than Ellie was. Mrs. Bigelow was on hand, in a long scarlet cloak, if not to celebrate the birth of Jesus, then certainly to take the opportunity to repeat her story about seeing a dark-haired woman with a bundle to anyone who would listen. She further embellished her account by declaring that she was sure the young woman was the very same one whose face was on the MISSING posters that had cropped up in the village.

“It was dark, wasn’t it, Mrs. Bigelow? And snowing?” Ellie couldn’t help saying. “That must have made it hard to see anything clearly.”

"Yes," she agreed, "but the church's porch light is bright, and I am directly across the street. There is no doubt in my mind what I saw." This theory quickly became conclusive evidence that the baby's mother was Anthea Davies.

"Why on earth would a young woman from Pidlington abandon her newborn child in Little Beecham? She has no family or ties here," said Mrs. Bell so angrily that her Christmas bell earrings jingled.

"It seems obvious to me. The father must be from the village," said Mrs. Bigelow, with her usual confidence. "By leaving the baby here on such a public occasion, he could hardly escape knowing about his birth. I'm sure there is a message in that."

Ellie had to admit this had not occurred to her. "Her birth," she said. "The baby is a girl." With the rest of the crowd rendered speechless by this exciting news, her words came out sounding too loud.

The looks that passed from person to person showed that each was calculating which men in Little Beecham might have had the opportunity to become involved with a beautiful Oxford undergraduate. But this was not something to discuss in church. Suddenly everyone needed to get back home. It was Christmas after all. No time to dawdle.

Ellie accepted Mrs. Bell's offer of help with the clean up, even though it meant listening to her indignant remarks about people who came to church as if it were simply a tourist destination and how Little Beecham was in danger of becoming uninhabitable like so many other Cotswold villages if it continued to be the subject of so much attention. Ellie nodded and boxed up the cups and saucers as fast as she could, her mind fixed firmly on getting home without saying a word she would later regret.

They had just finished and were putting on their coats, when a young woman with a parka over a white uniform came through the front door and headed straight for her.

"Hello, Mrs. Kent," the woman said, holding out a cool, pale hand. "I'm Vera Skinner. We haven't met, but I saw you at the hospital last night. I just got off duty and, you know, I couldn't go home without stopping to see where the little Christmas baby was found. I also hoped I might see you, so I could let you know that she is doing better. I know you were concerned about her."

"Thank you!" said Ellie. "That's so kind of you. I was planning to call the hospital this morning."

They walked over to the crèche, and Ellie pointed to the manger: "That's where she was left."

The young woman stared at the spot as if she expected all the figures to come to life under her gaze. "It really was a miracle, wasn't it?"

"Hmm," said Ellie, who did not believe in miracles.

"We don't see many abandoned babies at Kingbrook, but whoever left her here clearly meant her to be found. And the mother might turn up, you know. I've read sometimes they leave their babies on an impulse, because they can't cope, but then they want them back. Christmas is such a hard time for mums."

"Yes," said Ellie, picturing that newspaper headline about poor and homeless mothers.

"There was one odd thing though. When we unwrapped the baby's blanket, we found herbs on her. In her clothes. Like someone had put a spell on her or something."

Ellie felt the hairs on her arms rise. "Herbs?" Vera pronounced the word like the man's name.

The nurse nodded. “Matron thought it was some kind of preparation for death, but another sister who cooks a lot smelled it, and she said it was a herb.”

“Do you remember what kind?” asked Ellie, catching on.

She shook her head. “I’m afraid I get by on frozen ready meals, but it was a girl’s name, I think.”

“Rosemary?”

“Yes, that was it. Sister said she smelled like a roasting lamb. You can be sure we gave her a good bath, and now she smells like a baby ought, not like some. . . I don’t know what. Meat.”

“Rosemary is for remembrance,” Ellie said suddenly.

“What?”

“It’s from *Hamlet*. You know, Shakespeare. ‘There’s rosemary, that’s for remembrance’,” said Ellie, quoting the line. “Maybe that’s what the mother meant.”

“With all due respect, there was nothing—poetic—about finding those herbs wrapped into the baby’s clothes.”

Ellie wasn’t about to argue the point, but this first bit of evidence about the identity of the baby’s mother was certainly intriguing. What mother abandoning her newborn would leave her with such an enigmatic message? Someone who liked to think she was descended from Shakespeare? She would have to try to find out.

But first, they had to run the gauntlet of Christmas: the presents, the whirlwind of paper and ribbon, the roasting of the turkey with stuffing and sausage links, the bread sauce, the Christmas crackers, the paper crowns, and the flaming Christmas pudding. They sat in the seldom-used paneled dining room lit by candles, and Graham and Isabelle put on a good show for her, making her first English Christmas a splendid one. Although the bang when they yanked open their crackers made Hector howl, even he wore a paper crown.

Graham was delighted with his new fife and surprised that she remembered his story about losing his grandfather's fife in a pub when he was at Oxford. He played a dance tune, and Isabelle and Hector danced. Isabelle loved her earrings, and they all enjoyed poring over the pile of new books they had given each other. But Graham outdid them all by giving Ellie a gold bracelet engraved with "Let me not to the marriage of true minds admit impediments" and by getting the family a second used Mini Cooper. Now they had a blue one, as well as the red.

"Three drivers and one car is not an equation for a happy family these days," he said, by way of explanation, as he handed each of them keys to both cars. After they had eaten their fill, they took their new car for a spin through the snowy countryside, taking turns at the wheel, and then they headed home for tea and the Queen's Christmas message. More than anything else, listening to this made Ellie feel she had now become truly English.

By late afternoon, with Graham reading by the fire and Isabelle off on a ramble with Hector, she decided to make her Christmas call to her parents then go back over to the hospital.

For years her family had gone through the holidays without any reference to that unfortunate period—as her parents saw it—when her cousin Tom Shackford came to live with them. Because he was older than she was, they had always blamed him more than Ellie for the way their relationship "got out of hand." Ellie wondered if that time had been on her mother's mind this year because she'd moved so far away. Left them again, as it might seem to her. Or maybe she'd sent the ornament with Tom's name on it simply because he was Ellie's past, not theirs, and they had no desire to be reminded of it.

She listened to the phone ring and promised herself to avoid any potentially controversial topics, but slipped up almost immediately by mentioning the baby.

"You *found* a baby in the manger?" her mother asked. "A live baby?"

"Yes, Mom. Newborn, abandoned, but very much alive."

"I must say I hoped you'd start a family now that you've settled down, but I never imagined it would happen that way."

Her father laughed. "Ellie always does the unexpected, Mother, you know that," he said. "And are you going to solve the mystery of where she came from?"

"You never know, Dad. It's early days, as they say here."

"Well, keep us posted. We're on the edge of our seats."

"As always," said her mother.

Ellie promised she would, and they said their goodbyes.

After she'd hung up, it took a few deep breaths to bring her slowly back from California to England, Little Beecham, The Vicarage. The past to the present. Then she grabbed her bag, put on her coat, and headed out.

The hospital parking lot was jammed, and the wards bustled with visitors, no one wanting to let sick family and friends spend the whole holiday alone. On the Special Care Baby Unit, several families were visiting, and Ellie saw them looking at her surreptitiously though no one spoke to her. She supposed the new arrival's story had circulated among them.

She'd brought along a red bow that she tied to the baby's bassinet before she sat down and pulled the visitor's chair up close. This time, the baby grasped her finger right away when she touched her hand and stared at her with that all-knowing, unseeing new baby look. "Hello, little you," said Ellie, and the baby blinked.

A cheerful nurse from Jamaica wearing a Father Christmas hat over her neat dreadlocks came by on rounds to check on the babies, pronounced that her baby looked better, and laughed when Ellie asked if, by any chance, she'd had other visitors that day.

"This one? More like everyone, not anyone, come to see her," she said. "We've had no end of aunties and uncles wanting to get a look at her, but we knew she was in the news, so we sent them all away."

Ellie was shocked. "You mean like journalists? They're unbelievable. I was hoping, I don't know, I guess I was hoping the mother would come."

"No one owning up to that has been here, but she wouldn't, would she?"

"I suppose not. I heard she wrapped rosemary into the baby's blanket before leaving her."

The nurse's eyes widened. "Someone told you about that, eh? It's true. I saw it. I suspect she was trying to protect her."

"Protect her from what?"

"Evil spirits, of course," she said, dropping her voice low.

"Oh!" said Ellie, who instinctively placed her hand on the baby's head.

The nurse nodded. "There's no business as usual about that one," she said and bustled off.

Ellie pondered that encounter all the way home. She much preferred her own explanation for the rosemary to the one the nurse had put forward. Remembrance was benign, evil spirits were not. Still, she had to admit that mothers did not abandon their babies because all was well with them and their world.

She pulled into the driveway of The Vicarage just in time to see Graham loading a basket into the blue Mini.

"Where are you off to?" Ellie asked, when she had parked.

"I've been checking on elderly parishioners, and one of them said the neighbor who usually brings her Christmas lunch never showed up. I thought I'd drop by and bring her some of ours. Want to come?"

"I'd love to," she said, climbing into the front seat.

"To be honest, I'm glad to get out of the house for a while," said Graham, turning onto the B road away from the village. "There've been a lot of calls from reporters and a stream of people going into the church that I don't think came because it's Christmas."

"You never know. You once told me, bring the body and the mind will follow."

"Did I?" Graham laughed. "And has it?"

"I'm still a work in progress, but I envision a great increase in the size of the congregation soon. By the busload, in fact. Mrs. Bell's worst nightmare."

"Charles Bell wouldn't be glad about that either. He called this afternoon to complain about the wear and tear created by people who never put money in the collection plate. How's our new daughter?"

"She's attached to so many machines, it's a little frightening, but they say she's doing all right, and I heard some interesting things while I was there," said Ellie, who went on to tell him about the rosemary and the journalists.

"Protecting her from evil spirits? I've never heard that one before. Maybe her mother thought leaving her in the church would be a form of protection too. I wonder if we'll ever know," said Graham, as he passed through the village of Chadstone and turned down a single-track road that ran between tall hedges.

Mrs. Esther Daley's stone cottage was at the end of a narrow drive. It was draped with snow and, though one light burned, no smoke was coming from the chimney. As they pulled up, they saw the old lady waiting for them at the front door, wrapped in a heavy blanket.

Not only hadn't her neighbors arrived with her Christmas lunch, she told them, but also her fire had gone out, and the ground was so slippery she'd been afraid to try to get more wood. Ellie went quickly inside with her, carrying the food and supplies they'd brought, while Graham went to the woodpile for armloads of firewood to rebuild the fire in the woodstove.

Before long the little kitchen had begun to warm up and fill with the delicious scents of hot turkey and burning wood. The cottage had only two rooms downstairs and two up, and the wind rattled the windows in their frames, but everything was tidy and clean from the rag rugs on the floor to the dishes lined up on the sideboard.

Mrs. Daley, a tiny woman with a long frizzy tail of gray hair, asserted her role as hostess, making tea for Ellie and Graham and setting out a plate of homemade biscuits. But when they all sat down at her table, and she had a plate of hot food in front of her, Ellie could see relief relax the tight lines in her face.

As soon as she had eaten, she wanted to hear all about them and their Christmas.

"My goodness," she said, when Ellie recounted the story of the baby in the manger. "That's one of those tales that is both terribly sad and happy."

"Have you ever heard of someone using rosemary that way?" Ellie asked.

Mrs. Daley bobbed her head from side to side. "Not like that, but I am not surprised. It has many powerful associations. When I was young, you put rosemary into your wedding bouquet to ensure that your husband would be faithful." Then she added, with twinkling eyes, "Or maybe to ensure that you would be faithful yourself!" and they all laughed. "Anyway, God makes babies resilient, doesn't he, Father? It's the young woman who left her that my heart goes out to."

"I know, but maybe she'll turn up," said Ellie, taking Mrs. Daley's plate to the sink.

"Oh, don't spoil me," she said, getting up herself. "I can do that. But if you would do me a favor before you go, I wish you would check on my neighbors to be sure they're all right. It's very odd for them to go away without telling me. I usually take care of their cats."

"Of course," said Graham. "We'd be happy to. What's their name?"

"Woodman. Bill and his daughter Deborah. I'm sure you remember them, Father."

"I do. Though it has been years since I've seen them. Can we do anything else for you?"

The old lady shook her head, but Graham stoked the fire, while Ellie found her glasses and her book, and refilled her cup of tea, before they set off.

The Woodmans lived farther down that same single-track road. A handsome sign for Woodman Woodworks hung at the end of a drive leading to a large stone farmhouse with a new one-story workshop to the left and a barn behind. Ellie noticed that the drive showed only faint car tracks in the snow, and there was no car parked out front, although there were lights on in the house.

"You said you know these people?" she asked, as they got out of the car.

"They lived in Little Beecham about ten years ago, I'd say. There was a little boy then too, as I recall, but he died of meningitis, and the marriage split up soon after."

"So they'll be surprised to see us."

"Yes, but that's all right. Mrs. Daley sent us," said Graham, who knocked at a handsome raised panel door.

"I think they must be gone," said Ellie. Through the window to the right of the door, she could see into the well-appointed sitting room, where there was a decorated Christmas tree with a pile of unopened gifts under it. "My guess would be since yesterday. Or longer."

Graham knocked again and then tried the door, which turned out to be unlocked. "Hello?" he called, sticking his head in. "Is anyone at home?"

They immediately heard loud meows and the soft thud of running cat feet. Two big gray tabby cats raced down the stairs and circled their legs hungrily.

"See, I was right," said Ellie.

"Why don't you find them something to eat while I take a quick look around," said Graham.

In the kitchen she discovered signs that someone had been preparing tea, but the meal had never been eaten. The cats had polished off the butter on a plate and gnawed on a loaf of bread. A small jug that must have held milk had been turned over and was now empty. Apparently they were not hungry enough to eat just anything, because only the sauce from a pan of baked beans had been licked up. Ellie opened a can of cat food she found in the pantry and cleaned up the remains of the half-finished meal.

"There's definitely no one here," said Graham when he came downstairs.

"What should we do? Call the police?"

"I don't know. There's probably a simple explanation, although they obviously left in a hurry. I'll leave a note asking them to let us know when they get back, and we can follow up if we don't hear from them."

Before they left, Ellie refilled the cat dishes with dry food and fresh water, then they checked the outbuildings, but found nothing: the workshop was locked and the barn, empty. "I'm glad there are no cows waiting to be milked," said Ellie.

As they walked back to the Mini, she noticed that the air had become more humid. The snow on the ground was getting softer, almost mushy.

Graham noticed it too. "The weather is changing," he said. "I think it's going to rain tonight."

"So here endeth the white Christmas," said Ellie.

Saturday, December 26
Boxing Day
Chapter 5

The sound of pouring rain woke Ellie during the night, and when she looked out the window in the morning, she saw that the snow had been washed away except for the sagging piles created when they shoveled. The dreary scene added to her feeling of post-holiday let down, but in the kitchen she found Isabelle and Graham busily preparing sandwiches and a large thermos of hot sweet tea. To them, the disappearance of the snow was good news: it meant the Chipping Martin Hunt's Boxing Day meet could take place as usual.

"Why didn't you wake me up?" she asked, even though she knew she sounded grumpy. She filled a bowl with oatmeal from a pot on the Aga and sat down to eat.

"We thought you'd enjoy a bit of a lie-in after your long day yesterday," said Graham, giving her a kiss.

"Besides, today's a big day too. Your first hunt," said Isabelle, as she handed her a mug of tea.

"We're not hunting, I hope," said Ellie, who did not think the English love of hunting was one of their better traits.

"Of course not. We follow the hunt. It's part of the tradition."

"In the car," Graham added. "You'll see. It's brilliant."

"For everyone except the fox."

"Oh, you Americans," said Isabelle. "You always take the side of the fox. What about all the poor chickens, rabbits, pheasants, cats, and everything else that foxes eat?" She was looking very much the country girl today with her jeans tucked into her wellingtons, an Irish cable knit sweater, and her hair in one thick braid.

"Please. Don't remind me." Ellie pushed her oatmeal aside.

"Anyway there is no fox now. That was outlawed years ago. The hounds chase a fox-scented cloth instead."

"That seems really weird, but if there's no bloodshed, I guess I'm for it," said Ellie and, while she went upstairs to get an extra sweater, Graham and Isabelle loaded the car.

They set off for Chipping Martin under a low, dark sky, but at least it wasn't raining at the moment. They would not have to get drenched as part of their pursuit of the hunt.

The Chipping Martin Hunt had been a source of pride since 1835, Graham said, and the 300-year-old market square around the Victorian Town Hall was packed with eager spectators. Once she was there, with a cup of hot tea to warm her hands, Ellie had to admit that the scene was exciting to witness.

Many of the riders wore black velvet hunt caps and the scarlet jackets called hunting pinks, according to Isabelle. They sat high on their perfectly groomed horses, as the hounds milled around with their whip-like tails waving. A stout white-haired man circulated amongst the riders with a tray of small glasses of port, and they drank as if they were partaking of communion. Ellie figured they were praying for the resurrection of the Empire—or at the very least a reversal of the fox-hunting ban. She was surprised at the number of children, including some very young ones, riding small ponies led by their parents, who were intent on giving them a taste for the hunt. All were tense and excited, ready for their purpose.

When the Huntsman blew his horn, the spectators moved to the side so that the riders could form up behind the pack. At the second blast, they began a slow procession down the high street, and the clatter of horses' hooves on the street paved with setts overwhelmed all other sounds.

As soon as the last riders cleared the square and broke into a trot, the crowd began to disperse—some to pubs, but many others to their cars. "Come on!" said Isabelle eagerly, urging them into the stream of traffic heading into the country.

Like all true aficionados, Graham and Isabelle knew the route the hunt would probably take, so for the next hour they drove up winding roads and down muddy lanes, pulling over whenever they reached a spot where the hounds and riders would come into view. Then they stood in the dank air, staring across empty fields, straining their ears for the hounds' cries and the blast of the Huntsman's horn. When the baying hounds did appear, streaming across a field or through the bare woods with the string of galloping horses behind, there was a moment of excitement for the watchers, and then everyone got back into their cars to go to the next overlook.

Ellie kept reminding herself that no fox was being torn to smithereens by that pack of hounds, but she wasn't so sure that was true when she saw them pool up around something in the woods at the far side of the field where they stood. The first riders to arrive dismounted quickly and began pushing the hounds away from whatever it was they were after. As more riders pulled up, they too dismounted and joined the fray.

"Something's gone wrong, hasn't it?" asked Ellie.

The riders appeared upset by what had been found; one leaned against a tree and looked as if he were vomiting. Along the line of watchers, people stared through binoculars with serious expressions.

"I think I should go down there. Stay with the car, Isabelle," said Graham, as he climbed over a stile, and Ellie scrambled after him. They slipped and slid down the sloping field to the woods as fast as they could, and finally reached the spot where more riders were still pulling up.

"What's happened?" asked Graham. At the sight of him, the riders fell silent, their faces pale. Even without his clerical collar, they knew him. Some removed their caps, and others took swigs from their flasks. "Has there been an accident?"

"No accident," said a red-coated man whom Ellie was surprised to recognize as Dr. Whitcomb from the Chipping Martin Surgery. It was only then that she got a glimpse of what had attracted the hounds, and it had nothing to do with the hunt.

The body of a young woman was hanging by a rope from a branch of an oak tree. She was dripping wet, and her clothes looked as if they had frozen and thawed with the changing weather. It was almost hard to imagine that sodden figure with its discolored face as a living person, except for the dark hair, which clung to her cheeks. Ellie's first thought was: Anthea. And her second: she would surely want to brush that hair away, if she were alive.

The impression that here was the girl she had offered to help find was so strong that she was surprised when Graham asked quietly, "Does anyone know her?" The riders looked at each other, but no one showed any sign of recognition or offered up a name.

As Graham bowed his head to say a prayer, Ellie's brain whirled with questions. Why did this have to happen? And why here? Why now?

Afterward, she couldn't remember what made her approach the body, but she did. And that's when, looking up, she saw the tattoo. There was a delicate circlet of spiky green sprigs with purple flowers around the woman's left wrist. Rosemary.

Ellie lurched backward, nearly tripping on an exposed root, and might have fallen if Graham had not reached out to touch her shoulder and caught her. His eyes held a warning look, and he nodded toward the car, indicating that they should go.

She would have liked to stay until the police came, but he was right. They had no part in what would come next, and she could see Isabelle up at the far side of the field, watching through binoculars, impatiently waiting for their return.

The doctor and the Master of the hunt conferred and agreed that the hunt had to stop. The Master told the riders, "This may be a crime scene, even though the hounds and horses have already put paid to much of the evidence."

"I'm sure the police will want to speak with the riders who arrived first," said Dr. Whitcomb, and they came forward to wait. While the other riders quietly dispersed, the Huntsman began to round up the hounds.

Ellie and Graham slogged back up the muddy hill without speaking until they were some distance away. Then they paused, looking back. They could still see scarlet jackets flashing amongst the trees. The riders waiting for the police.

"Ellie, do you think that's Anthea?" Graham asked hesitantly, rubbing his chin.

"I don't know. It kind of looked like her. Don't you agree?"

He nodded and began walking again.

"Did you notice she had rosemary tattooed around her wrist? You know. As in the herb wrapped in the baby's clothes."

"No, I didn't. I was too caught up in thinking how ghastly it was that she'd been hanging there in all that weather—and how her parents will feel when they hear the news. So you're saying Mrs. Bigelow was right? She was the baby's mother?"

"I don't know, because if she is Anthea and she's the mother, and she was right nearby, what kind of situation was she in that caused her to cut herself off from everyone?"

"You're right, and we may never find out," said Graham. An answer that did not please Ellie one bit.

As if the day hadn't become depressing enough, the sky drew lower and darker and a cold rain that fell like nails began before they even reached the car. Back home, Ellie and Isabelle huddled by the sitting room fire, but Graham dried off and changed into his Morris whites. Beecham Morris was scheduled to dance at The Bull in Kingbrook in celebration of Boxing Day, a tradition carried out by sides across the country, and he wasn't about to let them down. The insistent jingling of the bells around his legs made an incongruously cheerful sound, but after he left, the silence was worse.

Isabelle had been subdued ever since she heard what they saw in the woods and took to the sofa in the sitting room with Hector and a book, once she was warm and dry. Ellie retreated to her study to think. She was supposed to meet with Mr. and Mrs. Davies at one o'clock. But what could she possibly say to them?

There was no news from Seamus in her email, so she reread the accounts of Anthea's disappearance and looked at the notes she'd jotted down after the first conversation with her parents. These bits of information only generated more questions, no answers.

For Anthea to abandon her baby and commit suicide, she must have felt terribly alone at the end of her life. So what happened to the mysterious friend who helped her move, and where was that person when these bitter events transpired?

Reluctantly, Ellie went down to the bedroom to change her clothes for the meeting. Her heart gravitated to black, but it seemed inappropriate. She was not the one in mourning. She was still mulling over the various options in her closet when her phone rang. It was Arthur Davies, and his voice sounded stretched to the breaking point.

"We have to cancel. Something's happened. The police want us to come to Chipping Martin." And then, without a goodbye, he hung up before Ellie could say a word.

She sat down on the bed with the phone still in her hand, picturing that trip, so full of dread and hope, but the voice in her head was her own father's saying: "I was afraid I would never see you again. Can you imagine what that was like?"

She could not. Not then, not now, but she suddenly felt as if she needed to see the baby before—what? Before she became someone else. Anthea's daughter. The Davies' granddaughter. No longer her "little you."

Not that it wasn't a good thing for her to find her family. It was what she wanted for her. Absolutely, without question. But she had to admit a part of her had enjoyed having people refer to her as "her baby" as if finding her had somehow made the infant her own.

She went down to the sitting room, where Isabelle had fallen asleep on the sofa. "Sorry to bother you," she said. "I'm going to run over to the hospital for a bit, but

I'll be back before tea. Will you take Hector for his walk?"

Hector lifted his head, going from sound sleep to wide awake in an instant at the word "walk." Isabelle was a little slower. She stretched, and her book fell to the floor.

"Sure, I have to get up anyway," she said. "But I won't be home for tea. I'm meeting some old school friends at the pub, and we're going to make a night of it. I think they're all panting to hear about our latest mystery."

"Is that okay with you?"

Isabelle shrugged. "I hate to say it, but in a way it's been brilliant. Blokes who steered a mile from me because I was the vicar's daughter now want to buy me drinks and pump me for information about the investigation."

Ellie laughed. "I don't think your father would be too delighted to hear that."

"Then isn't it a good thing that he doesn't know," she said with a saucy smile.

The nurses on the Special Care Baby Unit greeted her in a friendly way today. The holiday atmosphere continued with a plate of red and green biscuits on the nurses' station, and visitors coming and going.

The baby was still hooked up to the support systems, but she gurgled and burbled and wanted to suck on Ellie's finger. Ellie thought she seemed more alert than before, though mainly she couldn't help but be struck by the contrast between the faces of the sweet living baby and the dead woman she had seen that morning who might have been her mother. She found herself hoping there was no connection between them: that the coincidence of the rosemary was just that.

When the baby had drifted to sleep, she watched her for a while, then on an impulse, went out to the visitors' lounge and punched in the number of Detective Inspector Derek Mullane. They had only spoken once since the days when he had Ellie pegged as a murder suspect. She'd bumped into him while Christmas shopping at the bookstore in Chipping Martin, and Mullane had introduced her to his wife as if they were neighbors, not former adversaries. His wife was a tall, athletic woman with a friendly smile, and he had seemed almost human dressed in something other than a suit and tie.

Now she listened impatiently to the blurr blurr of his phone and had begun to expect she would get voice mail, when he picked up.

"DI Mullane?" she said. "This is Ellie Kent from Little Beecham calling."

"Hello, Mrs. Kent. I'd say it was a pleasant surprise to hear from you, except that it's not. A surprise, I mean."

Ellie was taken aback. "But it is pleasant."

"Of course."

"And why is it not a surprise?" she asked, although she suspected she knew the answer.

"Because I was called away from my family today to investigate a suspicious death, and I heard that you and your husband had already been there before me."

"A suspicious death? So you've already established that it wasn't suicide?"

"Mrs. Kent, why are you calling me? Isn't this a busy season for you at the church?"

"Christmas is over, and I do not work for the church. The reason I'm calling is that I might have some important information for you related to that death."

"Such as. . ."

"It's only relevant if the woman who was found dead had recently given birth. And I mean very recently."

"I'm listening."

"So she had."

"I didn't say that, but why do you ask?"

"Because, as you know, Graham and I were on the scene only minutes after the hounds found the body. We'd been watching the hunt from the road. So we saw her, and I noticed that she had a tattoo that might link her to the baby found at St. Michael's on Christmas Eve. You know about that, I assume?"

"Yes."

"Well, I found the baby, so I've been to see her, and the nurses told me that when they first undressed her there were sprigs of rosemary tucked in between the layers of her blanket."

"And you think this was a message."

"Yes. Rosemary is for remembrance."

"Is that an advert for perfume?"

"It's Shakespeare, Mullane. From a speech in *Hamlet* by Ophelia, a betrayed girl who kills herself."

"Well, if that's your theory you're off on the wrong foot. This young woman definitely did not kill herself."

Ellie drew in her breath sharply. "You mean it was murder?"

"I can't answer that, as you should know."

"But you've told her parents?"

"Once again, I have to ask you what your concern is in all of this."

"Mr. and Mrs. Davies came to see us. Graham and me. They asked for our help in finding their daughter. And then there's been this whole business with the baby. So certainly I'm involved."

"Mr. and Mrs. Davies. You're referring to the Anthea Davies who has been missing since October?"

"Of course. Who else?"

"Who else indeed. That is the question, as your Shakespeare would put it."

"He's your Shakespeare, Mullane. But what do you mean?"

"I mean we haven't spent our day eating leftover pudding, and we've already had Mr. and Mrs. Davies in to identify the body. Mr. Davies, I should say, since Mrs. Davies fainted."

"I'm not surprised. I can't think of anything more horrible. They desperately hoped she would come home."

"Well, she may yet, because the young woman found dead this morning was not Anthea Davies. She is still missing."

Ellie could hardly believe it. "So—"

"This one's identity is unknown."

"But she had recently had a baby?"

"That's all I'm going to say, except that I hope you're not going to get mixed up in this business, Mrs. Kent. It looks nasty."

"So you won't tell me, even for the baby's sake? If her mother's death was suspicious, she could be in danger too. Rosemary is also believed to protect babies from evil spirits."

"Didn't you hear what I just said? We have an investigation underway. Now you go back to your fireside, read one of those thick books you like so much, and be glad this isn't your job."

"All right. All right. Happy Christmas to you too, Mullane."

After they hung up, Ellie stood for a long time looking out into the darkness beyond the lighted hospital grounds. The rain had finally stopped, and she could see the villages scattered like constellations of stars in the night's landscape.

It was hard to sort out the jumble of relief and fear she felt. The whole scenario she'd been imagining since that morning had never happened. Anthea was not dead—at least as far as she knew—and this meant they had no new information at all regarding her whereabouts.

Ellie went back to the Unit and sat by the baby's bassinet. For the moment, no one else was there, and she was glad to be alone. She stroked the baby's belly and breathed in her warm baby smell. This news changed everything for her too. Her identity and history had become a blank once more.

Sunday, December 27
Chapter 6

In the media, the news about the body found on Boxing Day quickly became coupled with the discovery of the baby in the manger, despite a statement from the police that it was too soon to say anything about a link between them. Ellie was glad to see that the missing Oxford student was not put forward as the baby's mother. At least not yet.

Attendance at church was nearly equal to that of Christmas Eve, thanks to those who wanted to see the crèche and gossip. Ellie sat with Isabelle, who looked pale and rather hung over after her night of pub-crawling. She stared absently at her prayer book and only came alive when the doors opened, and she could be off. This time on a hike in the Malvern Hills, although the weather remained raw and damp.

After the service, Mr. and Mrs. Bell greeted this latest batch of visitors, exuding a chilly Christian forbearance. Ellie wondered if they really did prefer an empty church with the prayer books, hymnals, and kneelers all lined up neatly.

Priscilla Worthy had volunteered to help Ellie serve the tea and coffee, and she watched the Bells' royal progress through the congregation with ever so slightly pursed lips—her own sign of disapproval. To compensate, she urged everyone to take plenty of the homemade shortbread she had brought. They didn't need much encouragement for that.

Some visitors stared at Ellie, but none of them, she was amused to notice, seemed aware that the fluffy little old lady in layers of red and green Oxfam sweaters was one of Britain's most popular novelists. That was perfectly fine with Miss Worthy, who had only recently ceased to hide behind a pen name and was not entirely sure the change had been a good idea.

"You mustn't mind the Bells too much, you know," she said to Ellie, when there was a pause long enough for them to have their own tea and shortbread. "I believe they've both been quite unsettled over the past few months. It's not just your arrival, although they took a proprietary interest in Graham and Isabelle after Louise's death. I think Mary was very shocked by, well, let's just say, the events surrounding the man who died in the churchyard."

Ellie smiled at this example of Miss Worthy's modesty and discretion. "Their attitude bothers me more on Graham's behalf than my own," she said, observing that Charles Bell had cornered Graham by the front door—no doubt with more complaints about the unwanted publicity for St. Michael's.

"Exactly. What could he be on about now? He knows his role is to support the vicar, not harry him to bits—and you too. *You* didn't abandon that baby in the manger, after all."

Ellie laughed. "No, I didn't, and that's all I do know about her. That she's not mine."

"Well, then," Miss Worthy sipped her tea, cocked her head to one side like a bird listening for a worm, and added, "perhaps you might be thinking about how to find out more?"

Ellie smiled. "I'm as curious as the next person," she said.

"Of course. You know, I think it's been too long since we've had a good natter. Did you know that

Charlotte is working for me now?" Charlotte Worthy was her 17-year-old great-niece, who had a baby son named Dolphin. "She's handling something called my social media presence and does things like write a blog about what I do every day. None of it true, I might add. Except for bits like how I love to bake biscuits after hours of writing."

"Sounds like another anonymous novelist in the making."

"You might be right. You really should come and have tea with us, Mrs. Kent. You know Charlotte went to school with that missing girl everyone seemed to think was the baby's mother yesterday. Who knows what they think today."

"Is that so?" said Ellie. "When would you like me to come?"

"Would tomorrow at four be convenient? That's when we usually have a break."

"I'll be there," said Ellie, taking another of Miss Worthy's perfect buttery shortbreads.

On their way to Sunday lunch at The Bull—an old half-timbered pub in Kingbrook that served a great roast beef, Yorkshire pud, and three veg—Graham and Ellie stopped at the hospital to visit the baby. It was the first time he had seen her since she was rushed out of the church in Ellie's arms.

Her condition had continued to improve. Though she was still on oxygen and being fed by a nasal tube, they were both allowed to hold her briefly. Ellie was touched by how sweetly and expertly Graham nestled her against his chest.

"Do you have a name for her yet?" asked a smiling young nurse, who was changing the baby in the next bassinet.

Ellie blushed. “Do you think we should? Someone from her family might come forward soon to claim her.”

“Oh, that doesn’t matter. We usually name them if they don’t have one. It makes it easier. I’ve heard some of the other nurses calling her Rosie. Like for rosemary, you know?” she said knowingly.

“Rosie?” said Ellie, not sure this had a positive connotation in the baby’s case.

“I like that,” said Graham, who held her out to look in her face and began to sing softly, “Lo, how a rose e’er blooming from Jesse’s branch hath sprung. The tender floweret bright came in the cold of winter, when half-spent was the night.”

Ellie and the nurse fell silent, listening, and, when the nurse had left, Ellie said, “Okay, you’ve persuaded me. Rosie, it is.”

Graham set the newly named Rosie back in her bassinet and tucked the blankets around her. Then they both kissed her goodbye and left holding hands, almost as if they were her parents. But they weren’t.

Once they were outside, Ellie said, “I wonder how long it will be until we find out if the woman who died was her mother or not. It’s horrible to think of someone being murdered so soon after giving birth. What a legacy for Rosie.”

“Her mother might not be the murdered woman, despite your tattoo theory, but, if she were, you could also say that Rosie is the child of someone who fought hard to save her life—and succeeded.”

“You mean if the murderer had found both of them, he would have killed the baby too?”

“He—assuming it was a he—must have had powerful reasons for silencing the mother.”

“But the baby wouldn’t know anything about that. There would be no reason to kill her!”

"Indeed there would," said Graham. "A baby is a powerful piece of evidence, and he might not have wanted any such evidence to remain."

"That is a truly horrible thought, Father Kent. You do surprise me," said Ellie.

He smiled at her. "Looking for the light in people does not mean I can't see the dark."

That afternoon Graham had pastoral visits to make and left home in the red Mini before Ellie set off in the other car for her own pastoral call—her meeting with Mr. and Mrs. Davies. Pidlington was only 10 miles southwest of Little Beecham but there was no such thing as a direct route, and she had to turn around in narrow lanes three times before she found it. Except for the occasional bundled-up dog walker, she saw no one out and about and wondered how Isabelle and her friends were enjoying their hike. Most people seemed to have sensibly turned their backs on the raw, damp day in favor of dozing by the fire.

Villages in the Cotswolds generally have a prosperous picture-book exterior, but Pidlington was an exception. Its main point of interest was its pub, The George and Dragon, a down-at-the-heels establishment with a carved wooden dragon looming over its thatched roof. The dragon badly needed a touch up, as did the green paint on the shutters and doors. A few old buildings and a small church huddled around the pub, but they were surrounded by a sprawl of newer housing that aped the local architectural style while managing to have no personality at all. The Davies' house was one of these, and it took awhile to spot the number in the look-alike rows.

Mr. Davies opened the door when she rang, but he didn't look happy to see her. Since Christmas Eve, he seemed to have shrunk so that his clothes hung limply around him. He led her into what he called the lounge, where Mrs. Davies was seated in a rocker wrapped in a hot pink crocheted afghan that drained all the color out of her face. A Christmas tree stood in front of the window, blocking the light with its drooping branches, and the carpet underneath was littered with pine needles. Even the ornaments looked dispirited, and, if there had been gifts under the tree, they had been removed.

Frances Davies had gray circles under her eyes and looked at Ellie like a person coming out of anaesthesia, only slowly focusing on her presence. The hands resting on the afghan were papery and dry.

It was Mr. Davies who stirred himself, however reluctantly, to plump the pillow behind his wife and offer them both tea. Ellie suggested that she could help, but he refused, so she used the wait to take in the room's most notable feature—an array of framed photos of Anthea at all ages from chubby baby with a curled lock of dark hair sprouting from her head to Oxford undergraduate in her scholar's robe and mortarboard.

When they were alone with their mugs of tea in front of them, Mrs. Davies said, "I guess you've heard what happened. The police brought us in to view that body, and I thought I'd rather die myself, so it was Arthur who had to look at her. You can't imagine the dread and then the relief when it turned out she wasn't our Anthea."

"I don't think anyone who's never experienced it could," said Ellie quietly.

"But the worst time was when we got home. That's when I realized that part of me had actually hoped it would be her, so that the not knowing would be over. I wished for her to be found so badly that I didn't care anymore if she was dead."

"I'm so sorry. If you'd prefer to rest now, I can come back another day."

"No," she shook her head, suddenly vehement. "I can't sleep because I need to be doing something. I know now that I want Anthea found, no matter what that means."

Ellie swallowed hard. "All right. Then how would it be if you just talk about her and I'll listen. You'll be helping me to get to know her—and hopefully that will help us find her."

Mrs. Davies sighed and looked at the Christmas tree. "She's practically all I think about, and yet, the more I think, the less it seems I've ever really known her."

"I expect my mother would say the same thing," said Ellie. "But you probably do know her better than anyone else in the world."

A little color came into the woman's cheeks at her words, and she looked at her directly for the first time. "I'll tell you one thing. That baby is not hers. I saw her."

"You did?" said Ellie.

"Yes. Arthur doesn't know. He was very angry when he heard about her and that people were saying she was Anthea's. He said we should stay away, because our going there would only make people think the rumor was true, but I went anyway. I had to at least see her."

"So you went to the hospital on your own?"

Mrs. Davies smiled. "I did. And I walked right into that place where they have her with some other people visiting one of the other babies. No one sees older women, haven't you noticed that?"

Ellie suppressed a frown, not about being classed as an older woman, but because she had thought the Special Care Baby Unit had better security.

"She's nothing like Anthea," she repeated, as if this made it a fact. "Anthea was a lovely baby. Never sickly like that one. And for a long time she was never any trouble, but just so smart we had to stay on our toes to keep up with her. They wanted to push her ahead in school, but Dad and I felt it wouldn't be good for her to be singled out. We could give her what she needed at home."

"What was that like?" asked Ellie, who did her best not to show her annoyance at hearing Rosie described so negatively.

"Oh my. She had a new interest every week—and then she wanted to know everything about it. I had to take her to that library in Chipping Martin to get a stack of new books. The library van that comes around to the village wasn't good enough for her.

"Sometimes it would start with something she saw. Hedgehogs or badgers or stars. But she loved anything about our history early on. Other kids played with blocks. Anthea liked to play standing stones. By the time she was seven, she could recite all the kings and queens and their dates. That's what she was reading at Oxford. British history."

"Did she have friends who shared her interests?"

At this, her mother turned back to the window with its view beyond the Christmas tree of the identical stone cottages across the road.

"Not too many when she was younger. It was better when she got to the Grammar. That's where she met Sybil Bennett, and they were inseparable all through secondary school."

This was good news. "Are they still in touch?"

"You mean would she know something? About where Anthea has gone? No. She went to uni in America, and her parents told us she never hears from Anthea. I can give you their number though, if you like."

Ellie nodded. "Was it better at Oxford?"

"I hoped it would be, but I'm not really sure. She mentioned some names, but her focus was always her studies, and, you know, we tried, but we didn't really understand that. She didn't care about most things I thought a mother and daughter would share."

Ellie could imagine that Anthea wasn't interested in dolls or baking or shopping, whatever her mother had in mind, but she remembered the handkerchief embroidered "Mum" and thought: the girl did try. For the first time, she felt a real sympathy for Anthea, and her desire to find out what happened to her quickened.

Mrs. Davies picked up her tea mug, but her hands were shaking, and the tea slopped out onto the table as she put it down again. Ellie was about to say maybe it was time for her to leave, when it occurred to her that she would be missing an important opportunity if she did.

"Before I go, would you mind if I see Anthea's room, Mrs. Davies?" she asked.

The older woman looked surprised. After a moment of hesitation, she nodded. "The police did that, and they didn't find anything," she said, pointing to the stairs with a listless hand.

Ellie thanked her and climbed the narrow, photo-lined staircase, hoping she would not run into Mr. Davies. She didn't think he'd be keen on her poking around amongst his daughter's belongings.

At the top of the stairs, there was a narrow hallway with two bedrooms, a bathroom, and a spare room that had been used for storage. Anthea's room looked out over a small back garden and the rows of identical houses surrounding them. That was the conventional outside world, and the decoration of the room, with its rose-covered wallpaper, matching curtains, and cheerful white-painted furniture, was in keeping with that. With what, Ellie guessed, her mother thought a girl's room should be like.

But Anthea's contributions had turned it into something quite different. She had lined the walls with brick and plank bookshelves. Ellie's first reaction was to wonder how she had afforded so many books, but when she began to take them down, she saw that almost all had been bought used. Ellie personally thought a room without books looked barren, but in this small room they made the space feel like a fortress, a bunker.

There were no girlish touches. No pop star photos. No childhood stuffed animals or memorabilia from her teen years, although there was a row of oblong stones lined up on her desk that may have been the ones her mother mentioned. Her personal Stonehenge. Her desk drawers held nothing but pens and blank paper. No diaries, schoolwork, letters, notes, bills, receipts, business cards. Nothing. In her closet, there were some winter clothes in plastic storage bags and a few well-worn garments that had a left-behind look.

Except for the books, the room looked as if Anthea had moved out long ago, probably when she left for Oxford, and that reinforced Ellie's notion that her disappearance may have been planned. The next phase of her departure for a different life.

Would she be so cruel to her parents? Maybe. If she felt that was the only way to get where she wanted to go. She remembered her own blind desire to break all the rules and be free.

Ellie sat down on the narrow bed with its pink duvet and wondered how Anthea had ever been able to sleep in it. The conflict between herself and the surroundings in which she lived were that intense—and she seemed to have made no attempt to bridge the gap or hide it.

Beside the bed was a small chest with two drawers. She switched on the lamp with its rose-patterned lampshade and opened the top drawer. It contained the usual tissues and face cream, but there was one surprise. It had rolled to the back, and maybe that's why it had been left: a MAC lipstick in bright red called Perfect Score.

She thought this might be significant—a clue to Anthea's secret life—until she opened the tube and saw that it had not been used. So maybe it was a gift—but from whom? And had it been kept or forgotten?

In the lower drawer, she discovered a very worn copy of *A Child's History of England* by Charles Dickens and, underneath that, another surprise: the Kingbrook Grammar School yearbook from Anthea's final year. Ellie flicked through the pages to see what messages were written there and found none. Maybe that meant it was not their custom to write all over yearbooks the way it was at her school. Or perhaps Anthea had not asked anyone to write in her book. And yet here it was. Right by her bed. Ellie flicked through the pages again to see if the book opened automatically at any page. It didn't. But it had to be important. Everything about this room looked deliberately chosen. The very absence of other mementos argued that this had some special meaning.

She tucked the yearbook into her bag and went back downstairs. Mrs. Davies had drifted off, but she awoke immediately when Ellie entered the room. "Did you find anything?" she asked.

Ellie shook her head. "Not too much—a yearbook from Anthea's school that I'd like to borrow so I can look through it more carefully. Also if you could give me the phone numbers of any friends, that would be great."

Mrs. Davies couldn't hide her disappointment, but she got up stiffly and went to a telephone table, where she pored over an old address book, then handed Ellie a slip of paper with six names and numbers.

"Thank you," she said. "I'll let you know immediately if I learn anything new."

As soon as she got back to her car, Ellie checked her phone and found a text message from Graham: "Please meet me at Woodmans ASAP." This sounded like good news. Perhaps they had returned, and one little mystery would be resolved.

It took half an hour to find her way back to Chadstone in the gathering dusk. As she pulled into the drive, she saw welcoming lights in the windows up ahead and thought she must be right. But when she reached the house, it turned out that only the red Mini was parked in front, and Graham was the one who greeted her at the door. Inside the house was cold as if the heat had not been turned on for a long time. Ellie shivered and pulled her scarf tighter around her neck.

"Where are the Woodmans? I thought from your message they were back."

"No," he said. "I called Mrs. Daley, and, since neither of us had heard anything from them, she asked me to bring her the cats."

"That must have been a bit tricky," she said, but she liked the idea that Graham would consider his four-legged parishioners worthy of help.

"So why did you want me?" she asked.

"Because I looked around again, and there is something I want you to see," he said, leading the way upstairs, where Ellie had not been before.

He showed her into Deborah's room, which was one of several off a central landing. Unlike Anthea's room, there had been no motherly decorative hand here, but the walls were freshly painted white, and the bed and other furniture all looked handcrafted. It was also exuberantly cluttered with clothes thrown over a chair and books and papers piled on the desk. On the bedside table was a framed photo of the Woodman family when it had numbered four.

Ellie turned to Graham and said, "I don't see anything."

He nodded toward the bed, which was covered with a faded duvet decorated with trains. It had been pulled up hastily and threatened to slide off.

"That duvet looks like it must have belonged to her brother. It's not an obvious choice for a teenage girl, but maybe it had a sentimental value?"

He bobbed his head from side to side, as if this were not the point.

Ellie went over to the bed and peeked under the corner of the duvet. She was surprised to see that underneath there was nothing but a bare pillow and mattress. The bedding had all been removed, and on the edge of the mattress there was a dark smear. She wet her finger and rubbed at it. It came back red. She sniffed it. Blood.

She turned to Graham, who was watching her intently. "This could be nothing," she said. "That is, nothing out of the ordinary, if you know what I mean."

"I do know, and at first it was just the duvet that caught my eye as being odd, but then I saw that stain, and one thing led to another."

"What do you mean?"

"When I saw the bedding was gone, I looked for it."

"You never fail to amaze me," said Ellie. "And was it in the laundry?"

"No."

"So where was it?"

Graham looked embarrassed, but this was obviously the point of his asking her to come. Much to her surprise, he led her back downstairs and out of the house, across the yard to the barn. There he pulled open the creaking door and switched on the light. He pointed to one of the empty stalls where hay was heaped in the corner.

"I wondered about that hay when we were here the other day. It doesn't appear that any animals have lived here for quite a while, but that hay looks freshly tossed. So I poked about, and this is what I found." He pulled back the hay with an old hayfork, and there wadded up was a yellow striped duvet, heavily bloodstained and wrapped around something.

Ellie grabbed the side of the stall, bracing herself for the worst. But she was still taken aback when he carefully pulled open the bundle with the fork. Inside was the rest of the missing bedding and several towels, all stained, and, in the middle, a bloody mass and a pair of blood-stained scissors.

"Oh my God," said Ellie, who had never witnessed a birth or seen an afterbirth, but was nonetheless certain that's what she was looking at.

"Quite," he said, letting the hay back down to cover it. "Let's go back to the house."

In the Woodmans' kitchen, he put on the kettle, and that homey action added to Ellie's feeling of confusion.

"So what do you think happened here? I can't put it together. Is the Woodman girl Rosie's mother?"

"That could be one explanation," said Graham.

"But then where did she go? Where is her father? And why would she leave the baby?"

"I don't know." He set a mug of sweetened tea in front of Ellie. "There's one other thing though."

He disappeared and came back with a framed photo – much more recent than the one in Deborah's room. It showed a chubby girl of about 13 years old with long dark curls smiling at her father, a stocky, broad-shouldered man who had his arm around her.

It was hard to be certain, she might be mistaken, but Ellie thought she had seen her before. "Oh no," she said aloud. “We really shouldn’t be here.”

Graham nodded ruefully. “I know, but we have been, and I wanted you to see what I saw for yourself.”

They were no sooner home than their suspicions were confirmed. A touched-up photo of the young woman found dead during the Boxing Day meet was all over the internet captioned, “Identity of murder victim sought.” There was no question that this was an older version of Deborah Woodman.

“Will you call or shall I?” asked Ellie, putting her computer on sleep.

“I will,” said Graham, and he did.

When Isabelle came back from her hike, exuding energy and fresh air, Ellie and Graham were setting the table in the kitchen for a last meal of Christmas leftovers.

“What’s going on? You guys look totally down,” she said.

“The young woman found in Stevens Wood has been identified, and she’s most likely the baby’s mother too,” said Ellie.

“Who is she?”

“Her name was Deborah Woodman. She used to come to St. Michael’s with her family when she was a little girl,” said Graham.

“Oh, Dad. I’m very sorry to hear that.” She looked from Graham to Ellie. “So this means the other girl is still missing, right? There are two girls involved?”

Ellie nearly dropped the dish of creamed turkey she meant to put on the table. She didn’t know what made Isabelle link the two girls like that, but she had a terrible feeling that she might be right.

Monday, December 28
Chapter 7

Ellie had looked forward to this Monday as the day when life would begin to return to normal. The major hurdles of Christmas would be behind them. Mrs. Finch arrived, looking freshly starched and rested after her holiday with her sister in Winchester, and dove into her cleaning. The roar of the vacuum soon put every cowering dust bunny on notice. But it was not a normal day.

They had no sooner finished breakfast when the doorbell rang, and there were the police on their doorstep. Isabelle answered the door and rolled her eyes at Ellie and Graham as she invited Detective Inspector Derek Mullane and Detective Sergeant Alan Jones into the hall. Then she vanished up the stairs to her room.

"We're here to talk about the young woman found dead in Stevens Wood on Saturday. I believe you're aware she was identified yesterday as a Deborah Woodman," said Mullane, when they were all seated in Graham's study. Jones, who was the kind of young man best described as weedy, seemed awed by all the books everywhere and kept glancing from his notebook to Graham's typewriter, as if he had never seen one before, while Mullane sat on the edge of the sofa emitting pent-up energy and irritation. He had the capacity to make Ellie feel guilty with the least twitch of his eyebrows, but Graham responded to his manner by becoming preternaturally calm.

"We are aware of that," he said.

"Although the arrangement of her body was intended to make it appear she had committed suicide, the post-mortem has confirmed that she was strangled before she was placed in the tree. So we're dealing with a murder, and I know you appreciate the seriousness of that and will do everything you can to help us find the person responsible quickly."

Ellie waited to see if Graham would ask why coming to visit them was such a high priority, but he said nothing, and Mullane went straight to the point.

"Yesterday our investigators examined the home in Chadstone where Deborah Woodman lived with her father. There they found not only a handwritten note from you, Father Kent, but also your fingerprints. That is, both of yours," he said, looking from one to the other of them. "They proved to be the only recent prints other than those of the occupants, so naturally we're eager to hear your explanation."

The tips of Graham's ears turned pink. "How convenient that you happen to have our fingerprints on file. Of course I can explain why we were there," he said, in his most stiff and proper voice.

He went on to describe how they had visited the Woodmans' neighbor, a member of the parish, on Christmas night to bring her some food and make sure she was all right. It was she who had asked them to check up on the Woodmans, because she had expected to hear from them and she hadn't.

"So this was Christmas night? Friday? And what did you find when you went there?"

"No one was at home, and there were no fresh tire tracks in the snow. It appeared that no one had come in or out of the drive for some time, though I couldn't say for how long. We knocked and discovered the door had been left unlocked. We did not enter illegally, Inspector. Inside we were met by two very hungry cats, so we fed them. And yes, we walked around the house to ensure that no one was lying sick or injured, but we found no sign of Bill or his daughter."

"Bill. Do I take it correctly then that you know the family?"

"I did, years ago, when they lived in the village and attended St. Michael's."

"But you've had no recent contact?"

"None."

"What else did you do while you were in the house?"

"We looked around to see if there was any sign that could explain why they had left—and when they might be back. The lights were on, and the kitchen looked as if someone had been interrupted while preparing tea. Since their Christmas presents were unopened under the tree, we assumed they had probably left the day before. That is, on Christmas Eve."

"But there was nothing specific that suggested whether they left together or separately or if they had left even earlier?"

"No. I assumed they were together."

"And there was no sign of any violence. Nothing was disturbed."

"No. As I said, it looked as though the occupants had been interrupted suddenly, causing them to leave without making any preparation for the care of their cats, which they normally would do, according to Mrs. Daley. They left despite the fact that someone had obviously been preparing a meal, and they were anticipating the celebration of Christmas at their home."

"Very good. So you left everything as it was and put the note on the kitchen table."

"Not exactly," said Ellie. "I did clean up the kitchen, as well as feeding the cats."

Mullane and Jones exchanged glances. As if she had destroyed critical evidence by washing out a pan of baked beans.

"We were also there again yesterday," said Graham. "Since the Woodmans hadn't returned yet, Mrs. Daley asked me to bring their cats up to her cottage."

"I see. All very neighborly. But you say you've heard nothing from either of the Woodmans during all this time?"

"Correct. On our second visit, we did, however, discover something that might point to an explanation for their hasty disappearance."

"I say. What is that?"

"There were signs that someone had recently given birth at the Woodmans' home."

The two detectives looked surprised. "Really? Such as what?"

"Deborah's bed had been stripped, and I found the bedding, as well as the, um, afterbirth in the barn under a pile of hay."

DI Mullane looked sharply at DS Jones. "This is the first I've heard of that. Didn't our people find this? I thought you said the entire property had been searched."

"Sir, we did find traces of blood in the daughter's room and in the barn, but there was no bedding or anything else. We thought the blood might be evidence of the crime scene, but Forensics is still working on it."

Ellie and Graham exchanged glances.

"What time did you say you were there?" Mullane asked.

"About three thirty," Graham said.

"And the police arrived when?"

"It was just gone five," said Jones.

"Leaving ample time for someone to come and remove evidence. Was there anything else you noticed on this second visit? Something that might have changed since the first time you saw the house?"

Graham paused for a long time. Then he said, "No. Not that I noticed."

"But still, someone had to be close by watching the house to slip in between four and five o'clock," said Jones.

"Yes," said Mullane, looking annoyed. "We all see that."

"Father Kent, I can not imagine these discoveries occurred unless you were making a concerted effort to search the property. I am very surprised that you took that initiative. I know Mrs. Kent has a tendency to think she should involve herself in our investigations, but I hope you are not developing the same trait. Why didn't you call us with this information right away?"

"Nothing I found was indicative of a crime, Inspector," said Graham, equally annoyed. "I can't imagine you're suggesting I should report the private activities of my neighbors to the police."

"Murder is not a private activity," said Mullane.

"There was no question of murder at the time."

"Are you saying that the murder took place in the house, and the murderer was watching us while we were there?" asked Ellie.

"I can't comment on where the murder took place until all the forensic tests are completed, but I would guess that our suspect was very nearby."

"So you have a suspect?" Graham asked.

Mullane cocked his head and didn't reply. Instead he asked, "Do you know where Bill Woodman is, Father Kent? Because I assure you, I won't hesitate to charge either or both of you with obstruction if you withhold any information about this case."

Graham paled. "You don't think he had something to do with his daughter's death, do you?"

"Until we can talk to him, he is certainly a person of interest. So I'll ask you again. Do you know where he is?"

"No. I already told you that."

"All right. You'll both need to come down to the station in Chipping Martin to sign statements detailing your movements later today. And if you think of anything you might have forgotten to mention, be sure to let me know." Mullane got to his feet, and Jones followed.

"Inspector, you will find out soon if Deborah Woodman was the mother of the baby we found on Christmas Eve, won't you?" said Ellie. "She could be in danger too, you know."

"That is being taken care of," was all he would say, and then they left.

"I can't believe the murderer was out there watching when we were in the Woodmans' house—and I certainly don't think it was her father," said Ellie, when she and Graham were alone. She gathered up the empty teacups, eager to be rid of this reminder of the detectives' visit.

"I can't either. Which is not to say that some men don't kill their daughters. I just don't believe Bill is that type of person, and I don't think what we saw was the crime scene."

"So you think, if Deborah is Rosie's mother, that she left her at the church, and then met the person who killed her somewhere else?"

"All I'm saying is Bill and the house are not the only possibilities. We—I mean, the police—should keep an open mind. Which is more than I expect from Charles Bell, who is supposed to be here in ten minutes to discuss what he calls 'some issues.' That usually means money—and probably how much we didn't make over Christmas."

"As long as it's not me! In any case, I will make myself scarce," said Ellie, "and get back to the problem of Anthea Davies. I promised her mother I would talk to her friends."

But first, she looked to see what information had been released about Deborah and found only a short announcement: "The young woman whose body was discovered in Stevens Wood on Boxing Day was Deborah Mary Woodman, 18, of Chadstone. A lifelong resident of the area, she was a sixth-form student at the Kingbrook Grammar School. Her death has been ruled as suspicious." A school photo accompanied the story that made her look terribly young and innocent.

The fact that Deborah was a student at Kingbrook was a surprise. This was a definite link between her and Anthea despite their differences in age and circumstances. She picked up the Kingbrook yearbook and began to pore over it, page by page.

It was hard for her to see past the lovely campus with its Tudor-style half-timbered building and lush green playing fields; the smiling groups of uniformed students at work and play in their well-appointed facilities. She had gone to the large, diverse, and rambunctious Berkeley High, but she knew from the countless novels she had read that the reality behind the yearbook photos was probably very different. England's schools were fraught with as many tensions and troubles as any American high school.

Whatever Anthea's experience at Kingbrook had been, she had received the education she needed to win a place at Oxford, and she had enough positive memories to have kept this book in her bedside table more than two years after she left.

She studied the photo of Anthea herself. The students were permitted to select their own settings for their photos, and she had chosen the library. Dressed in black, she stood against shelves of books with her arms crossed. Her expression was serious, even a little fierce. It was a lonely, defiant image, very different from the one on the MISSING poster. It was also very unlike the photos of the other girls in her year, which leaned toward pastoral scenes or portraits with their favorite cats, dogs, or horses. Except for her friend Sybil Bennett. Sybil had chosen a graffiti-covered brick wall as her setting, and, like Anthea, she stared into the camera. No wonder they were friends. The photos made Ellie want to laugh. She would like these two.

Anthea appeared in only one group photo: the Drama Club. Ellie studied the faces of the 15 students arrayed around the obvious show-offs who sat on a sofa making silly faces. Anthea stood behind the sofa at one end of the group. She was looking away from the camera, her posture relaxed, perhaps bored. Despite the school uniform, with its silly clip-on necktie, she had a kind of unconscious elegance that was arresting. Ellie looked at the image for a long time. Where are you? she wanted to ask. What are you up to?

Finally she turned to the rest of the group, examining the pea-sized faces and their corresponding names. And there she discovered a dark-haired girl who was "D. Woodman" and a pretty slim blonde who turned out to be none other than "C. Worthy"—Miss Worthy's great-niece, Charlotte.

She looked back at the date on the cover of the yearbook: these photos would have been taken nearly three years ago. It was hard to believe that the lives of three of the girls in this one group had taken such dramatic turns. She studied the club's advisor too. Mr. D. Pettibone was young with a shock of straight blond hair and wore Sixties vintage clothes. She would need to find out more about all of them.

To that end, she took out the list of Anthea's friends that Mrs. Davies had given her and called every number on it without reaching a single person. She sighed and looked at her watch, thinking that whoever called detective work fast-paced had obviously never tried it.

Ellie filled in Graham on what she had learned from the Kingbrook yearbook as they hurtled along the narrow road to Chipping Martin. A pale sun cast the familiar fields and villages in soft greys and browns like a watercolor, but the air still held its biting edge.

She was speculating about how well Anthea, Charlotte, and Deborah might have known each other as members of the Drama Club when she noticed his preoccupied expression. "By the way, how did it go with Mr. Bell?"

Graham glanced sideways at her. "I shouldn't talk about it while I'm driving," he said.

"That bad?" she asked.

"I think it was Mary talking really. You know. Like a ventriloquist. Charles looked embarrassed."

"So he said he's worried the village is going down the tubes and will soon be fit for nothing better than vacation photos on Facebook," she said.

Graham laughed. "Something like that. But I'll tell you more later," he said, as he pulled into the parking lot of the Chipping Martin Police Station.

The waiting room was crowded, so Graham answered email on his mobile phone while Ellie wandered around looking at the various posters. There was a bland police poster about Anthea's disappearance that was clipped together with notices about other missing people. Some of them had been missing for years and age-advanced photos had been created to try to make identification easier. Ellie fervently hoped that Anthea would not wind up amongst those cases.

There was also one of Mrs. Davies' posters—a larger version than the ones she had hung up on the streets. Ellie studied the smiling girl with outstretched arms, whose mood here was so different from that in the other photos she had just been looking at. She could see now that the photo had been taken outside the Ashmolean Museum in Oxford. The trees on St. Giles had begun to lose their leaves, but it was sunny and she wore her sweater tied around her neck, jeans, and knee-high boots. Around her wrist there was a watch or close-fitting bracelet that Ellie had not noticed before.

Very close fitting, she thought, as she peered at the photo. In fact, it might not even be a bracelet at all. It almost looked like a tattoo, but no "identifying marks" had been recorded on either this poster or the police version.

DS Jones appeared then and called them into an interview room to review and sign their statements. The police station reminded Ellie unpleasantly of the times she had been there as a suspect. She felt jumpy, even though Graham was with her, and this was a routine visit. She barely glanced at her brief statement before signing it in her eagerness to get out of there. She wanted to call Mrs. Davies and ask about that tattoo, if that's what it was.

But her attention shifted quickly when they were saying goodbye, and DS Jones said casually: "By the way. That baby you found. Deborah Woodman was the mother, but we didn't find any other DNA on the scene that matched."

Ellie was so taken aback that she didn't even respond until they were outside. Then she exploded. "How could that useless little twit say that? As if Rosie were a glove turned in to the lost-and-found. He just told us that her mother was murdered, and she'll probably never know her father."

Graham put his arm around her shoulder. "Don't let Jones get to you. He's a prat, but he told us one thing he may not have intended that's good for Rosie. Bill Woodman is not her father."

Ellie pulled away to look at his face. "Is *that* what you've been thinking?"

"It was certainly one of the possibilities," he said ruefully.

"You're right, and I am very glad we can cross that off the list."

Ellie called Mrs. Davies from the car, tapping the button to turn on the speaker so Graham could hear both sides of the conversation as he drove.

Frances Davies answered on the first ring. "Is there news?" she asked, her voice urgent and insistent.

"Nothing concrete, I'm afraid," said Ellie, "but I do have a question. It's about something in the photo of Anthea that you used for your poster. Could you email me the original?"

"I suppose Arthur can do that, but what's the question?"

"It looks as if she has a tattoo around her left wrist, but nothing was mentioned under identifying marks."

"Oh, Lord. If that awful thing has anything to do with her disappearance, her father will have a stroke."

"So it is a tattoo. And is the design a yellow flower?"

"I'm not sure—to be frank, I haven't seen it very often. Arthur was that mad she kept it covered when she was with us. But she did that years ago. How can it have anything to do with what's happened now?"

"Do you remember when she had it done?"

"It was right before she left Kingbrook. She was

eighteen, she told us, and old enough to do what she wanted. But you mustn't judge her by that. She really isn't that kind of girl."

"Did she ever say why she wanted a tattoo—or why she picked that particular design?"

"No. It was just some bit of rebellion, but it was so unlike her. That was as upsetting as the fact that she did it."

"Did anything else uncharacteristic happen around that time?"

"No," she said firmly, "and I really hope you won't be sidetracked by that. It was not important."

Ellie rolled her eyes at Graham, but didn't argue. In her opinion, Mrs. Davies' reaction showed more than ever how important it was. "That's fine," she said. "There's one other thing you might be able to tell me more about. I saw in the yearbook that Anthea was a member of the Drama Club. Did she enjoy that? Was she friends with the other people in the group?"

"I never heard her mention any friends, and she usually disliked the musicals and things they chose to put on, but as a group they sometimes did scenes from old plays, and she loved that. She said it was like being alive centuries ago."

"You mean old plays like Shakespeare?"

"Yes, she's read all his plays, and whenever the school took them to Stratford, she'd go around spouting bits for days afterward. So you see, that's what she was like. Not one of these girls with tattoos and spikes all over their bodies."

"I understand, and thank you, every bit of information is helpful," said Ellie.

"I suppose, but do you still want that photo? I'll have to give Arthur a reason, and I can't say it's about that."

"Just tell him I asked for a copy and didn't say

why."

"All right," she said, but she was still hesitant.

"Mrs. Davies," said Ellie, "I probably should have asked you this first thing, but what do you personally believe has happened to Anthea?"

There was a silence on the other end of the phone. Then she said, "She was a beautiful girl, full of life. Some men hate that, you know. They're like people who pluck a flower for no reason and then drop it on the ground. That's what I think happened." With that, she rang off.

"Whew," said Ellie, putting her phone away. "I didn't expect that."

"It was probably good for her to say it out loud. I doubt if she really believes that though."

"I don't agree," Ellie said, thinking of her own parents. "I know I'd rather believe the worst and be surprised if something better happens than hope for the best."

Graham looked at her sideways. They were passing down the high street of Little Beecham and, at that moment, Ellie found all the twinkling lights and evergreens—those symbols of light and everlasting life—exceedingly depressing.

"What? You think that shows I have no faith?"

"Whatever faith you or anyone else has is a totally private matter," Graham said evenly.

"But you'll pray for us," said Ellie, unable to resist.

"I pray for everyone," he said, pulling the car into the drive, "You don't have to worry about it."

Ellie got out of the car and zipped up her coat. Maybe it was just her overheated emotions, but the temperature seemed to have dropped.

"Hey," she said, grabbing the arm of Graham's jacket as he walked past her to the house. "I'm sorry. This has been a crappy day, but I don't need to fling it at you, and I don't mean to make jokes about your work. Your faith. Any of that."

"Ellie, I might get annoyed with you sometimes. I might even get angry at you. But it will never be about that." Then he pulled her into a hug.

Ellie tried to put herself in a better mood before going to tea with Miss Worthy and Charlotte. She changed her clothes and put on the new gold bracelet Graham had given her for Christmas. Still, as she walked across the village, she couldn't help noticing that the MISSING posters, so hopefully placed on the telephone poles along the high street a week ago, had disintegrated or blown away.

What were the odds of a person missing for three months turning up unharmed? She'd read that more than 300,000 people go missing each year in Britain. She only wanted to find one of them. Surely that was not too much to ask. And if that counted as a prayer, so be it.

Miss Worthy's thatch-roofed cottage was at the end of Chapel Lane, named for the former Methodist Chapel, which was now the home of a London stockbroker. Charlotte answered the door, dressed all in black, and she had dyed the ends of her blonde hair blue since Ellie last saw her at the Crib Service. Miss Worthy was nowhere to be seen, but the tap-tapping of her typewriter could be heard coming from upstairs. She was another one, like Graham, who didn't like to write on a computer.

Charlotte led the way back to the kitchen, where she now had a desk with a computer set up in a corner and her son Dolphin in a playpen full of stuffed toys. "Auntie will be down for tea in a minute," she said. "She sets the timer for four, and sometimes she stops even if she is in the middle of a sentence. But sometimes she doesn't."

Ellie watched Dolphin grab toys and toss them down again, while Charlotte prepared the tea tray with cups and saucers and a plate of Miss Worthy's homemade ginger biscuits. She looked older than her 17 years—maybe as the result of being a mother or maybe she'd become a mother because she'd had enough of being a girl. Ellie had never heard anything about Dolphin's father, and Charlotte did not seem to feel the need for him or anyone else in her life other than her baby son.

Ellie had gotten to know her when she worked at the Little Beecham Library, and she told her she missed seeing her there. "I expect your job here is more interesting than shelving books though."

"Much," said Charlotte. "It's brilliant. My blog *Ramona Speaks* has ten thousand followers already. The baby and I are probably going to move in here after the holidays."

"That sounds like it will be nice for all of you."

Charlotte shrugged. "Auntie enjoys having a baby about more than my Dad does, that's for sure. And it helps her for me to answer the door. People keep showing up looking for Ramona Blaisdell-Scott, and when they see me and Dolphin they don't know what to think."

Ellie laughed. "That's great. Maybe you'll become a novelist too."

Charlotte shrugged again. "I could if I wanted to."

"Do you ever think about going back to school?"

"No. I hated school," she said flatly and reached down to pick up Dolphin. He had begun fussing at the sudden harshness of her voice.

"I thought Kingbrook Grammar was supposed to be one of the top schools in this area," said Ellie, who was struggling to find a way to ask about Anthea like a climber fumbling for the next handhold on a cliff. She guessed Charlotte was not about to give her a hand up.

"Schools like Kingbrook train you how to divide and conquer the world. Not to be or think, much less feel."

Ellie decided to laugh, which caught Charlotte off balance. "I was looking at the Kingbrook yearbook this morning, thinking how idyllic it looked compared to where I went to school."

"The Kingbrook yearbook? What were you doing with that?"

Ellie took a biscuit off the plate casually. "The parents of Anthea Davies, that former student who went missing in October, loaned it to me. I'm trying to help them find her."

"What do you think you can do that the police can't?"

Ellie stirred her tea. "I can talk to people, and I notice different things than they do."

"I bet she's not really missing. What does that mean anyway—except that she's not where someone else wants her to be. I'd guess she'll turn up when it suits her."

"You think so?"

Charlotte set the baby back into his playpen. "I do. I didn't really know her, but she always seemed very sure of herself."

"What about Deborah Woodman? She would have been in your class, and you were all in the Drama Club together."

"Were we?"

"I saw you in a photo with both Anthea and Deborah."

"Was I? It must have been a long time ago. I stopped thinking about Kingbrook and the people there the day I left school."

"It was so awful?"

"No, but it's the past. I live in the present," she said, picking up the tea tray. "I hear Auntie coming down now, we should go to the sitting room."

Ellie had hoped Charlotte would join them, but she set down the tray and went back to the kitchen. To Dolphin and the computer.

Miss Worthy closed the door before sitting down. "I'll pour out, shall I?" she said. Today she was wearing blue sweaters over an old gray tweed skirt that had what looked like an ink stain on it. Her white hair was pulled about in different directions as if she had been twirling it while she wrote, but her dark eyes were as bright and sharp as ever.

"How did you make out with Charlotte? I tried to give you a bit of time together before I came down." She smiled her impish smile.

"Not too well actually. She didn't seem to know Anthea or any of the other members of the Drama Club that I was interested in. She lives in the present, she said. Apparently that means the past vanishes behind her."

Miss Worthy laughed. "Now that was very naughty of her, and no more true for her than anyone else. I don't know how friendly she was with the other students, but she was very active in the Kingbrook Drama Club and seemed to enjoy it even when she had nothing good to say about her studies or anything else. Unfortunately she decided to turn her own life into a drama in which she could play the lead. The old Charlotte is quite hidden behind all that baby weight and blue hair. All that mystery about her child's father. Not that that matters to me. Dolphin is a lovely boy."

"It's interesting that you put it together like that."

Miss Worthy sipped her tea with a noncommittal expression. "I write about romance and mystery. It's not all made up."

"Did you ever meet Mr. Pettibone, who ran the club? He's another person I'd like to know more about."

"I didn't, but I have seen him. It was at a production of *The King and I.* Charlotte's hair was black for that one. She was a Siamese wife and ran around with her midriff exposed the whole summer afterward. Her father found it very upsetting, but then Jack inherited all of the worst conventionality of the Worthys."

"He is quite good looking, Mr. Pettibone," Ellie remarked.

"Yes, I remember that and well liked by the students from what I've heard." She regarded Ellie thoughtfully. "Are you still looking for Anthea Davies? Or is it the father of your baby you're interested in now?"

Ellie blushed. "I guess the full answer to that question is both."

"Yes, I can see why. I heard the murdered girl was also a student at Kingbrook. That must be very distressing for everyone associated with the school. Did Charlotte know her? She hasn't said a word to me about it."

"She acted as if she didn't."

"Acted as if. Now isn't that just the way with girls."

"I've found a link between Anthea and Deborah that makes more sense now that I know they were in the Drama Club. It could indicate they were both involved with the same person at different times. Someone who would have been there when both girls were at the school."

"You mean a teacher, such as Mr. Pettibone? I always had the impression from Charlotte that he was gay."

"That could be an act. Camouflage. He is the drama teacher after all," said Ellie.

"Even so, it's one thing to have flings with students––which is bad enough to cost him his job if he were discovered—and quite another to become embroiled with both a disappearance and murder."

"It could be two murders, for all we know."

"True, but perhaps you've read too many of my books," said Miss Worthy. "If something like that has been going on, you'll have an extremely hard time finding out anything. Secrecy will have been essential for all parties. Of course, that's also very stimulating to romance, and the students would probably enjoy it. Something similar is central to my new book *Death of Desire*," she added, and since she seemed to want to change the subject, they did.

"My publisher wants me to do public readings now that my identity is known. Do you think I have to? Jane Austen never did. Not that I'm comparing."

"Jane Austen might have liked it. Her family adored putting on theatricals."

"Yes. I remember reading that. Perhaps I could get Charlotte to do the readings for me. I think she would enjoy playing the role of Ramona Blaisdell-Scott. It would be a change from Unwed Teenage Mother."

They both laughed, and Ellie walked home with a lighter heart even though she'd learned nothing that would help her find Anthea Davies.

The day was not without tangible progress though. At the hospital, she found that the nurses had begun trying to get Rosie to take a bottle, and Arthur Davies did email her the photo from the poster. She could see from zooming in on it that the tattoo was indeed a circlet of tiny yellow flowers and feathery greens. She quickly checked each of the herbs and flowers in Ophelia's speech to see what they looked like—and there it was. Fennel.

Her excitement increased as she delved into the lore about fennel, which was even more thought provoking than what she had read about rosemary. A 10th century

Anglo-Saxon medicine recipe called the Nine Herbs Charm claimed that fennel stood against pain, poison, noble scheming, and the enchantment of vile creatures. When Shakespeare wrote *Hamlet* 600 years later, he had Ophelia say: "There's fennel for you, and columbines." Columbine was frequently associated with foolishness, which suggested that, in the play, she regrets being enchanted by the noble, scheming Hamlet. It was easy to imagine a girl who gave her heart to a false lover identifying with that idea.

Ellie took a deep breath and leaned back in her chair. Did 21st century girls, members of the Drama Club, still know this story and identify with the betrayed and broken-hearted Ophelia who loved the indecisive and unavailable Prince Hamlet of Denmark? Of course, they must. But where did that get her? Who starred in the role of Hamlet in their tragedies? That's what she needed to know.

Tuesday, December 29
Chapter 8

The police investigators who were trying to trace Deborah Woodman's movements on the last day of her life showed up in Little Beecham the next morning. They endured cold, blowing rain as they went from house to house asking if she had been seen, alone or with anyone else, in a car, on foot, and so on. DI Mullane telephoned to inform Ellie and Graham that, in addition to the routine check, a Scenes-of-Crime Officer would be coming by to examine the crèche where Rosie was found.

While she had him on the phone, Ellie asked, "Have you found Bill Woodman yet?"

"No, there's been no sign of him," he said, "but, if he's still in the country, we will."

"What about the baby's father? Is he a suspect too?"

"I can't comment on that," was all he would say before ringing off.

Ellie looked at the phone in her hand and said to no one, "I guess you don't want to hear about what I've learned."

The SOCO turned out to be a young woman about 30 years old with an air of self-importance who was introduced to them by DS Jones as Jane Perkins. They followed Ellie and Graham across the churchyard to the church, bent against the storm, and they all shook themselves off like dogs once they were inside. The empty church still looked and smelled like Christmas, and Ellie was struck by how she could never have imagined this moment when she and the other women put up the greens and holly decorations.

"We'd like you to take us through the discovery of the baby," said Jones, who had taken out his notebook. "It would be helpful if you would both think back to that night and whether—in addition to the baby—you noticed anyone unusual. Anyone you might not have expected to see or who might have been paying special attention to the crèche and your discovery there."

Graham shook his head and said, "I have to admit, I didn't see anyone or anything. The church was packed, and I was concentrating on the service, rather than individual faces in the congregation. Unfortunately that service is one of the biggest of the year, and many people come who are not familiar to me."

"I can't be of any help either," said Ellie. "I noticed the few people I know, but a stranger would never stand out for me. I haven't lived here long enough."

"So you had no sense of anyone around you watching to see if and when the baby was found."

"I didn't. Even the people on either side of me didn't notice her until I went to the crèche and picked her up."

"And what exactly made you do that, Mrs. Kent? If no one else noticed, why do you think you did?"

Ellie resisted the urge to react to his tone. "Impossible to say for sure. I was likely the only one who'd been at the earlier Crib Service and knew what a scrum of stuffed animals the children had put in and around the crèche. I thought the noise I heard might be a kitten, and then I also noticed the difference between the baby Jesus who had been in the manger earlier and the one who was there."

Jones wrote hurriedly, nodding as he went. "And the church was open the whole time between services? That is, about four hours? You didn't happen to see anyone coming or going during that period?"

"No, it was dark and snowing, and we were busy," said Ellie.

"One of your neighbors—a Mrs. Geraldine Bigelow—reported seeing a dark-haired young woman with a bundle go into the church about seven o'clock and a silver car driven by a dark-haired woman passed her house a short time later, but she couldn't be sure it was the same woman."

"She couldn't? I'm surprised. Her powers of observation usually border on the extraterrestrial," said Ellie, on hearing this new version of what her neighbor had seen. Jones did not smile, and the look he gave her made it clear he was taking Mrs. Bigelow's account seriously.

"You're hoping to establish that this person was Deborah Woodman?" Graham asked, as he watched Jane Perkins dusting the crèche for fingerprints.

"We're looking for any evidence that shows where she was on Christmas Eve," Perkins said.

"Do you really think you'll find fingerprints? It was very cold, and I expect she would have been wearing gloves," he said.

"Possibly, but she could also have taken them off. She might have sat here with her baby for some time before leaving. Didn't you say the baby was pretty quiet? If she's anything like my kids were, then her mother must have nursed her before she left, as difficult as that would have been."

Ellie was taken aback by the image of Deborah nursing Rosie then kneeling by the manger to say goodbye in the same spot where she herself had later been. "So where did she go after that? Do you know what happened?" she asked.

"She was killed," said Jones, with his usual tactfulness. "We're still working out the timetable—and any fingerprints from the principals would be helpful.

"You don't have to wait for us though. We'll lock up and bring you the latchkey. The Detective Inspector said he would send someone over with your statements when they're ready to sign, so you don't have to come to the station this time, but Father Kent will need to testify at the inquest about what you saw at the Woodman house. That will be tomorrow at eleven in Oxford."

Walking back to The Vicarage, Ellie grumbled not only about the insensitivity of the police but also about not being asked to testify herself. After all, she was the one who found Rosie, but Graham assured her it was better for him to do it. There was no need to call broader public attention to her role.

"You mean no reason to add to my reputation as that American magnet for trouble and publicity?"

Graham smiled. "I'm afraid so. Didn't I tell you? Charles suggested it would be a great benefit to the parish if you would start helping with the Sunday School and take a more active role in the Women's Institute."

"He thinks I should learn to make orange marmalade? I am not even going to dignify that proposal by asking what you said."

"Not to worry, but there's something else I've been meaning to tell you."

"Yes?" said Ellie, crossing her arms over her chest. "I can hardly wait."

"We're invited to a New Year's Eve party at Castor House."

"You mean we're going to ring in the New Year—our first new year—with the Bells?"

"It has been rather a tradition, I'm afraid, and the party is not as bad as you might think," said Graham. "Lots of people are there, and the food is excellent, I promise."

"Then I guess that settles it. But you owe me! I'll have to think what."

In this age of social media, email, cell phones, ubiquitous cameras, and texting, it was hard to believe that any relationship could be kept secret. Nonetheless, Ellie had been unable to turn up any information about Anthea suggesting that she was in a relationship, much less involved with someone who could have turned out to be dangerous. Secrecy had obviously been a prerequisite, but even given that, could she really be certain there was a man in the story? And could she further assume that his invisibility was actually a measure of his importance?

She took out the list of names and numbers that Mrs. Davies had given her and called all of Anthea's friends again. She still didn't reach any of them, but she left messages, and then opened the Kingbrook Grammar website to troll through the online photos and information about the school.

The names of the teachers in each department were listed, but only with honorifics and first initials. There were no photos. She did an internet search on each man and found a few on social media, but none who looked like a candidate for the role of Hamlet—with the possible exception of Mr. D. Pettibone, an English teacher and the Drama Club advisor.

David Pettibone had his own website, because he was also a professional actor. Studio portraits showed the glossy-haired blond in a variety of poses and production shots that demonstrated his skill in roles from the antic to the tragic. According to his bio, he was about 35 years old and had studied at the Royal Academy of Dramatic Art. His acting career had begun with promising stage and television roles, but, reading between the lines, she saw that it had devolved more than evolved. His recent work had been with small repertory companies.

Talking to him was her next most obvious step, since he had known both Anthea and Deborah, and it took only a short but dogged search to find his phone number. She considered different ways of approaching him—after all, why should he want to meet her—and decided it was best to be straightforward. She left a voicemail saying she was helping the parents of a former student, Anthea Davies, who had been missing for several weeks. Although it was a couple of years since she'd left Kingbrook, she was talking to various people who could provide background that might shed light on the present situation.

Much to her surprise, he called her back a few minutes later. "You're not from the police, are you?" he asked in a well-trained and mellifluous voice.

"Nothing like."

"Thank God for that. I've already been interviewed about that student who was murdered, and I'd rather hoped I'd seen the back of them for a few lifetimes. Is it true that Anthea is still missing? I did hear something about it a while ago, but not recently."

"Yes, and I'm interested in anything you remember about her," said Ellie. "I'd also like to know more about the Drama Club."

"The Drama Club?" He sounded surprised and seemed about to say something more, but then didn't. Instead, he offered to meet her for coffee if she could come to Oxford, where he lived, and they made a date for the next morning.

It was only after she'd agreed to this plan that it occurred to her she might be meeting a kidnapper and murderer, who would find her interest threatening. Still, he couldn't strangle her in the pub, and she'd just have to make sure he wasn't following her when she left.

The detective business was hopping for a change: the phone rang two times in short succession. Melanie Thomas, one of Anthea's roommates from Oxford, was the first caller, and all she wanted to express was how annoyed she was that Anthea had stiffed them for the rent by her inconvenient disappearance. The second was Anthea's friend from Kingbrook, Sybil Bennett.

"I don't see how I can be of any help," she said. "I didn't even know Anthea had gone missing until I received your message. We haven't spoken for more than two years."

"I understand," said Ellie, unable to disguise her disappointment. "But I've never met her, so if you could describe her at the time you were friends that alone would be helpful. Her mother said you were very close. Is that true?"

"Yes, and I suppose nothing essential about her has changed. She's a very unusual girl, and I was pleased that she picked me to be her friend," said Sybil, in an oddly formal tone. "We wanted to be different from other girls and made a point of talking about books and ideas, never boys or clothes or make-up, you know? We both said we'd have nothing to do with boys because they were usually thick as planks and narrow-minded. But I thought that meant one thing, and it turned out to mean something else to Anthea."

"You mean she became involved with someone who was not a boy? A man?"

"I don't know for sure, because she never told me anything, but I began to suspect from little things. When we were in Year Eleven, she started to act different. Not like she lorded it over me or anything—but she had the air of someone who'd been let in on a secret, and she kept it so well, you wouldn't ever guess there was one, unless you knew her as well as I did."

"This started when she was sixteen?"

"That sounds right. People at school began calling us the lezzies. I mean it was unusual for a girl as pretty as Anthea to go through secondary school without ever having a boyfriend. Without a crush or a great romance or something. For me, it was different. I am a lesbian, though I was slow to grow up and realize it. I'm making up for it now," she said with a laugh.

"So you think all that time she might have been in a secret relationship?"

"Yes, but I think it ended around the time we left school. Her composure never cracked, but she went out and got this tattoo, and I was pretty shocked. It seemed so unlike her. She told me it was a school-leaving present to herself. 'It's fennel,' she said. 'You remember what that symbolizes, don't you, Syb? False flattery. This is to remind me never to be taken in by it again.'"

"It could have referred to anything. She received a lot of praise from people at school. Maybe she was feeling anxious about going to Oxford, you know? It's one thing to be the smartest girl at a place like Kingbrook, and another to be competing with the most brilliant people in the world. It didn't have to be about a man."

"No, but the choice of fennel is suggestive."

"You mean, the Ophelia thing," said Sybil, in an offhand tone that made the back of Ellie's neck prickle. "I'm surprised you heard about that."

She waited not wanting to lead the conversation but rather see whether Sybil would say anything more. If the key would be placed in the lock and turn, and it did.

"That was sort of an inside joke with us. Ophelia was our special anti-heroine. Or rather victim. The one let down by all the men around her."

"Was it a private thing just between you or did other people know about it? Other girls?"

"They could have. It wasn't a secret. We joked about it. We used to call girls who'd been dumped or were flaunting their broken hearts 'Ophs'. And if anything bad happened, we would say, 'I'm not going to do an Ophelia over that'."

"Really. You said that?"

"Sure, why not?"

Ellie didn't reply. Instead she said, "And you never challenged Anthea about the meaning of that tattoo? You never had any sense of who might have been the Hamlet to her Ophelia?"

"No. As I said, she was secretive about it—and there was no talk in a school where secrets were virtually impossible to keep—so I assumed it was someone I didn't know. Not connected to the school. But regardless, I never challenged Anthea about anything. I would say now that I was in love with her, but I didn't know it then. Not like I would know it now."

"And after you left Kingbrook, you lost touch?"

"I went to college in New York, and things happened fast for me there. I came out, and I tried writing to tell her, but every time I felt I just couldn't get the words right, and I threw the letters away. As close as I thought we had been, I had no idea how she would react. She could be very cutting and judgmental, and I couldn't bear having that spoil the memories of our friendship, so I let the whole thing slide away. I only moved back to London this summer because I transferred to uni here. No offense, but I've had enough of Yanks for a while."

"When you were at Kingbrook, did you know a younger girl named Deborah Woodman? She would have been three years behind you."

"No. The name rings a bell, but I don't know why. Who is she?"

"She's the Kingbrook student who gave birth to a

baby and then was strangled last week."

"Oh, right! I saw that on the telly," said Sybil. "It was awful."

"What hasn't been in the news is that she had a rosemary tattoo around her wrist."

"Rosemary. Really? And you're thinking there might be a link? Between Anthea and that girl? I don't see how there could be. I mean, they were years apart in school."

"But they were both in the Drama Club."

Sybil was unimpressed by that. "I suppose she could have heard about the Ophs. In fact, maybe that's where Anthea got the idea about Ophelia to begin with. Shakespeare is not my thing; I'm reading biochemistry. But you think that girl wanted to imitate Anthea for some reason?"

"Possibly. I'm also wondering whether there was a man from the school who was involved with Anthea as a student, and if he might have later become involved with Deborah."

"Some kind of philandering teacher at Kingbrook? That sounds kind of far-fetched. You have no idea how dull most of the teachers are."

"What about David Pettibone?"

"The drama bloke? I would have said he loved himself too much to notice anyone else. Listen, I don't know about this Deborah, but I can't believe Anthea would ever have fallen for him."

Her tone was emphatic, but Ellie wondered. Sometimes your best friend is the last person you want to know about the guy you've fallen for.

"By the way, are you sure she's really missing? I mean, her parents used to raise the alarm if she was an hour late getting home from school."

"That's interesting," said Ellie. "They made a point of telling us that they had been trying hard not to hover—and that's why they didn't report her missing right away. She'd spent the summer in London, and there was a mix-up afterward where her parents thought she was in Oxford, and her roommates thought she was with her parents. So although there's evidence she did return from London, no one has heard from her since the beginning of October. She has simply vanished."

"God, that's so creepy. But it also seems typical of her parents that they would overshoot the mark in the opposite direction," she said unsympathetically. "You know, ever since I got back to the UK, I've been thinking about her. Planning how and when we would meet again. What I would finally say."

"There's a rumor she met a man and went off with him. Perhaps is underground until she has a baby."

"No way! That doesn't sound like Anthea at all. She would never let anyone or anything get between her and finishing her degree. She's been dreaming of a first from Oxford since she learned to read. If she did fall pregnant, she would have an abortion. Unless, of course, she's completely changed."

"True. You've changed, after all."

"No, I haven't. I'm exactly the same. I just understand who that is now."

"Point taken. So is there anyone else you can think I should talk to? Someone she might have been in touch with during the past couple of years?"

"Not offhand. I'd say she went to Oxford and didn't look back."

Remembering Anthea's room, Ellie was inclined to agree. Except for that yearbook.

After lunch, Ellie took Isabelle to visit Rosie. On the way, they stopped in Chipping Martin to buy her some books—which they both agreed were the perfect gift for a five-day-old baby—and a little teddy bear. Isabelle was proud to be the first person ever to read her *The Tale of Peter Rabbit.* “Even though she won’t remember, I’ll never forget it,” she said, when they had tucked the baby back into her bassinet.

“I’m sure it’s like what they say about hearing Mozart in the womb,” said Ellie. “Good literature changes your cell structure for the better.”

“Just think,” said Isabelle, as she drove them through the narrow streets of Kingbrook, which was built into the side of a hill. “If I’d gone to Kingbrook Grammar, Rosie could be my daughter.”

“What a thought!” said Ellie. “Was it ever a possibility? That you would go there?”

Isabelle shook her head. “Mum had her heart set on my going to the school she went to in Oxford. All girls. Hardly a male in sight. Kingbrook is nice though. Did you ever see it?”

No, Ellie said, she hadn’t, at which Isabelle made a sharp right that led out of the town and down a road lined with tall beech trees and a high stone wall. At a handsome wrought-iron gate, she pulled up, and they got out of the car.

“There it is,” she said. “The den of iniquity, it would seem.”

The gates were locked since the school was closed for the holidays, so all they could do was peer in through the bars. Lush green lawns surrounded the main half-timbered building with its leaded windows and tall brick chimneys, which had obviously been a home at one time. The modern buildings were tucked behind it so as not to spoil the first impression of a gracious, intimate school. Ellie studied it for a long time, trying to match up what she had heard of the students’ experiences there with the image it projected of a wonderful place to go to school.

The rain had stopped, but a brisk wind rattled the

bare branches, and heavy clouds promised to unleash more rain soon. Not interested in the school, Isabelle watched the sky impatiently, and finally said: "Had enough? I'm freezing."

"I guess," said Ellie, reluctantly, and returned to the car.

"Do you really think the school is connected to the murder? And even Anthea's disappearance?" Isabelle asked, as she tore confidently along the road.

"There's no firm evidence," said Ellie. "Not from the police's point of view. So you probably shouldn't say anything to anyone about that."

Isabelle grinned. "Oh, don't worry. Theories abound that you wouldn't believe. My favorite is the notion that the headmaster selects students to be his sex slaves. He usually dumps them when they leave school, but he couldn't get over his obsession with Anthea so he kidnapped her and brought her back."

Ellie grimaced. "Very funny," she said, and Isabelle laughed.

"Don't you read the *Daily Mail*? That's nothing. A commonplace."

Isabelle wanted to be left off at a friend's house a couple of miles from Little Beecham, so Ellie continued on alone. She was nearly home when she saw Seamus MacDonald plodding along the side of the road. The rain had begun again, and he looked very happy to see her, when she pulled over and called out: "Want a ride?"

"I am so glad to see you!" he said, holding his gloved hands up to the heating vent. "You would never believe what hard work it is trying to bump into people casually. I've prowled Chipping Martin and Kingbrook from end to end, as well as the Whichester Mall—and getting from place to place on the bus takes so long, I decided to walk home."

"You are amazing. And did you find out anything interesting?"

He wrinkled his nose. "Not about Anthea Davies. She's too much older than my friends, but I found kids who were eager to talk about Debbie Woodman. The story I heard was that she was bullied a lot for having too many fat cells and not enough brain cells, until suddenly she got, you know, boobs instead of blobs. That's a quote, by the way. I would never say that."

"I'm glad to hear it."

"Anyway, then all the blokes were interested, and quite a few took advantage, if you know what I mean. She went along with everything thinking she was finally liked, only they, you know, thought she was a slapper. When she wised up, she shut them all out. The girls too. For a while she was still beautiful, but last summer she got fat again. End of story. Not one person guessed she was pregnant, though I think a couple of blokes were counting backwards when they heard about the baby. A surprising number of people insisted she must have killed herself, even though the police say it was murder. It's just too hard to imagine something like that happening to a kid you know."

"That's a terrible story, but it rings true unfortunately," said Ellie, and they both fell silent, watching the rain wash across the windshield.

When they reached Morag's cottage, she pulled over. "I have another question, if you're interested," said Ellie, and Seamus eagerly took out the notebook he always kept in his inside coat pocket. "It's an easy one, I hope. I need to know where kids from around here would most likely go for a tattoo."

"You mean a scratcher, who won't ask for your ID? Or a legal place."

Ellie considered that. "I think legal."

"It's not my area of expertise, of course," said Seamus, "but I have heard of a shop called Beezlybub's. In Oxford. That might be a starting point."

"Super, thanks. And how's your mom? I haven't laid eyes on her since Christmas Eve."

Seamus scowled. "Who has. She's so busy bonding with Crispix. I got home from Gran's last night, and there was no food in the house at all. Speaking of which, I'm starving. I hope there's some tea in my future."

Ellie laughed. "Give her a break, Seamus. This phase doesn't usually last long."

"That's fine, as long as the next phase is when she dumps him. Did you know he teaches at Kingbrook?"

"No, I didn't. I don't think I've ever heard his last name."

"It's Souter. Crispin Souter. And the kids say he's really tough. That's a side Mum doesn't want to see," he said, and with that, he hopped out.

Wednesday, December 30
Chapter 9

While Graham attended the inquest at the Oxford County Council Coroner's Court and Isabelle shopped for a dress to wear on New Year's Eve, Ellie met David Pettibone at The Eagle and Child pub on St. Giles. They sat at a table in the Rabbit Room that was wedged in next to a bricked up fireplace and surrounded by photos of the pub's famous literary patrons. She suppressed her desire to dwell on the idea that J.R.R. Tolkien might have sat at the very same table and focused on the man sitting across from her.

He was not handsome in a conventional sense, but he had charisma. He knew how to use his assets, for example, calling attention to that shock of thick blond hair by running his hands through it, and Ellie thought his clothes were simply wonderful: colorful and obviously chosen with care from his green tie and flowered shirt down to his blue patent leather shoes. She could see why Charlotte might have pegged him as gay, but he gave off a very sexy energy when he leaned his elbows on the table and smiled at her. So the first question that came to her mind was why every girl at Kingbrook Grammar hadn't joined the Drama Club. She certainly would have.

She could tell that she wasn't what he was expecting either. She'd explained on the phone that she became involved because she was married to the vicar who Mr. and Mrs. Davies had asked for help. That plus the American accent had confused him. He took his time to assess her, a woman of about his own age, dressed in black jeans and a black turtleneck sweater, before turning on the casual, practiced charm of a trained actor.

"We were all very shocked to hear about Deborah. It's hard to fathom that happening to someone you know. Someone so young. And at Christmas too," he said, as he carefully stirred two sugars into his tea.

Ellie wondered to whom the 'we' in that sentence referred, but all she said was, "Yes. I think you mentioned that the police interviewed you about the murder."

He pulled back slightly with his hand over his heart. "About the girl, yes. Not about the murder. They talked to all of us from the school, even though I understood they believe her father did it."

"I'm sure they don't want to jump to conclusions too quickly," said Ellie, watching him closely.

"I suppose you're right. In that case, I hope they catch the one who did it soon because my own alibi is none too good. I was waiting for Father Christmas at my parents' house in Cheltenham, where Mum and Dad go to bed by nine, and my sister was ill and had knocked herself unconscious with cough medicine."

"Between DNA and Father Christmas's witness statement, you should be able to clear yourself," said Ellie.

"DNA. . . oh, of course, the baby. My God." He cleared his throat and sipped his tea. "But that isn't why you wanted to talk to me—Ellie, isn't it?"

She nodded. "The police have drawn a complete blank in their search for Anthea Davies, and her parents are quite desperate for any new leads."

"So, Yanks to the rescue. Is that it?"

Ellie caught herself before scowling, but she hated that expression. Sybil had used it too. It was amazing how much disdain for its successful former colonies a Brit could pack into those four letters.

"Why do you think her disappearance has something to do with Kingbrook, rather than the back alleys of Oxford or somewhere else?"

"There are reasons to believe the present events are linked to the past," she said. This was pushing the truth to the limit, but she wanted to see how he would react.

He lifted an eyebrow—that very English mannerism that conveyed superiority but no meaning. "I see. A lot of students have been over the dam since then, but I do remember Anthea. She was an unusual girl with a great deal of presence and determination. Definitely a Juliet," he said.

"What?" said Ellie, splashing her tea as she set down her cup.

"Sorry. I didn't mean to imply anything about her fate. It's just a little theory of mine. I think of teenage girls as either Juliets or Ophelias. The ones who know how to get what they want and the ones who don't."

"Really. That's very interesting. And is this something you talk about—in the Drama Club, for example?"

"Absolutely. When we do scenes we try to come up with entry points to the characters that are easy for the kids to grasp. For example, is a character a Romeo or a Hamlet? Impetuously decisive or a sensitive brooder."

"Have you ever had the impression that the students were applying these categories to each other outside of the club?"

"No. Have you?"

"Yes."

"In what way?" For just a moment, his poise slipped.

"Anthea and some others apparently took to calling girls 'Ophs' if they dramatized their broken hearts too publicly."

He laughed, and Ellie thought he looked relieved, as if he expected something worse. "That's very clever, but I find it hard to believe it led to the dire consequences we've been discussing."

"Hard to say, if you think about where bullying can lead. Would you have called Deborah an Ophelia?"

"Oh, yes. I'm afraid it is not all that difficult to draw a line between her behavior and the outcome. Not that she committed suicide. I appreciate that."

"But Anthea was a Juliet?"

"Without question. If Anthea disappeared, I'd expect her to be carrying out some very specific plan of her own. She was remarkably smart and deliberate. Totally lacking in the spontaneity required to be an actress, but she could learn lines faster than anyone I've ever met."

"Did the students ever act out scenes from *Hamlet*?"

"Of course, and a lot of the girls have a go at Ophelia. Both *Hamlet* and *Romeo and Juliet* are great for kids. Think about it. The two things that most obsess teenagers are sex and whether to obey their parents or not. Add some great sword fighting and weepy endings, and you've got everyone's attention."

Despite herself, Ellie laughed, and he relaxed a bit more. "So what role do you play in all of this?"

"Me? I'm an actor. A chameleon. Tell me who you want me to be, and I'll be it. I play a very good secondary school teacher at the moment."

"Mr. Chips?"

"No. To be honest, I aim to give a good dollop of entertainment to make the learning go down, but I don't much go for the role of confidant."

"So you would have had no idea if Anthea were carrying on a secret relationship with a teacher or that Deborah was pregnant."

"Anthea, no. I never heard a hint of anything like that. In her case, there were a number of people who liked to take credit for how well she did, but beyond that, nothing. There has been talk about Deborah after the fact. How we could all have missed that—but teenagers do change a lot physically, and I'm afraid I do my best to block out the students' personal stuff. It's too draining.

"Do you really think a teacher was involved?" he asked. "That's quite an accusation. I hope the police don't agree with you."

"I'm just fishing. I have no idea what the police think."

"No worries," he said, unconvincingly. He drained his cup of tea and looked at his watch. "Now it's my turn for a question, don't you think? I know why I teach in a secondary school at the moment, the theater world being the chancy place it is, but how did a woman like you end up as a vicar's wife in an English village?"

"I fell in love," said Ellie, and he laughed, almost genuinely.

"Oh dear, the source of all our pleasure and our pain. Someone must have said that somewhere, but it does appear you've found something meatier in the role than arranging the flowers on the altar. I wish you luck, and, of course, I do hope you'll find Anthea safe and sound. Now I must run, I've got an audition in London for what may be my next role."

When he had gone, throwing his scarf over his shoulder in a perfect imitation of Sebastian Flyte, Ellie put the money for the bill down on the table. Then on an impulse, she looked around quickly, put David's teacup into her purse, and hurried out onto St. Giles with her heart pounding. She didn't know whether his DNA could be captured from the cup, by why waste the opportunity?

She didn't stop to pause for breath until she realized that she was in the exact spot by the Ashmolean

Museum where Anthea's photo had been taken on that October day just before she disappeared. The day when she'd been happy, smiling at the person who held the camera. Could that have been David Pettibone? She didn't think so, but why? The self-confessed chameleon had skillfully presented himself as an entertainer-cum-teacher, making sure she saw only the colors he wanted her to see, and nothing more. Nonetheless, she didn't see him in the role of Kingbrook's Hamlet.

When she left St. Giles to head toward the train station, it did not take long before the University seemed worlds, as well as centuries, away. On a dingy narrow street, she found the shop with the sign that said Beezlybub's tucked in next to a brick hotel whose name was missing a few letters.

She pulled open the door and launched into her story to the bored, colorfully tattooed girl at the counter, who listened as she stared at Ellie with suspicion.

"You're not a mum or something, are you?" she asked, when Ellie had laid out the rosemary and fennel designs on the counter.

"No, and I'm not the police either."

The girl laughed. "I could tell that, and anyway I keep clear of them. This is a strictly legit tattoo business. Did you want one?"

Maybe it was frustration at the lack of concrete results she'd gotten from her first interview, but she was determined to do better this time. "No," she said. "I'm trying to locate the girl who had this design—fennel—tattooed around her wrist."

"Fennel—what's that?"

"An herb," said Ellie.

"A what? Do you mean a herb?" The girl laughed again. "There's only one herb we get asked about here."

"So you didn't do a tattoo with yellow flowers like this?"

"I didn't say that. Are you sure you're not a mum?" Her face grew more suspicious.

"Yes, I am sure, but I think you should try harder to help me," said Ellie. "The girl who has that tattoo has been missing for three months. The one who got this one"—she pointed to the rosemary—"was murdered last week."

The girl blanched. "I thought you said you weren't police."

"I'm not."

"So, what. You're a private detective?"

"Something like that. And I'd very much like your assistance. You can start by telling me if you've ever done this design as a tattoo, and, if so, was it for a girl who looked like this?" She slapped down the photo of Anthea. "Once we've covered that, you can tell me if you've ever done any of these others." She laid down pictures of daisies, violets, rue, columbine, and pansies.

Now the girl looked genuinely panicked. She wet her lips. "I know I haven't done all of those."

"Okay," said Ellie, trying to stay cool. "Tell me about the ones you have done. Tell me about her." She pointed to Anthea's photo.

The girl looked at it for a long time. "She came in ages ago. Going on three years. I wouldn't remember except that it was my sister who wanted me to do it, as an exchange like, for some girl she knew at Kingbrook Grammar who was going to help her swot for her A levels.

"The girl brought in a picture of what she wanted. I never heard the name. Fennel, you said? It was an odd sort of flower for a tattoo, so tiny, and yellow, which doesn't show up that well, but believe me, in this business you learn fast not to make any comment. You'd be amazed what people want."

"More than amazed. Shocked."

"Anyway, it was actually quite pretty. Delicate. She wanted it to be like a bracelet going around her wrist. I told her that could be painful because the skin is so thin there, but she didn't care. In fact, she seemed to want it to be painful, which I usually consider a warning sign that I'm dealing with a nutter. It went okay though. I never saw her again, and my sister never did sit her exams. She ran off with a drug dealer instead."

"Anyway I forgot all about it, but a few weeks ago another girl came in, who wanted the same kind of bracelet design with a tiny flower. Funny, isn't it?"

Ellie didn't reply except to say, "Was it one of these?"

"I don't know. It was purple."

"Don't you keep a photo record of your work?"

"Only if the customer agrees. Are you saying the girl who got that tattoo was murdered?"

"Yes." She set down the photo of Deborah from the newspaper.

"Oh, God. That could have been her." She stared at the photo then she said, "There was someone with her."

Ellie's heart lurched. "A man?"

"No. Another girl. I think she would've liked to get the same design, but she was too young. She asked me about how to find a custom-designed temp. Red-haired, she was. You know that really amazing color."

"A redhead. Do you remember anything else about those girls?"

"No. I mean, when I'm working, I'm concentrating on the tat. Not on the person. So what do you think this all means?"

"I wish I knew. But all of these flowers and herbs are mentioned in the same speech from a play."

"A play? Blimey, that's a new one. So you think they're connected, and that's where they got the idea?"

"Possibly. And you don't remember anything more

about that first girl? The one with the yellow flower tattoo?"

She shook her head. "Sorry. It's a fluke I remember her at all."

Ellie thanked the girl, who smiled. "My pleasure," she said. "And if you decide you want a tattoo, come back any time."

"I'll keep that in mind," said Ellie, scooping the designs and photos back into her bag.

As she walked back across Oxford to meet Graham and Isabelle, Ellie came out onto Cornmarket Street, which was so crowded with shoppers taking advantage of the post-Christmas sales that you could hardly see where you were going. She did not find it a comforting sign of home that American chains like The Gap now existed there cheek-by-jowl with Oxford's ancient buildings, but the locals didn't seem to mind.

She tried to sum up what she had learned that morning—but what she hadn't was more evident. Nothing David Pettibone said or did and no sixth sense supported the idea that he enjoyed inappropriate attachments with his students, though he had probably provided the inspiration for the Ophelia imagery. At least she hadn't made up that link. She supposed she could be pleased about that.

The news that Anthea and Deborah had gotten their tattoos at the same shop did not really advance her investigation very much. Ellie was surprised to find out that a younger, red-haired girl had been there with Deborah and did not like the thought that it might have been Sarah Henning. It hadn't occurred to her until now that Sarah could have also joined the Kingbrook Drama Club.

Then she realized that if Sarah had been close enough to Deborah to accompany her on the excursion to Beezlybub's, she might also know the name of Rosie's father. The one who made Deborah want that tattoo. Her Hamlet. And suddenly the whole mystery seemed to shift toward resolution. If only the redhead turned out to be Sarah. And if only she trusted Ellie enough to tell her everything.

She quickly dialed Sarah's number and waited while the phone rang, but there was no answer, and she decided it was best not to leave a message. She'd have to try again later or go by the Hennings' house. She was long overdue for a visit to the family anyway.

The century-old Blackwell's Bookshop took her mind off solving mysteries as soon as she climbed the two steps to the front door, crossed the creaky wooden floor, and inhaled the fragrance of thousands of books. When she decided to leave San Francisco for Oxfordshire, Blackwell's ran a close second to Graham in terms of the advantages her new life would offer.

She was browsing through the British literature section, when she heard a voice call out "Ellie!" and looked up to see Morag MacDonald approaching with a man a few steps behind.

"How funny to run into you here. What are you doing in Oxford?" Morag asked. She had an armload of books, and her face was flushed and happy.

Ellie held up a thick just-released biography of Charlotte Brontë she'd been looking at, and said: "I'm bankrupting myself—or I will if Graham and Isabelle don't get here soon. How are you?"

"Fine. Crispin, this is Ellie Kent, my friend from Little Beecham."

Ellie smiled at poor Seamus's rival, a tall and strikingly handsome man with thick chestnut hair and gray eyes. He managed to look both comfortable and elegant in an expensive gray tweed jacket and faded jeans. He shook her hand with a warm, firm grip, and said, "I've been looking forward to meeting the woman who singlehandedly managed to turn a village Christmas service into a major media event."

Ellie blushed. "It wasn't intentional, believe me. But it's nice to meet you too. I guess this is where you two met," she said, hoping to shift the focus away from herself. "Here at Blackwell's?"

Morag laughed. She looked beautiful out of her usual gardening clothes and with silver clips holding back her dark curly hair. "Sort of. We knew each other when we both taught at Shepherd's Hill School years ago, but then Crispin went off to teach in China." Turning to him, she said, "The first time we saw each other again was last summer. You were with your nephew and didn't remember me."

"Impossible," he said, putting his arm around her shoulders and giving her a squeeze. Ellie thought she saw a flash of annoyance cross his face, but Morag didn't see it.

She rolled her eyes at Ellie. "Possible," she said, laughing. "But a few weeks ago we met again, and, um, connected."

"So I see," said Ellie, who thought the word connected had never before sounded so sexual. She had always found it annoying when new lovers seemed unable to keep from touching each other all the time, and she was glad to spot Graham and Isabelle coming up the stairs.

"How is that baby, by the way? I've been meaning to call and ask," said Morag.

"Still at Kingbrook Hospital, but she'll be fine. Look, I'm sorry but I have to go. I see Graham and Isabelle heading into the cafe, and they'll be wondering if I've gotten lost if I'm not there. Let's get together, when you have time."

"Sure," she said. "Crispin starts back to school next

week, so any day then."

On the way home, Graham reported that the inquest was uneventful. Deborah had been formally identified by her GP, and her cause of death was described as manual strangulation. In the end, he had not even been called to testify. The verdict was murder by a person or persons unknown. Ellie found this predictable result very depressing, and her own progress report did little to dispel that mood. Everything about Deborah and Anthea seemed clouded over by that word: unknown.

But Isabelle cheered them by describing her shopping adventures and how she had managed to find an incredibly skimpy red silk dress at half price, thus leaving her enough money to buy red shoes as well. Listening to her, Graham kept glancing away from the road as if to make sure this was the daughter he'd set out with that morning, which made Isabelle laugh and say: "Just you wait and see, Dad. . . .It's brilliant."

Ellie was still not able to reach Sarah, so she went to visit Rosie. Snow flurries foretold a change in the weather as the afternoon faded into darkness. This time around they no longer struck Ellie as festive.

When she arrived at the fourth floor, she discovered that the baby had been moved to a private room with a constable posted at the door, who would not let her in.

"I'm just following orders, love," he said. "No one but hospital staff can go in since the incident today."

"What do you mean? What incident?" she asked, alarmed.

"I'm not at liberty to give out any details," was all the officer would say.

Ellie looked up and down the corridor, hoping to see a nurse she knew, and spotted the Jamaican woman who had told her rosemary offered protection from evil spirits.

"Anna," she said, glancing at her nameplate. "Do you know what happened to Rosie? Is she all right?"

"The man you were expecting came," she said.

"What man was that?"

"The one you imagined when I told you her mum wanted to protect her from evil." They looked into each other's eyes, remembering that moment. How Ellie had instinctively covered the baby's head with her hand.

"And did you see him?" she asked.

"No," said Anna, "but the others told me they felt there was something wrong. He looked like he was wearing a disguise and waited around as if he hoped to get into the Unit when no staff or visitors were there. To be sure the babies were safe, they locked the Unit and called for help."

"Did they say what this disguise was?"

Anna ran her hand over her dreadlocks. "Tall, fair-skinned, but with black hair, all slicked back flat, glasses, and a Scottish accent."

"I see," said Ellie. That certainly didn't sound like Bill Woodman, who had broad, strong shoulders and a stocky build in the photos she had seen at their house. So who was it? "Do you know when he came?"

"An hour ago? I was on my break, so that's all I know."

Ellie thanked her for her help and was about to tackle the constable again, when DI Mullane came striding down the hall. "Hello, Mrs. Kent,' he said. "I heard you were here, so I came to see you and the famous baby."

"Well, if that's the only way I can get to see her, let's do it," she said, with a frown at the constable.

They went into the room where Rosie's bassinet had been set up with a chair for the nurse assigned to care for her. She was glad to see the teddy bear and books they'd bought her had been moved too, but Rosie looked pale and her dark eyes had lost their sparkle. When Ellie picked her up, she was fretful and anxious, which made her wonder if the baby could have sensed some danger had passed close by.

Mullane watched without saying anything, as Ellie rocked her until Rosie relaxed and fell asleep. Then he said, "She's a lovely one. Takes after her mother."

"Can you tell?" asked Ellie. "To be honest, I've tried not to notice, except for her fingers." She carefully opened the tiny hand to show him how her fingers were delicately tapered. "They're so pretty and already distinctive. At least that's my opinion." She smiled and then remembered to whom she was speaking.

She set Rosie back into her bassinet, saying "Now you've seen her. What was it you wanted me for?"

"I'd like to have a little chat. Shall we have a coffee?"

Ellie picked up her coat and bag. "All right," she said and followed him to the hospital cafeteria without speaking.

When they were settled, he said: "I know you've heard about the man who tried to get access to the baby today and how the hospital called us. Unfortunately he got away before we could talk to him, but we've reviewed the security tapes, and we're certain he was not Bill Woodman.

"He also doesn't appear to be any of Deborah Woodman's other contacts that we've interviewed, so I'd like to know if you have any ideas about this man's identity."

"What makes you think I would?"

"As you yourself told me, you have been in the middle of this investigation from the start. From even before the start. And, I know you, you find out things."

"I wish I had found out more. I have no idea of that

man's identity. I've been trying to help Anthea Davies' parents, and I'd like to help Rosie too, but all I know is that there are some links between Deborah and Anthea. Whether they are really related to what happened to them is not clear."

"Tell me about the links anyway."

"Both of them went to Kingbrook Grammar and participated in the Drama Club. They were both attractive girls who had a penchant for keeping their romantic relationships a secret from everyone they knew. In the Drama Club, they did scenes from Shakespeare, and *Hamlet* was popular with them. Girls who were heartbroken were joked about in the club as 'Ophelias' or 'Ophs'—and both Anthea and Deborah chose to get tattoos of the flowering herbs mentioned in Ophelia's mad scene. Anthea did this at the end of her final year at Kingbrook—choosing fennel, an herb that symbolizes false flattery, and Deborah got hers only a few weeks ago. As you probably remember, she chose rosemary 'for remembrance.'"

"That's it? All you have?" He looked disappointed.

"The rest is supposition: that both girls followed this similar pattern because they were involved with the same man. Not a student, but someone older who would have been at the school when they were both there. In other words, probably a teacher. I'm not aware of any other situation where their paths crossed so they would meet the same man."

"And in your theory of parallels, have you deduced that Anthea has also been murdered, although her body has not yet been discovered?"

Ellie drew back, but she nodded. "That does seem a likely scenario, given what happened to Deborah. It doesn't explain the time lapse though. After all, Anthea left Kingbrook well over two years ago."

"True. It may come as a surprise to you, but we have

also thought about the possibility that Deborah was involved with someone at the school. However, we've interviewed everyone and checked their alibis, and they all seem to be in the clear for the murder. As far as the baby is concerned, to hear them talk, she must be the result of immaculate conception."

"Are you going to do DNA testing?" Ellie asked, thinking guiltily of David's teacup, which was still in her bag. Under the circumstances, this did not seem like a good moment to mention it.

"No DNA from the killer has been found," said Mullane.

"But if you knew who the baby's father was, you would have a suspect, wouldn't you?"

"At the moment, the baby's father is not a suspect. We're still looking for Bill Woodman. We finally located his car, so we hope to trace him soon."

"And I suppose you won't tell me where it was. Fair enough, but what about the man who came to the hospital today? If he wasn't Woodman, he must have been Rosie's father. Who else would care?"

"We're working on that. Now listen to me, Mrs. Kent. I'll admit you've helped uncover some useful information in the past, but you must not interfere with murder investigations—and it's looking like that will include the missing girl."

"So you want me to tell Anthea's parents I can't help them."

"Yes. You know, people disappear all the time, and there's usually some trace. On the other hand, bodies disappear quite easily."

"So the police now believe Anthea is dead?"

"Nothing is that certain. But you yourself have highlighted the links between the two girls and, if they are dead, it's also possible that Bill Woodman is dead."

"Oh my God."

"Exactly." Mullane's phone rang then and, when he saw who was calling, he got up quickly, saying he had to go. Over his shoulder, he added, "I told you from the start this was a nasty business, and you really should keep out of it."

Ellie was driving, when her own phone rang, but she couldn't answer it. Instead she listened to the voice of David Pettibone.

"I think I told you we do a lot of scenes from Shakespeare in the club, and I encourage everyone to pick one they would like to do for the group. I can't believe I forgot this until now, but last term Deborah Woodman volunteered, and she chose one of the songs Ophelia sings in *Hamlet*. Even though she didn't have a particularly good voice, her performance was so moving it took everyone by surprise. We were gobsmacked, to put it in the vernacular. It was the one about St. Valentine's Day, do you know it?"

"Young men will do't if they come to't
By Cock, they are to blame.
Quoth she, 'Before you tumbled me
You promised me to wed.'
'So would I ha' done by yonder sun
And thou hadst not come to my bed.'"

"I think that says it all, don't you?" Then he rang off.

Ellie pulled over and listened to the message again. She was familiar with the song, and she was sure he was right. Rosie's father had promised to marry Deborah and then reneged. But there must have been love before that, at least on her side, and perhaps that's what she wanted to remember. What she wanted to pass on to her daughter.

Ellie had re-read the scene in *Hamlet*, where Ophelia scatters a bouquet of flowers and herbs, describing their meanings as they fall to the ground. She says, "There's rosemary, that's for remembrance; pray you, love, remember."

Pray you, love, remember.

That was quite a goodbye for her newborn child, whom she left safely tucked in the manger on Christmas Eve. Then she must have tried one last time to make her Hamlet change his mind, but, instead of wedding her, he killed her.

Thursday, December 31
Chapter 10

"He classifies girls as Juliets or Ophelias?" said Graham, when they were lying in bed, arms around each other. It wasn't that early, but the sky was still dark, and the room cold and shadowy. They wanted to put off leaving their warm duvet, turning on the lights, and starting the day as long as possible. "Why would anyone want to be Ophelia? Hamlet barely says a civil word to her in the entire play," he went on. "I would have thought Juliet would have much more appeal to young women."

"I think most girls go back and forth between the two," said Ellie. "They want to be rebellious Juliets, but they're afraid to be. Ophelia is the classic obedient daughter. On the other hand, I've always found *Romeo and Juliet* boring. I mean, what's their story? They fall in love at first sight, are in love throughout, and die due to a series of mistakes. The end."

Graham laughed. "So says the professor of English literature."

"It's true. There's no comparison. *Hamlet* is much more romantic and tragic because he's so erratic: now loving and attached, now indecisive and unavailable. Nothing drives a woman wilder. The play tracks the unraveling of their relationship, and Ophelia can't understand how everything could go awry so quickly when she's just trying to do the right thing. The men in her life all abandon her in different ways, and her future is destroyed, so she kills herself."

"And this relates to our present circumstances in what way?"

"I think love puts people in untenable situations now every bit as much as it did five centuries ago."

"I suppose so," he said.

"You know so," she said. "Or anyway, I do."

"Then I'm glad we have been given a different script."

"Me too," Ellie agreed, snuggling closer to him. But at that moment, they heard the patter of feet followed by an insistent scratching at the door. "And this is where it says 'Enter the dog.'"

While they were dressing, they heard on the radio that William Woodman's abandoned car had been found. Apparently it had been in the Oxford train station's long-stay car park since six p.m. on the 27th of December, and no one had noticed it, despite the police asking for help in locating that car. This oversight was attributed to holiday staffing. Evidence linking Mr. Woodman to his daughter's murder was found in the car, and the police requested anyone with information about his whereabouts to contact them.

"My God," said Ellie, pulling on her heaviest sweater. "Six p.m. would be just about right. If he were at the house after we left and before the police arrived, he could have removed the evidence of Deborah giving birth there—and whatever else he thought was incriminating—driven to Oxford and taken off for anywhere in the world."

"I suppose, but I would have thought he'd already be long gone, if he were the one who killed Deborah. Which I do not for one minute believe."

"So who's your suspect?"

"Your chameleon?"

"I don't think so. He claims he was with his family

in Cheltenham—and Mullane said all the people from the school have been cleared."

"He was more or less on his own though. I'd say his alibi was pretty flimsy."

"Okay. So let's say Deborah knew where he was and showed up there after leaving Rosie at the church. They quarreled, and he killed her to prevent the relationship from coming out. Why would he then drive all the way over here to Stevens Wood, in a snowstorm, to dispose of the body—and then drive back? And where does that leave her father? Waiting for her at home?"

"I don't know. But the only way Bill ever could have killed her would have been in an act of rage—and where and when would that have happened? There was no sign of it at the house."

"The police haven't let on where it happened, and, you know, strangulation is not messy."

A stricken look crossed Graham's face, so Ellie said, "Come on, let's not discuss this any more on an empty stomach."

Sarah still did not answer any phone, email, or text messages, and no one was at home when Ellie went by the Hennings' house, so she visited Rosie and then took Hector for a long ramble. It was a quiet day with crisp air and a milky blue sky that looked as if it would turn gray before long. Yesterday's flurries had not amounted to anything but more snow was predicted.

For now, walking on the dry, frozen ground was easy. When they reached the woods beyond the village, she decided not to go on her usual walk through the fields, but to take an unfamiliar path that followed a brook. Although ice had accumulated along the banks, water bubbled over the rocks in the middle, making a cheerful sound.

Hector trotted beside her, his tail an antenna

broadcasting his pleasure. She had paused to let him track the scent of some bird or animal when a splash of color on the far side of the brook caught her eye. It appeared to be clothing stuck in the ice, and she climbed gingerly down the bank to see what it was: More than clothing. Although it was obscured by the overhanging branches, it looked like a body. Possibly female.

With shaking fingers, Ellie took out her cell phone and called Detective Inspector Mullane. The phone rang several times as she waited impatiently, then the familiar laconic voice said: "Mrs. Kent. I can't say I expected to talk with you again so soon."

"I am sorry to bother you, Inspector, but I've seen something worrying stuck in the brook that runs close to the B road out of Little Beecham."

"Something. What kind of something."

"Well, I can't get close enough to tell for sure, but it's definitely clothes and sort of body shaped."

There was a silence on the other end, before he said: "All right. Tell me again where you are."

She described her location then waited shivering and stamping her feet until Mullane arrived with DS Jones. They both wore wellingtons and had brought a long pole with a hook on the end of it.

"There," said Ellie, pointing.

Jones looked skeptical, but he gamely slid down the bank to the edge of the brook. The ice broke immediately under his weight, and water rushed around his legs as he splashed across to the other side. From where Ellie and Mullane stood at the top of the bank, they still couldn't see much, but Jones turned to them and said, "It's nought, sir," barely hiding his annoyance.

"Well, it's obviously something, man," said Mullane. "So what is it?" and Ellie was grateful that he didn't simply turn on her with an accusation of wasting police time.

"It's not a body, sir. It's a sort of guy like you see on Bonfire Night. A bunch of old clothes and straw," he said. "It's stuck in the ice, so I can't shift it. What with the changing weather, I'd say it's been here a few days."

"Take a photo for me, Jones," ordered Mullane.

"Sir," said Jones, moving in closer. "There is something around the neck." He pulled it up and turned to them holding an envelope sealed in a plastic bag.

Both Ellie and Mullane leaned forward as if they would see what it was by doing so, but they couldn't.

"Bring that here when you're done with the photos."

"Yes, sir," said Jones, starting to make his way back across the brook and up the bank.

When he reached them, Mullane took the envelope in his gloved hands. There was no writing on the outside, but it was carefully sealed in two plastic bags with a string that must have gone around the figure's head.

Mullane took out the envelope, while Ellie hovered, waiting to see what was inside. It was a half piece of paper with a message written in block letters:

"Oh woe is me, t'have seen what I have seen, see what I see."

Mullane glanced at Ellie as if ready to say, "Nonsense," but she cut him off.

"It's Ophelia again."

"Very interesting," he said, putting the paper back in the envelope. "I had no idea so many people in these parts spouted the Bard the way you do. So I guess this figure is lost property from a play."

"I doubt it. Attaching a note. That's not part of the play. May I look at the photos?"

Begrudgingly Jones handed her his phone, and Ellie

flicked through the pictures he had taken. The figure was dressed in a long flowered skirt with a shawl wrapped around the upper body. The straw arms were folded across the chest and had clutched the envelope in gloved hands. The face was blank straw, but a wreath of holly had been wrapped around the head.

"It definitely portrays Ophelia, who drowned herself in a brook."

"So what we have here is a suicidal guy," said Jones.

Mullane laughed. "I must say, you drag us out on some wild goose chases, Mrs. Kent, but they aren't boring. Agreed, Jones?"

Jones looked as if agreement were the last thing on his mind. He was emptying the icy water out of his boots, while hopping on the frozen ground in his stocking feet.

"Sir," he said. "Next thing we'll be bringing in a scarecrow for murder."

"Very funny," said Ellie. "You should be glad it's not another body, but you must admit the repeated references to Ophelia have to be significant and linked."

"Our job is to find a murderer not some Shakespearean phantom. But do let me know if your theory takes on 'too, too solid flesh'".

"Well said, Mullane. You surprise me."

"I did go to school once upon a time," he said.

"So you're just going to leave that there?" she asked, looking back at the straw woman.

He shrugged. "Our remit is pretty broad, but it doesn't include trash collection." And with that, they unceremoniously departed.

They had not bothered to take the note, so Ellie put it in her pocket. She was sure the straw figure was a clue and slid gingerly down the bank to cross the icy brook herself. The water numbed her legs almost immediately, and she was unable to free the figure, which was both waterlogged and frozen. Anyway, she realized, it was much too big to fit in the Mini, so what would she do with it once she got it out of the brook?

She made her way back across the water and up the bank, shivering, and wondered if Michael-John Parker was at home. He had a van that he used to pick up antiques, and he had helped her figure out how a book of Italian poetry was linked to the dead man she'd found in St. Michael's churchyard last fall. Maybe he'd be willing to help again. She punched in his number and was pleased when he answered right away.

"Hello, Michael-John. Happy New Year! It's Ellie Kent."

"Mrs. Kent, how nice to hear from you. I take it you survived Christmas."

"I did. . . and it already seems like ancient history."

"Isn't that the way with most of our worries. So what can I do for you now?"

"Actually, I was wondering if you might be able to take a break from the shop to help me with something. A rescue."

"A rescue? *Moi*? Is it an antique we're rescuing?"

"Not exactly. But it's something that needs to be picked up, and my car isn't big enough. I think your van is."

"My van? My dear Mrs. Kent, this is the most exciting proposition I've had in weeks. But tell me first, is this the vicar's lovely new wife calling—or my favorite detective?"

"I'll explain when you get here."

"I see. . . then it must be the detective."

"I'm on the B road where it runs along that brook—about a mile outside the village. I recommend wellingtons—and it would be great if you could bring some kind of tarp and an axe."

He laughed. “All right,” he said, “I will do as you bid. Whistler and I will be at your service as fast as we can. Otherwise I will surely die of curiosity.”

“Thank you, because otherwise I will surely die of hypothermia.”

While she waited, Hector ran up and down the bank, stopping periodically to look at Ellie with dark, questioning eyes. He was done with this spot. Why were they not continuing their walk?

“Sorry, Hector, the walk is over,” she said, as she stamped her own feet to keep warm and re-read the message attached to the figure.

Who could have taken the trouble to re-enact Ophelia’s suicide in this way? Was the figure supposed to be Deborah? Or was it someone else?

She was still circling around these questions when Michael-John arrived, looking large and competent in a capacious waterproof coat and boots. Hector gave Whistler, his Golden Retriever, a happy bark of greeting, and they ran off together, leaving Ellie and Michael-John to the less enjoyable task at hand.

“I should know by now not to get involved with your projects. The last time I saw you, you’d turned a plaster Jesus into a live baby. What alchemy are we up to now?” he said, when he saw the straw woman in the icy rushing brook.

“That figure is related to the mystery of the baby and her murdered mother, as well as a missing girl named Anthea Davies,” said Ellie, as they spread the tarp on the ground.

“How can you tell?” said Michael-John, as he slithered down the bank after her.

Ellie handed him the note that had been attached to the straw woman before splashing across the brook with his axe.

"Woe is me?" he read aloud. "Let me guess. *Hamlet*."

She glanced back at him with a broad smile. "You see, I knew I was right to ask you for help."

Then she attacked the ice with the axe, freed the figure, and pulled it across the brook to where Michael-John was waiting to help her drag it up the bank.

"So this, I presume, is Ophelia?" said Michael-John, looking down at the bedraggled, faceless figure.

"Exactly," said Ellie.

"I can't wait to learn more, but not until we get somewhere warm and dry," he said, heaving the straw woman, wrapped in the tarp, into the back of the van.

Once she was stowed in the barn behind his shop that he used for storage, and he, Ellie, and the dogs were comfortably situated in his office at the back of The Chestnut Tree, Michael-John said, "I have a great deal of faith in you, Mrs. Kent, but I am mystified about how Ophelia in straw or in any other medium plays a role in last week's murder."

Ellie explained while he brewed his favorite *Mariage Frères* tea with a dash of brandy to drive out the cold.

"So if Deborah has been killed, and Anthea is still missing, who is the Ophelia who has now symbolically committed suicide over the woe she has seen?"

Ellie sipped her tea and looked out the window with its view of the high street. The expected snow had begun, and snowflakes swirled in the blue dusk, creating again that illusion that the picturesque village was a perfect world.

She hadn't known until that moment, but suddenly she was sure she knew the answer. "Sarah," she said. "I'll bet it was Sarah Henning."

"The sister of that dreadful little yob who was killed not long ago?"

"Yes. I think she and Deborah Woodman were good friends."

"And what do you think she was trying to accomplish with Our Lady of King Brook?"

"King Brook?"

"Yes, that's the name of the brook. It runs right through the town and ends in a lake there. Haven't you ever noticed?"

"No. But that could explain why the figure was there—to point at the school and to hint at why Deborah had committed suicide, which is what everyone first thought had happened. If I am right, and Sarah did it, she must have been wanting to explain her friend's death."

"Well, it's ironic that the one person in the world who would understand the message found it."

"Oh no, I'm not the only one. I'm sure she hoped the person it was meant for would hear about it."

"And that would be. . . ."

"Hamlet, of course."

"Hamlet? You've cast him as the villain of this piece? I've always adored him—he's my favorite of all Shakespearean characters. Of course, it has long been my theory that he was gay and loved Horatio much more than Ophelia."

"You are not alone in holding that theory," said Ellie. "But some would also say that there is evidence throughout the text indicating that Ophelia was pregnant. And, while I have always loved Hamlet too, you must admit, he was a total disaster where she was concerned."

Michael-John sighed. "All right, the villain. I guess he deserves it. But 'Good night, sweet prince' will always make me tear up anyway."

"'And flights of angels sing thee to thy rest,'" said Ellie. "but I have to go to a party now. Thanks again for your heroic help."

Ellie filled Graham in on what had happened while she took a long hot shower. He sat on the edge of the tub and shouted out his questions.

"I still don't see what this has to do with Anthea's disappearance. That's where we started from, remember? It seems like you've gone rather off track."

"I think it's like putting together the border of a jigsaw puzzle. Until you have a complete edge, you can't begin to define the middle."

"You're kidding, aren't you? The middle is the whole picture. When you have the edge you have nothing."

"No, you don't. You have a defined universe. What we had a week ago was nothing. A person who disappeared and could be anywhere."

"So you're still convinced Anthea and Deborah's mysteries have a common source."

Ellie poked her head around the shower curtain and wiped the water from her eyes. "I'm not convinced about anything. To switch metaphors, I'm chasing after breadcrumbs that I hope form a trail to somewhere. Do you want me to leave the water on for you?"

"Me? No, I'm English, remember? I prefer a bath."

"Right-ee-oh," said Ellie and shut off the taps.

"I have some news too," said Graham, when he had filled the tub. Ellie had put on her bathrobe and taken his place on the edge. The bathroom was steamy and cozy, and she had no desire to leave it for the chilly bedroom, where the black velvet pants and white silk shirt she planned to wear to the Bells' party lay waiting on the bed.

"What's that?" she asked, as she filed her fingernails.

"Sarah Henning came by while you were out with

Hector."

"You're kidding, I've been trying to reach her for two days."

"I know. Her father has gone back to work, and her mother decided to take all the children up to her brother's for a couple of days. Apparently it's somewhere in the Lake District with no mobile phone or internet reception."

"At least that's one mystery solved. So is she going to call me? Come back?"

"Actually, I had a feeling she had something on her mind right then, so I invited her in, gave her a cup of tea, and we ended up having a very good talk."

"What did she say?"

"She told me all about her friendship with Deborah, which started after Jackie's death. She said Deborah was the only one at the school who was kind to her and understood what it was like to lose a brother. That was their bond. She never knew a thing about the pregnancy or what was really going on for Deborah, and she's very hurt about that. She also said she couldn't believe Bill Woodman was responsible. She told me that just a couple of weeks ago they all spent a wonderful day in his woodshop making Christmas gifts together."

Ellie sighed. "Poor Sarah. Did you ask her about the tattoo?"

Graham nodded. "She said Deborah told her it was to remember her brother by. That's why Sarah wanted one too, and Deborah promised to get her a temporary one. Now she thinks that was all a lie."

"But does she know who Deborah was involved with? The person to whom she was sending the message of the straw Ophelia?"

"You can't be sure it was Sarah who did that, but no." He stood up in the tub, water running down his pale, lanky body. "She said she has no idea at all about who that was."

At eight o'clock, Graham, Ellie, and Isabelle drank a family toast to the New Year by the light of the Christmas tree, before Isabelle left with multiple reminders to call if she needed to be picked up, and they had to leave for their party.

"Tell me again who's going to be at this shindig?" she asked Graham, when they got in the car for the five-minute drive to the Bells' home, Castor House. It was snowing harder now, so there was no way Ellie was going to walk in her good wool coat and four-inch heels.

"Old people," he said, grinning when he saw her expression. "Actually, there are usually some of Charles' Oxford friends there. Not just villagers. Charles read history at Balliol. I'll bet you didn't know that."

"I didn't, but it sounds like it was a good decision not to wear my black satin pants with the slits up to my thighs."

"When have you ever worn them?" he asked.

"Never. But I like owning them, and after seeing Isabelle in her little red dress, I was wavering. The idea of shocking the Bells has so much appeal."

Ellie thought Castor House was an unlikely setting for a New Year's Eve party, which she associated with bad singing, spilled champagne, inappropriate kissing, and spats between otherwise congenial couples. But tonight, the candles in the windows made even this forbidding Georgian stone house look inviting, and the coldness of its high ceilings and very correct décor were offset by the scents of wood fires, beeswax, roasting beef, and perfume.

Mr. and Mrs. Bell greeted them in the front hall as if they were the receiving line at Buckingham Palace, and

Ellie half-expected a butler in black tie to announce them as “The Reverend and Mrs. Graham Kent” when they moved on to the drawing room. No such novel thing happened though, and they found themselves in the usual, if more polite, party scrum of people juggling drinks, food, and conversation.

Ellie caught sight of a few people from the village, but talking to them made New Year’s Eve feel like an after-church tea, and she scanned the crowd for new faces of interest. Like boats in a storm, she and Graham were quickly separated, and she wound up face to face with a man of about 60 years old, once good-looking and still vain, an academic type wearing a red bow tie. An Oxford don, he informed her, name of Alastair Thicke-Smythe.

Ellie asked him about himself and his work out of politeness more than genuine interest until she discovered that was on the Faculty of History at Anthea’s college. Suddenly she forgot that her feet hurt when she wore. high heels and even that she was hungry.

“I wonder if you know a student named Anthea Davies from there,” she asked. “My husband and I are friends of her family.”

“Oh certainly,” he said. “She was a very promising student. It was a terrible shame she decided to go down.”

“Decided?” said Ellie.

“Well, naturally, I assumed it was her decision to leave. Her academic standing was excellent.”

“It might have been, but it’s unclear what role she played in her disappearance.”

“Pardon me?” he said.

“I guess you didn’t know. Anthea disappeared from Oxford at the beginning of October.”

“And you think the college was somehow

involved?" He sounded alarmed and defensive.

"No, no. I'm not saying that. I mean no one knows what happened. From all I've heard about Anthea, she was a very dedicated scholar."

"Indeed she was. How very strange. I read a paper she co-authored on the importance of the Venerable Bede to the development of the English identity only the other day, and I was very impressed. But, with students, you come to accept that they are unpredictable."

"Did Anthea take a course from you?"

"She attended my lectures, but I don't get involved in students' affairs, if that's what you're asking. What they do outside of the work of college is not my responsibility," he said and took the first opportunity to begin talking with someone else.

Ellie caught a glimpse of Graham in an animated discussion with three other men at the far side of the drawing room and decided to venture on her own into the candlelit dining room, where a buffet was laid out on the lace-covered table. Everything about the scene made her feel like a fraud, an actress who'd wandered onto the wrong movie set. Last New Year's Eve, in San Francisco, she'd skipped the party where her latest ex-lover was expected to be and drank half a pint of bourbon while she wrote a letter to her ex-husband Vito Ruggieri, detailing what a despicable human being and lousy poet he was. Fortunately she didn't have his address, and in the morning she took four aspirin and threw the letter away.

Now she picked up a Wedgwood plate from the stack at one end of the table and, ignoring the standing rib roast, filled it with slices of smoked salmon, black caviar on triangles of toast, asparagus with hollandaise, crab puffs, shrimp, and crescents of melon. She took a tender shrimp and pulled it away from its tail with her teeth in the full understanding that life is not fair. She didn't deserve her good luck in meeting Graham and finding this new life any more than Deborah deserved the bad luck that separated her from her sweet baby and left her hanging in a tree on a winter's night.

She thought she'd found a quiet place in the library to enjoy her food and browse through the Bells' collection of books, but she was soon joined there by two women who were deep in a discussion about the problem of getting reliable childcare. When one of them recognized her as the person who found the baby in the manger, nothing would satisfy them but to hear the story, and more women drifted in to gather around and provide their judgments on everything from teenage girls who had sex to Rosie's dim prospects of health or happiness.

"I don't know what these girls think is going to happen when they have sex," said a skinny woman wearing an unfortunate shade of orange velvet.

"Orgasms. Lots and lots of orgasms," said another woman who looked tipsy. Her plate kept tilting and all the food would slide together before she would suddenly notice and right it.

"The reality is eighteen years without sleep," said a woman whose plate was piled with desserts, "and that's if you're lucky. For me, it's twenty-five and counting."

"Deborah was not lucky," Ellie couldn't help saying. These women seemed to forget she had been a real person who did not deserve to die for the crime of having sex, but they didn't even notice.

"Someone will snap that baby up, even though it is a girl," said Orange.

"That's true. Newborn white babies are hot commodities even when their background is dodgy," said Desserts.

"I could never adopt, but then I can't even face

buying used books," said the tipsy one as blancmange slipped off her plate and down the front of her dress.

There is a God, thought Ellie, as the fussing this disaster produced gave her a chance to slip away. She finally found Graham cornered by an earnest woman who was wearing a clerical collar even on New Year's Eve, and the look he gave her showed he was having as much fun she was.

Nonetheless, Ellie made it through the obligatory conversations with both of the Bells, as well as several other people whose names she forgot as soon as she heard them, and at last midnight came. Then all of the guests crowded around to witness the ceremony of opening the back door to let the old year out, followed by toasts to the new. Many people used the snowstorm as an excuse to leave promptly, and Ellie was hunting through a pile of coats for her own when Alastair Thicke-Smythe came in.

"Oh," he said, "I'm glad I found you. I was afraid you'd already left. I haven't been able to stop thinking about what you said. That Miss Davies has disappeared. Are the police trying to find her?"

"Yes, although they have drawn a blank so far. I'm trying to help her parents do a bit more. Informally, you know," said Ellie.

He nodded. "I don't think it would be out-of-bounds for me to say that I believe one of my colleagues might know a bit more about her situation than I do. If you like, I can ask him if he would be willing to speak with you."

"That would be fantastic. Thank you. Her family would be grateful for any information that might shed light on what happened." She scribbled her name, phone number, and email address on a page of the notebook she always carried, put on her coat, and went to meet Graham.

At home, they lit the fire in the sitting room and turned on the Christmas tree again. It was hard to believe that Christmas Eve had only been a week ago. They drank more champagne, toasting each other, and Ellie, forgetting the hours of hard social labor at the Bells, was convinced that this was, hands down, her best New Year's Eve ever.

She had drifted into a sound sleep when she suddenly woke up with the realization that Graham was still awake, lying rigid in the bed beside her.

"What is it?" she asked. "What's wrong?"

"It's Isabelle. She's not home yet."

Ellie rolled over and looked at the clock. It was nearly three a.m.

"I don't know what it's like here, but where I come from, no self-respecting teenager would dream of getting home before three on New Year's. It means you had a good time, no matter how miserable it actually was."

"I know. But I can't help worrying. What with everyone drinking and the snow."

"Do you want to try to call her?"

"No. I'm sure she'll call us if anything's wrong."

"You're right," said Ellie and hoped he was. It didn't always happen that way.

She sighed and resettled her pillows. Now she wouldn't sleep either until Isabelle was safely home. The room was dark but lit by the falling snow. Under the covers it was warm and cozy but the air was freezing. Her nose was cold, so she pulled the duvet up as far as she could without suffocating herself.

She wanted to think about something other than young women who failed to come home when they were expected, including herself, but no other topic came to mind.

They lay there listening to the silence, which was broken occasionally by a burst of firecrackers lit by some late reveler and a soft yelp from Hector, who was under the bed.

"I've never told you the story about Tom, have I?" she said.

"No. I've only heard about Vito," said Graham, his voice muffled by the duvet as well.

"Tom was my cousin, but he came to live with us when I was sixteen, and I fell madly in love with him."

"Is this a Romeo and Juliet or a Hamlet and Ophelia story?" he asked.

"Neither. We both survived. At least as far as I know."

"Good. So what happened? Your parents were none too pleased, I expect."

"No, they were not." And Ellie was about to continue when the lights of a car swept across the ceiling. They heard it pull in, and the thump of the doors as the occupants got out. Then, after a suitable interlude for farewell, the car departed, and they heard the sound of Isabelle creeping up the stairs to her room. Graham was asleep before her door shut, and Ellie, with the sense of having received a reprieve, soon followed.

Friday, January 1
New Year's Day
Chapter 11

Graham was up early and remarkably cheerful, Ellie thought, considering how little time they had spent sleeping. While she drank tea and watched the winter birds peck the birdseed he had scattered on the snow, he prepared them a full English breakfast, including fried eggs, bacon, baked beans, grilled mushrooms and tomatoes, and fried bread.

It was a tradition, he said, that went back to the early days of his marriage to Louise. "One of my New Year's resolutions was always to help more with the cooking, so she thought I should start off on the right foot."

"And did this resolution ever last beyond New Year's Day?" asked Ellie, as she got up to set the table.

"What do you think?" he said, turning the eggs.

"I hope not, since I'm always happy to find that men of God are merely human like the rest of us."

"I should think you knew all about my cold feet of clay by now."

Isabelle straggled in with her bathrobe mis-buttoned, as Ellie was pouring orange juice. "Oh Dad," she said, wrinkling up her nose at all the food smells. "I can't believe you did this." To Ellie she added, "Every year he pretends he makes this huge New Year's Day breakfast to be kind, but it's really a ploy to remind me I shouldn't drink on New Year's Eve.

"I can't eat anything," she said, slumping down on the bench that ran along the wall. "I need water.

Dispirin. A gun. I think I drank four martinis before the champagne."

"In that case, you deserve to feel awful," said Graham. "I hope the person who drove you home was more sober."

Isabelle gave him a baleful look. "Actually, Dad, unlike in your day, there were three kids at the party who didn't drink at all so they could drive everyone home. I think they had more fun than the rest of us."

"They're probably tucking into their breakfast at least," he said, putting a full plate of food down in front of her.

"But you did have fun, didn't you?" asked Ellie.

"Did I? I can't remember. No, really, the guys were great. If only I knew their names, I'm sure there was at least one I'd like to have sex with again."

Graham turned sharply from dishing up his own plate of food, but Ellie laughed and nudged her. "Come on, Graham. She's just teasing you," she said, and he made a good effort to join in.

"The truth is, I spent the evening discussing climate change with the most boring jerk from Magdalen I've ever met. His obligatory kiss at midnight tasted and smelled like algae. And I hate martinis. Full steam ahead to the next rite of passage." She picked up her fork and began eating.

Graham was about to comment on this goal when the phone rang. Isabelle answered, saying "The Vicarage" and then handed the receiver to Ellie.

At first she didn't realize who it was, since he referred to himself as "Alastair." Then, sensing her hesitation, he added stiffly, "Professor Thicke-Smythe."

"Oh, of course," said Ellie. "Good morning."

"I've spoken to my colleague, and he would be glad to meet you. I thought he might be worried by my call, but he seemed relieved that someone is looking into the matter. His name is Richard Crowley, and he's expecting to hear from you. Here is his number."

Ellie thanked him and hung up. When she turned back to the table, she saw Graham and Isabelle waiting expectantly to hear what she'd been talking about. She picked up her toast and ate a bite before saying, "That was one of the Bells' friends I met last night. Alastair Thicke-Smythe. It turns out Anthea Davies was a student of his at Oxford, and he gave me the phone number of a colleague who apparently knew her well."

"Perhaps you should give that information to the police," said Graham.

"I will if it's relevant, but I understood that he will only talk to me in confidence, so I'll see what he has to say first."

Isabelle stretched and stood up. "Well I plan to do absolutely nothing today. Save no lives or souls. Simply let the hours flow over me."

"That's fine, as long as you carry out your traditional role in the New Year's breakfast—the washing up."

"Right-oh," she said, taking her plate to the sink.

"Somehow this tradition seems to hark back to a time when I would have been the one slaving in the kitchen for days to get ready for the holidays. Since that has hardly been the case, thanks to Mrs. Finch and you, Isabelle, I will wash up," said Ellie.

"And I will take Hector for a walk. Don't forget we have the New Year's Evening Prayer service at five. Next to Dispirin, it's the best cure for a hangover," said Graham, at which Isabelle rolled her eyes.

As soon as she was finished cleaning up, Ellie called the number Professor Thicke-Smythe had given her. Although she had no expectations about what he would say, she was surprised to conclude from Richard Crowley's shaky voice that he had been crying. He told her he did not want to talk on the phone. They should meet in person that afternoon, and he suggested a pub in a village she'd never heard of.

"All right," said Ellie, looking at the clock. She would barely have time to visit Rosie on the way and get back for Graham's service, but she did not want to risk his having second thoughts if she put him off. Suddenly the day had become a busy one.

Ellie was scraping last night's snow off the blue Mini when her cell phone rang. She fumbled to remove her mittens and get the phone out of her pocket, only to drop it in the snow. By the time she had retrieved it and dried it off, the call had ended.

"Oh good," said Seamus, when she called him right back. "You won't believe it, Guv, but I finally have some news about Anthea Davies for you."

"That's wonderful. What is it?" she asked with only a cursory thought about Mullane's order that she drop her investigation.

"You remember I told you the older brother of one of my friends was in love with her, and she wouldn't even speak to him?"

"Yes," said Ellie, even though she didn't.

"Well, I kept asking Jack if he knew anything else, and he finally admitted that Gerald's crush was so bad that he was practically stalking Anthea for a while."

"Really. Did he say what this stalking consisted of?"

"Mostly stupid stuff, but a couple of times he followed her into Oxford on the bus, and he saw what she did there."

Ellie felt the hairs on her arms rise. "And what was that—"

"She would carry a rucksack like everyone does, but she'd go into Debenham's, go straight up to the ladies', and come out a few minutes later in disguise."

"Seriously?"

"Cross my heart. That's what he said. When she came out, she'd be disguised as a boy with her hair tucked into a baseball cap, and she'd walk over to the bus station to meet up with a guy who Gerry says looked disguised too. Then they'd spend the day together."

"And when was this?"

"When she and Gerry were both in the sixth form. So, something like three years ago."

"Did he say what this guy looked like?"

"He was tall, with dark slicked back hair, and glasses."

"Really," Ellie said again. "But Gerry didn't recognize him?"

"I don't think so. Jack didn't mention anything about that. Gerry was mostly interested in Anthea, and he said she made a very convincing boy. If he hadn't seen her change, he wouldn't have noticed that she was someone he knew because she walked differently and everything."

"And he didn't happen to notice what bus this guy arrived on?"

"He didn't say anything about that, but I can ask him. The weird thing, Gerry said, was that they just larked about going into shops and eating lunch. They never touched each other or anything. At least not in public. And in the afternoon, she would go back to Debenham's, turn back into Anthea, buy some tights or lipstick or something, and take the bus home."

"Lipstick? Wow, Seamus. This is great."

"Is that important, Guv? I mean, the lipstick?"

"It's all important. Incredibly important. This is the first information I've heard that connects Anthea to a man, and obviously this was a secret relationship of some kind."

"Right. Well, it sure put Gerald off his feed, though I

guess he followed them more than once."

"Great work, Captain! Let me know if you find out any other details. Especially about the man." Then she wished him Happy New Year and hung up, but she stood there so long with the snow scraper in her hand that she saw her across-the-street neighbor Mrs. Bigelow pull aside the curtain of her sitting room window and stare.

On the way to The Sheep Dip in Redhill, Ellie wondered if she should have warned Seamus that a man of the same description had come to the Kingbrook Hospital only yesterday and tried to see Deborah's baby. She thought not, at least for now, but she was very excited that the man in the story had come on stage again—and she felt certain it was the same man. She was so exhilarated at this progress that she stepped on the gas and nearly skidded through a stop sign. After that, she settled down, made it to the hospital safely, gave Rosie a good cuddling, was polite to the constable guarding her, and left with enough time to make her rendezvous with Richard Crowley.

Redhill turned out to be little more than a crossroads but The Sheep Dip was surprisingly crowded with people enjoying a New Year's pint. She stood in the doorway and scanned the crowd until she spotted a gloomy-looking young man sitting alone in a corner with a half-pint in front of him. She guessed he was the one she was supposed to meet.

Before approaching him she tried to assess whether he might be the tall dark-haired man with the slicked-back hair and glasses who had known Anthea when she was at Kingbrook, but this man's whole demeanor was wilted, like old lettuce. This could be faked, of course, so she intended to be watchful.

"I think you might be waiting for me," she said, as she came up to his table. "I'm Ellie Kent."

He nodded, looking at her quickly from under shaggy hair and thick dark eyebrows but did not offer to shake her hand.

"Yes, I can tell," was all he said. "Thicke-Smythe said you were American, but perfectly all right. I find, though, that I have to judge for myself. With Americans, it can be so hard to get past the accent to the person."

Ellie would have liked to return the compliment, but there was no use in reciprocating with more rudeness. She had driven nearly 40 minutes to get there, and she hoped to learn something from this. . . jerk.

"How very English," she said and hung her coat over the back of her chair. Since he was obviously not going to get her a drink, she squeezed her way to the bar and ordered a pot of tea.

"Sorry," he said, when she returned and settled herself. He managed to look at her this time as if he were coming out of a thick fog. "It's one of my shortcomings. Forgetting what shouldn't be said aloud. I know I should be thanking you for coming."

"So you should," said Ellie, feeling like his mother. "But I wanted to come, and whoever you are, I would like to hear what you know about Anthea Davies and where she might be. Her parents have been worried sick for months."

He blushed, an unattractive red flush creeping up his neck. "In that case, I'm afraid there's been a bit of a balls-up. I don't know anything about where Anthea is. I'm sorry if you were led to believe that."

"I see. Professor Thicke-Smythe seemed to think you knew her well. Better than most."

"I did know her," he said, tearing bits off an Old Speckled Hen beer mat with his pale fingers. "At least I thought I did. To be perfectly frank, I was in love with her, and I thought, I hoped, she felt the same way. I mean she acted as if she did."

"What do you mean by that?"

He flushed again. "We spent a great deal of time working together on a paper, but it was more than that."

"You mean she slept with you?"

He practically turned purple and drank quickly from his glass. Watching him struggle to hold onto his composure all Ellie could think was, what was Anthea doing with someone like this? He didn't seem her type at all.

Finally he managed to say, "Yes, we were lovers. But it happened just the once."

Ellie said nothing. She sipped her tea and waited for him to go on. It was clear that he wanted to tell someone the details, and she was sure this was why he had agreed to their meeting.

"We were working on some research together, you see. It involved a lot of late nights and that led to talks about our lives and so on. She was extraordinarily mature for a young woman, barely more than a teenager, and I found myself falling in love with her."

"What did she tell you about her life?"

"She talked mostly about her ambitions, but I heard a little bit about her parents, her background. That they were not well off at all, but that they could trace their lineage all the way back to Shakespeare. That's why she'd become so passionate about history."

Ellie leaned forward and covered her mouth with one hand, so she wouldn't laugh when she heard that, but Richard Crowley had obviously bought the whole tale.

"After a while I did wonder why she never mentioned any kind of love life, but then neither did I.

In my case though, it was because I had no past love life to tell her about.

"I had such fantasies. It's terribly embarrassing to think of them now. I imagined, you see, that maybe this beautiful, brilliant girl had never fallen for a man. Like me, she'd been isolated by her intelligence. She too had been in a cocoon until we met.

"You probably think it sounds daft, but I could tell she had definitely felt cut off from other children growing up, and there was something remote, something incomplete, about her.

"When we had submitted our paper, we decided to celebrate, and one thing led to another. I'd never so much as even kissed her and suddenly, you know, we were taking off our clothes."

"Sounds like your dream come true," said Ellie, adding more sugar to her tea.

"It was," he said, not noticing her tone. "But it wasn't anything like I imagined. I mean it very quickly became clear that Anthea was far more experienced than I—more than I ever could have thought possible."

"So, you suspect you weren't the first after all."

"Hardly." And the bitter disappointment and self-pity that he couldn't hide—that poured out of him—made Ellie's small well of sympathy dry up.

"How did the evening end?" she asked briskly.

"When it was over, she got up and left, and I never saw her again. It was the end of term and she was going to London. I was sure we would continue to be in touch, but she never replied to my messages, even when we were informed that our paper had been accepted for publication."

"When was that?"

"In October. But the last time I saw her was in May."

"You tried to reach her?"

"A few times. Not often. She owed me an apology for misrepresenting herself, and we both knew it."

"Why do you think she slept with you?"

"I've spent many hours thinking about it, and the only conclusion I have come to is that she did it because she was angry at someone else. I think she used me to get back at someone. That's what hurt the most. She slept with me, but it wasn't about me. It was a performance. She was flaunting all she knew, but I was not the audience. She was showing off for someone else who wasn't there except in her mind. Believe me, it was not an experience I will ever forget."

"If it's any comfort, I think you're right. The nearest I've come is to get a glimpse of a man who loomed large in her life—and may still. Even her closest friends have not been let in on the secret of his identity, which leads me to believe that he's someone who has no business being involved with her."

He turned pale and sighed. "You mean a married man. I was afraid it might be something like that." He looked out the window, where clouds had moved in, and the snow had begun again. "So do you think she ran away with him? Packed in her whole education and career for a man?"

"I don't know," said Ellie. "She hasn't been in touch with anyone since October, and the police have found no activity on her phone or credit cards."

His eyes widened. "You mean she really is missing? I mean, like that. With the police involved?"

"I guess you don't read the paper." She took out the photo from the MISSING poster and showed it to him. "This is the last known photo of Anthea. It was taken right before she disappeared."

He stared at the photo for a long time. "She looks happy," he said, pushing it back toward her. "You know all this time I thought she was making herself scarce because she didn't want a confrontation with me. I guess that shows what a prat I've been. I've been too proud to ask anyone about her."

"I think it's safe to say that her actions have not been a response to her relationship with you," said Ellie, "but I appreciate your sharing your story with me. Meanwhile, if for any reason you should happen to hear from her—or of her—her parents would be very grateful to know about it. You have my number."

She said goodbye then and left him to nurse his ale and his wounds.

The story of his romance, as he thought of it, added new details to her picture of Anthea and her evolution from the 16-year-old who underwent a sudden change and began meeting a man while disguised as a boy to her callous demonstration of her sexual experience with Richard Crowley. Was the absent lover he sensed the same man whose false flattery enraged her enough to get a tattoo as a lifelong reminder? Had the passionate child, hungry for knowledge, grown up to be the type of woman who falls in love once and for all and never wavers no matter what it costs her? And could that happy photo in front of the Ashmolean come from a moment of reconciliation with her old lover that ended with her disappearance?

The most chilling detail in Richard Crowley's story was that even when their research was accepted for publication, he had received no response to his messages. No matter where she was or with whom, wouldn't that have been important to her, if she knew about it?

Ellie called Mullane and left a voice mail, promising that she was going to steer clear of his investigation, but wanted to give him an update on what she had learned that day: that, when Anthea was in the sixth form, she had been seen in Oxford on more than one occasion with a man who was disguised very similarly to the man who tried to get in to see Rosie at the hospital. Although more than two years had passed since those sightings, they might be significant.

Even as she said this, she could imagine Mullane's reaction: call me back when you have news from this century. Nevertheless she soldiered on, adding that he should let her know if he wanted to contact the boy who saw them and have him look at the hospital's CCTV footage.

Lame, she told herself, as she hurried back down the lanes to Little Beecham. Incredibly lame. She was still trying to connect dots that were too far apart, so she'd better forget her investigation, focus on being the vicar's wife, and get to church on time.

Graham's prediction was right: the Evening Prayer service on New Year's Day was a good antidote to the excesses of the holidays. There was no music, but the banks of lighted candles and the fragrance of the evergreens created a soothing atmosphere for those who needed time to pause and reflect before charging into the fray of a new year.

Ellie felt herself slowing down for the first time in more than a week as the soft drone of the prayers filled her head, and she was listening with only half her attention until Graham's words suddenly echoed her own question:

"Who knows where a new road will lead? No one," he said. "But every mother who gives birth, every king who sets out to follow a star, each of us beginning a new year, steps out on a road to an unknown destination.

"If you wonder about your capacity for faith, consider how you rise each day and you will know that you don't have to question whether you have it. Like your heartbeat, faith moves you forward with strength and steadiness, and God is with you in the same way. Our English word "confidence" comes from the Latin word *confidere*—"with faith"—and that is how I hope each of you will follow your path this year."

A hush fell, in which everyone in the church seemed to take a deep breath and release it, refreshed and renewed, and Ellie felt a shift in her heart. No matter how things turned out for any of them—for good or ill––there was power and magic in this place, and Graham was its minister. That he had chosen her and she had chosen him was all she really needed to know about what was to come.

When he ended the service with "Wolcum Yule!" the congregation was ebullient in its reply, "Wolcum Yule!"

Ellie was putting out candles when she noticed Sarah Henning sitting on a kneeler by the crèche. "Hey, Sarah," she said, pulling up a kneeler for herself and sitting down beside her. "It's nice to see you here. I'm sorry I missed you the other day, but I hope Graham was helpful."

Sarah nodded then reached out to touch the baby Jesus in the manger. "I had to come," she said. "I've just been thinking so much about Deborah and her baby. How she left her in this place. You know people are saying it was because the father is from Little Beecham?"

"Yes," said Ellie.

"I don't believe that. I think it was because she knew I was going to be here that night. She said she'd try to come to the service, and I thought about saving her a seat, but then I was embarrassed, so I didn't—and when she didn't show up, I was glad I hadn't. And all that time I had no idea what was really happening.

"But she knew that I would be taking Jesus from manger when it was time to say the *Magnificat*, so if she left her baby there, I would find her."

"That sounds right," said Ellie. "And it shows how important you were to her and how she trusted you. So wouldn't you like to see the baby again? To meet her?"

Sarah bit her lip. "I guess so," she said, though she glanced quickly up at Ellie and then away.

"I'd be happy to take you with me tomorrow, if you have time."

She nodded, but then stood up to leave. Ellie would have liked to hold her back, to ask her so many questions, but she could tell it was not the right time, so she simply said good night and watched her go.

Saturday, January 2
Chapter 12

"Can you come over for a coffee?" Morag asked, when she called first thing in the morning. "We've been so out of touch. I'd love to catch up."

"Sure," said Ellie. Anything would be more fun than sitting at her desk endlessly reviewing the list of unanswered questions produced by her investigation. She hoped Crispin Souter would be there too; she wanted to get to know him better—and perhaps even ask him some questions.

It had continued snowing all night, a quiet, gentle snow, but as she walked down the high street, Ellie could tell from the expressions of the people trying to park cars, shovel walks, and do their weekend errands that the unusual weather had worn out its welcome. Every storm was predicted to be the last until the next one came along. She chose to enjoy it along with the Christmas decorations that still clung to the houses and shops. Soon they would be gone too.

Morag's neat stone cottage was decorated with evergreen branches over the front door and red candles in the windows. Bells on a strip of red leather jingled as Morag opened the door, but Ellie was immediately aware of a tense atmosphere in the home.

Crispin was not there. He was out doing errands, Morag told her in a way that implied that he was pretty much living there. When they had settled in the book-lined sitting room with coffee and Christmas cake, they exchanged the customary questions and replies without the conversation getting off the ground. Ellie felt increasingly uncomfortable as she waited for the real reason Morag rang her to surface.

Finally, it did, when she said in a voice that feigned casualness, "Do you remember the night we saw the mummers' play, and Seamus went on and on about searching for that missing girl?"

Ellie nodded, trying not to show that this was what she had feared was coming.

"I think he's been doing it," said Morag. "I found one of those little notebooks he carries around on the floor in his bedroom earlier today, and it was full of notes about people and dates. I recognized the girl's name, and I'm afraid I said something to Crispin about being frustrated that Seamus doesn't obey me anymore. Then, when I explained what it was about, Crispin became upset too and lashed out, telling Seamus he should mind his own business. Needless to say, Seamus was livid and left the house. It was all very unpleasant."

"I can imagine," said Ellie.

"Has he told you anything about this? I mean, you said you weren't going to get involved. So is he doing this all on his own?" Morag asked, but Ellie sensed she knew the truth.

She would have liked to lie, but she couldn't. She'd known from the beginning this moment would come. "You're right. I never intended it," she said. "But Mr. and Mrs. Davies came to us for help, so, yes, I have been involved."

"Us? You mean you and Seamus?"

"No, no, no. They came to Graham—and to me—for advice about dealing with the police and other issues related to the search for their daughter. They can't afford professional help, so I said I would do what I could. Talk to people and so on."

"But you're not a detective. How can you find out

anything? And who are all these people Seamus is talking to? Is that related?"

Ellie blushed and said, "You know how much he wanted to help."

"But he's fourteen years old! And I told him not to."

"All he's done is talk to some of the kids he knows from Kingbrook Grammar."

"Well, he shouldn't even be doing that. It could be dangerous. And what good is it doing? Have you actually found out anything?"

Ellie licked her lips before admitting, "Very little."

"Exactly my point."

Then she took a chance. "What we have learned is that, while it's always possible Anthea was snatched off the streets of Oxford by a stranger, it's more likely that she went away with someone she knew—probably the person who helped her move back after her summer job in London. No one has been able to find out who that was—not the police, not her parents, not me. None of her friends or family were aware of her having a relationship, but there are indications she was involved secretly with someone when she was at Kingbrook. And then there's this friend, whose name she wouldn't give to her parents, who was with her just prior to her disappearance."

"And you think it's the same person? Still in her life years later? That's an awfully big leap, Ellie. And why would the kids Seamus knows have any idea about any of this since it was a secret even then?"

Ellie sipped her coffee slowly. "He actually has found out some things from talking to the younger brothers of boys who were in school with Anthea."

"Like what?" said Morag, who was on the verge of getting angry, when the door opened and Crispin Souter walked in. He was still wearing his outdoor coat with a knitted cap, and his cheeks were pink from the cold, giving him a boyish look, but his eyes, as he glanced from Morag to Ellie, were serious. Even stern.

"Still at it?" he said, without a greeting, and Ellie realized he had left, in part, so Morag could have this conversation with her. She felt set up.

Morag flushed, embarrassed. "You have no idea how long Ellie and I can talk," she said. "There's cake and coffee in the kitchen, if you'd like to join us."

He smiled then, but the warmth did not reach his eyes. "Sure," he said. "I'll unpack the shopping first."

When he disappeared into the kitchen, Ellie got to her feet. This was clearly not an opportunity for her to ask him any questions, and she'd had enough of being on the hot seat herself.

"Actually, I should be getting home. Graham's expecting me back to help him," she said, although she couldn't even come up with anything specific she was supposed to help with.

Morag looked as if she were not finished talking, but her eyes slid toward the kitchen where they could hear cupboard doors opening and closing. When she turned back, there was something in her expression that made Ellie wonder if it were her or Crispin who didn't like Seamus talking to the students from Kingbrook. Certainly she wanted her son to be safe, but she used to find his passionate pursuit of his interests, even detecting, very entertaining.

"Of course," she said finally. "I'm sorry I got off on that topic. There's so much else I want to hear about. Your Christmas. The family."

"Short version is that all went well," said Ellie, picking up her coat. She wanted to apologize to Morag for not discouraging Seamus, but resisted doing it while Crispin was within earshot. Instead, she gave her friend a hug. "Let's talk more soon. It has been too long."

Morag hugged her back. Just then Crispin returned

carrying a mug of coffee. "You have to leave?" he asked. He didn't look disappointed.

Ellie nodded. "Nice to see you again though," she said, with a smile as forced as his own.

She had just turned the corner from Crooked Lane, where Morag lived, onto the high street, when suddenly Seamus appeared from between two houses.

"Gee, Guv, I was beginning to wonder if you'd ever leave. I suppose my mum told you what happened."

"She did. And she was in the right, you know. She did tell you not to get involved, and I was wrong to encourage you."

He snorted. "I started my investigation all on my own; it wasn't your doing. Anyway, Crispix was the one who was mad when he heard I was talking to people about his school. I don't see why. No one knows we're connected, and I hope it stays that way."

"I'm sure everyone at the school is touchy these days. It's not good publicity to have a pregnant student, much less one who gets murdered—and Anthea's disappearance is probably also worrying for them."

"The police interviewed Crispix about the murder, you know. I overheard him telling Mum about it. He said they talked to all the teachers and kids who had anything to do with Deborah."

"Really," said Ellie. "Did you hear anything else?"

Seamus grinned. "That's not our case, is it, Guv?"

"No," she said, "but tell me anyway."

"He said naught. He told them she was a quiet, unremarkable student about whom he remembered almost nothing. Then he gave his alibi."

"Which was. . ."

"What do you think? He was in my house shagging my mum."

"Come on, he didn't say that."

"No, but he did say he was at our house. And how would I know? I was at Gran's."

"True. Well, he was at church on Christmas Eve, when the murder took place. I saw them there together. So what about our case? Anything new?"

"This could be my last report," he said grumpily. "Mum took my notebook and wouldn't give it back, but there was nothing new in it anyway. Gerry didn't pay much attention to the man with Anthea, and they separated on the street, so he didn't see what bus he took."

"I'm not surprised. That was a super long shot, but do me a favor and write down Gerald's name and phone number," said Ellie.

Seamus looked surprised, but he did as she asked.

"Now look," she said, "keep a low profile for a while. I think that's best for both of us. Mullane read the riot act to me too."

He sighed. "I really thought we'd crack this case before the holidays were over."

"Since the police have been working on it for three months, and we've only had a week, I think that was a bit over-optimistic." She patted him on the back. "Go home and have your tea. The Christmas cake is very good. You look frozen."

Ellie could hear Graham typing behind his closed door, no doubt working on his sermon for the next day, so she fixed some tuna sandwiches for lunch and then went in to see him.

"Nearly done," he said, his fingers flying over the clacking keys. "What's up with you?"

"Oh nothing," said Ellie, flopping down on his sofa. "I'm just discouraged. I set out to help the Davies find their daughter, and all I've done is cause a row with Morag."

"A row?"

"She's upset that Seamus has been trying to ferret out information from his friends about Anthea."

Graham laughed. "I can't imagine they know anything anyway."

"That's what she said too. It's more the idea of it. Also it makes her new squeeze uncomfortable. He teaches at Kingbrook."

Graham's bushy eyebrows rose. "Who's that? I suppose he's had the police around and hoped to have heard the end of it."

"Yes, apparently. His name is Crispin Souter, and he teaches English. That's all I know about him, super sleuth that I am." She stretched and yawned. "Maybe the Women's Institute really is my future."

"Ellie, there's no either or about that and you know it."

"No. Of course not."

"I did warn you at the start that our job isn't to solve problems, it's to help people bear them."

"I know, but that's just not good enough!" she said.

"It's the reality though."

"Reality is not as immutable as it's cracked up to be. By the way, I made sandwiches. Are you ready for lunch?"

Sarah had to help her mother with housework, so they agreed she would not go with Ellie to visit Rosie until the next day. Graham needed to edit his sermon, and Isabelle had gone to the movies, so Ellie bundled up and set off to visit Rosie on her own. She didn't like the baby to be alone, with no visitors, all day.

She hadn't noticed until she was on the road that the snow had begun to accumulate, and sharp squalls made the visibility poor. By the time she arrived at the hospital, she was sweating from the concentration required to drive. Apparently most other people had chosen not to venture out, because the parking lot was nearly empty.

Ellie was glad she'd made it, but she felt her efforts were not very well rewarded, since Rosie was in a cranky mood and cried no matter what she did to amuse, appease, or comfort her. This only added to the feelings of frustration and failure that had been mounting all day.

On the way home, she drove as slowly and carefully as she could, peering through the snow that flew into her windshield, but she made a wrong turn without realizing it, and then couldn't find a place wide enough to turn around. She knew she had to resist the urge to touch the brakes, but when a pair of dog-sized muntjac deer suddenly leapt across the road in front of her, her instinct took over, she braked, and went into a skid. Turning the wheel did nothing to stop the momentum. Instead the car began to spin and, within seconds, she had gone backwards into a ditch.

It took a moment to register what had happened. She released her seat belt, struggled to open the door, and climbed out. Once she was on her feet, she could tell she wasn't hurt, only shocked and dismayed because there was no way she would be able to get the car out of the ditch on her own.

She took out her phone to call the AA emergency breakdown number and found she had no signal. This was not uncommon in that area, but today it was a problem. Already new snow was covering her windshield. In the vain hope that she might somehow drive the car up and out, she tried to restart it, but the engine only whined and sputtered.

So. She couldn't wait for help in the car, and she wasn't sure exactly where she was. What was the last signpost she had seen? She had no idea, and the blowing snow obliterated all the landmarks. Normally she had a good sense of direction, but, in this whiteout, she was not at all sure she could find her way back to the hospital or get home on foot.

She tried to start the car one more time. Nothing. She was beginning to feel cold.

Walking, she could keep herself warm and hopefully come to a house or village where she would be able call for help. She zipped up her coat, glad of the warm Barbour parka, slung her bag across her chest, and grabbed Hector's blanket from the back seat along with a half empty bottle of water. Then she left a note on the dashboard saying that she was walking home and locked the car.

The cold of the snow bit through her corduroy pants as she scrambled out of the ditch onto the road and shook herself off. She began to walk in the direction she'd been going, trying hard to remember what landmarks to look for. The snow soon coated the blanket she'd wrapped around herself like a shawl, but she wasn't going to die. This was the Cotswolds, after all, and she wasn't Dr. Zhivago walking across Siberia in winter. She was well dressed, well fed, and on a road that must lead somewhere.

Ellie had probably walked two miles—which seemed like 20—when a car came crawling along behind her. She stepped as far off the road as she could to avoid being hit and waved her arms until the driver ground to a halt.

"You look like you need a lift," said the man, who had leaned over and rolled down his window. "Climb in."

"Thank you," said Ellie, as she clambered into the car. "I'm sorry I'm so snowy."

"No worries. I guess you've been walking for a while. Was that your car in the ditch back down the road?"

Ellie nodded, her teeth chattering. The warm air blasting from the heater felt almost painful on her cold skin. When she pulled back the blanket and her hood, the man stared.

"Why it's Ellie Kent, isn't it?"

Ellie looked at him with surprise. She'd been so preoccupied with getting out of the cold that she hadn't really paid attention to her rescuer. It was Crispin Souter.

"Yes, of course. And here I was beginning to think I would never see another human being again, much less someone I know."

"I guess it's your lucky day," he said. "Here I am. Your knight in shining armor."

Ellie smiled, as she was meant to. "Are you headed to Morag's now?" she asked.

"Morag's? No," he said, gunning the engine slightly to get the car moving again. It slewed to the right then went forward. "Where are you going?"

"Home," said Ellie, surprised that he would ask.

He laughed. "Well, you were walking in the wrong direction for Little Beecham. I've just come from there. I'm on my way to my place to take care of some things, but I can take you home afterward. What I have to do won't take long."

"Thank you," said Ellie, who thought this very unexpected turn of events was a gift: an opportunity to question Crispin when he was feeling magnanimous and in control. "It's certainly lucky for me, but it's too bad you have to travel back and forth between houses on a day like this."

Crispin took his eyes from the road for an instant to look at her. She had turned toward him and was watching him closely too. “I don’t live with Morag, you know, though Seamus seems have gotten it into his head that that’s my intention. We’ve only recently got together, and I do have my own life. A rather complicated one, in fact.”

“You mean your teaching and all,” Ellie said blandly.

Again he turned to her then looked quickly back at the road. The blowing snow was making the hedges and ditches nearly impossible to distinguish.

“That’s right. Morag told me you used to teach, so you know how consuming it can be. I must say I don’t blame either of you for getting out of it. I only wish I could.”

“Kingbrook is a beautiful school though,” said Ellie. “It must be a good place to work most of the time.”

“I suppose you mean when we aren’t all caught up in the kind of terrible events that have happened lately. But, if you want my opinion, the only surprising thing is that more such tragedies don’t happen. I mean, teenagers. They’re like nitroglycerin in human form.”

“They can be fun though. If you like living dangerously.”

He glanced over at her again and chose to laugh. “I take it you do,” he said. “Like to live dangerously, that is.”

Ellie shrugged. “Not really. I was just exploring your metaphor. My students were in college and obsessed with their egos and ambitions. As long as I wasn’t directly in their path, I was pretty safe. Secondary school must be harder. I imagine a lot of the girls fall hard for you.”

Again that quick look and the confident smile of a man who knows how attractive he is. “Boys too,” he said with laugh. “But only until I grade their first essay," he said. "I am a terrible stickler and that usually snuffs out any romantic imaginings."

Ellie thought "snuffs" was a particularly tasteless choice of words and couldn't help replying, "You mean you never let them forget the difference between lay and lie."

She thought a shadow crossed his face then, but maybe it was just the failing light. They had turned down a narrow lane that ran through thick woods and ended with a small clearing where a stone cottage stood.

"Here it is. My hideaway," said Crispin, suddenly cheerful. "I'll just be a few minutes. You can wait here where it's warm. The cottage will be an icebox." He reached into the back and grabbed a rucksack, then got out, leaving the engine running. Snow swirled in through the open door, reminding Ellie to be grateful that she was no longer out in the storm.

She watched him make his way to the front door and saw the lights go on. It felt very strange to be sitting in his car surrounded by the thickening darkness, tall trees, and blowing snow. She tried to reach Graham by phone again, but, of course, there was no signal.

For something to do, she opened the glove compartment. Glove box, as Graham would say. She found Crispin's car registration, which explained where they were: Alder Cottage, King Lake Road, Chipping Martin. She hadn't noticed any lake, but then she hadn't really been able to see anything beyond the headlights. She'd have to look it up when she got home.

There were maps of Oxfordshire, Gloucestershire, and London; a greasy chip bag; a packet of Kleenex, and a lipstick. Her heart beat a little faster as she took this last item out and examined it. MAC Perfect Score. The same kind of lipstick that Anthea had in her bedroom at her parents' house. Well, so what? She personally did not like red lipstick, but millions of women did.

She thought back over her conversation with Crispin and concluded that all she had learned so far was that he was rather conceited, cynical about his young students, and didn't get along very well with Seamus. In other words, nothing much.

Thanks to the blasting heater, her wet clothes had gone from cold and wet to warm and wet, and she felt increasingly uncomfortable in the now snow-covered car. She looked at her watch and saw that it was already five o'clock. Crispin had been gone for 20 minutes, and the gas gauge was down to one-quarter of a tank. She hoped they weren't going to run out of gas on the way back to Little Beecham.

After five more minutes, she decided to get out of the car. An icy wind whipped at her coat and snow blew in her face as she hurried across to the cottage. When she reached the door and peered in through the glass panel, she saw Crispin coming down a ladder from the attic with a Monopoly game under his arm.

A look of annoyance flashed across his face when he caught sight of her, and he seemed to deliberately ignore her as he closed the hatch and picked up his rucksack as if he had all the time in the world.

Ellie went back to the car and waited, trying not to be impatient, while the lights inside the cottage went out, and he locked up. He got back into the car without speaking, and the silence soon made her feel embarrassed.

"I'm sorry you have to make this trip again on my account," she said.

"It's all right. Morag will be glad to see me, though I expect Seamus will not be best pleased."

"I gather you had a confrontation with him today," she said, wondering if this line of questioning would lead her anywhere.

He gave a wry smile. "Yes, we did. Boys who've had their mums wrapped around their little fingers have a tough time when another man comes on the scene, no matter what. And this whole detective thing he's into. I can't see how Morag ever let that get started."

Ellie said nothing. She didn't know if Morag had told him that Seamus's detecting had only gone from fiction to reality since he'd gotten to know her. The look he gave her then said she had.

"So you're a fan of Monopoly?" she asked, shifting ground again.

He shrugged. "I thought it might be a good gesture on behalf of family life."

Ellie laughed to try to lighten the atmosphere, which had become unpleasantly tense. "In my family, it always brought out our most cutthroat competitive instincts."

"Not a good choice for our situation then, eh?"

"I don't know. You'll find out, I guess."

They didn't speak again until the lights of the village could be seen haloed in the swirling snowflakes, at which point Ellie mustered her good manners—and real gratitude—to thank him for giving her a ride home.

"My pleasure," he said, as he pulled up in front of The Vicarage. "I'm glad to get to know more about someone Morag holds in such high esteem."

"Likewise," she said. "Thanks again."

When Crispin had driven away, Ellie turned to the house and was surprised to notice an unfamiliar car in the driveway. The amount of snow covering it suggested the visitor had been at The Vicarage for a while.

She hurried in, thinking she would be greeted as a long-lost traveler, but the scene she found was not what she expected. In the sitting room, Graham was in his leather armchair looking solemn, while Isabelle sat on the hearthrug holding Hector, and Detective Inspector Derek Mullane perched on the sofa, his hands clasped between his knees. They were deep in conversation and barely noticed her arrival.

Graham looked surprised when she pulled up a chair to join them. "There you are," he said.

"What's going on?" she asked. "Has something happened?"

"Yes, love," he said then he looked at his watch. "You've been gone a long time. Is Rosie all right?"

Ellie nodded. "Yes. She's fine. I'll tell you everything later. I want to hear your news."

"Inspector Mullane came to tell us that Bill Woodman has been found."

"And—" she said.

"He's dead," said Mullane. "We won't know for how long until the pathologist's report is in. Ostensibly he drove his daughter's car into King Lake—and who knows how long it would have taken to find him if another car hadn't gone into the lake on New Year's Eve. That driver survived, but he told us he was sure his car had hit something big under the water, so we searched, and it turned out to be Deborah Woodman's car."

"Do you think it was suicide?"

"I might as well tell you that we doubt it. We won't know for certain until all the tests have been completed, but we suspect he was dead when he went into the lake."

"You mean he was murdered too."

Mullane nodded. "How does that fit with your Hamlet theory?"

"I guess since Graham has said all along that Mr. Woodman would never kill his daughter, it fits perfectly. But it certainly makes the other person involved sound a lot more dangerous."

"Yes, which is why you must stay out of the whole thing, including the search for Anthea Davies, until we have caught him. There'll be time enough to look for her later."

"You still don't think they're linked?"

"The police have spent three months looking for a girl who vanished. I think my time will be better spent looking for a killer who's killed twice in the past week. If they are linked, that may be good news or it may not."

"On a happier note, we have finally located Woodman's ex-wife in America, and she and her husband are on their way over to deal with the various estate issues and take custody of her granddaughter."

"Oh—" said Ellie, taken aback. "That's good," she said, swallowing hard to get down a wave of ifs and buts.

Mullane left soon after, and Graham said, "I'm sorry, Ellie. I was so caught up in Mullane's news that I haven't asked you again where you've been—and where is the blue Mini?"

Ellie blushed. She had practically forgotten about the car, thanks to her own preoccupation with Crispin.

"In a ditch, I'm afraid," she said, "and I hope it's not damaged. I'm not even exactly sure where it is, the snow was so blinding. Somewhere between here and the hospital."

"So how did you get home?" he asked, suddenly alarmed.

"I was very lucky. Morag's friend Crispin came along and offered me a ride, but he needed to go to his cottage first, and that's why it took so long."

"I put the red Mini in a ditch during my first year of driving," said Isabelle. "It's part of the baptismal rite for Kent family cars. And then we only had the one. Isn't it a good thing we have two now?"

"It is," said Graham, "but it's an even better thing that Ellie was not hurt and got home safely in time for tea."

Sunday, January 3
Epiphany Sunday
Chapter 13

Cold rain dampened the enthusiasm of St. Michael's parishioners on the Sunday after Christmas, and few people came to mark the arrival of the three kings in Bethlehem. Technically they were three days early—since Epiphany fell on Wednesday the sixth of January–-but their parish was celebrating on the Sunday before, like many others, and Ellie put the kings into the crèche herself. From her perspective, the end of the 40 days of Christmas was in sight, and no foul weather was going to bother her.

Graham included a prayer for the Woodman family, former members of the parish, and the talk after the service centered on the weather, of course; the discovery of William Woodman's body; and the news that his ex-wife was returning to claim the baby found in their very own manger on Christmas Eve. Ellie was surprised how many people preferred to believe that Mr. Woodman had committed suicide after killing his daughter, rather than accept the disturbing notion that they had both been murdered by the baby's father.

Ellie poured tea and said little, although she saw Miss Worthy eyeing her as if she wanted the chance to speak. When most people had buttoned their coats and ventured back into the rain, she offered to help with the clean up, and Ellie accepted.

"I wondered if I might have a word with you about this new discovery," she said.

"Of course," said Ellie, who poured them both fresh tea and sat down in a pew with her feet on a kneeler.

"I was terribly sorry to hear about Bill Woodman," said Miss Worthy with genuine sadness in her voice. "Somehow I kept hoping there would be an explanation for what happened that didn't involve him. I remember the family from when they lived in the village, and no one could have imagined that life would turn out so badly for them! I'm glad Daphne is coming for the baby though. Are you?"

Ellie sipped her tea before answering. "Yes," she said. "I'll be honest—I've had moments when I thought I would love it if Graham and I could keep her, but that really wouldn't be fair. In a small place like this, she would never escape her history. It's much better for her to go to America."

"You're hoping that she may never have to know about any of this, I suppose," Miss Worthy said, looking thoughtful. "I only wish Charlotte and Dolphin could do that too. Get away."

"What do you mean, Miss Worthy? I thought Charlotte was very happy working for you."

"She is, but she doesn't have a lot of foresight, does she? None of these girls do, who plunge into motherhood when they're not even grown themselves."

"But isn't that just why it's lucky she and Dolphin can live with you?"

"In some ways," she replied. "But have you never considered the possibility, Mrs. Kent, that the man you've talked about—your Hamlet—might also have been the one to take advantage of Charlotte? She was a lovely young girl too."

"No," said Ellie, taken aback. "I was under the impression—I'm not even sure why—that Dolphin was not conceived locally."

"Charlotte has worked hard to foster that idea, despite the obvious problem of the timing involved. Dolphin was born in July. She left school after the holidays a year ago. She did go to Brighton for a weekend that October, and she claims she met Dolphin's father there, but it has always seemed unlikely to me. Charlotte is not that impetuous or flighty, and as this whole drama about Deborah Woodman—and even Anthea Davies—has developed, I have lain awake at night worrying and wondering . . . why just those two girls? Why not others? Such a man might have a long history of victims."

"Good Lord," said Ellie. "Charlotte doesn't have a tattoo around her wrist, does she?"

"No. And we have all tried to find out the name of Dolphin's father without the least success. The other fear that keeps me awake is that if all the girls were involved with the same man, and he was the one who killed Deborah, my Charlotte knows who the murderer is and may be in danger."

"Has she had any contact with Dolphin's father?"

"I don't believe so, and I'm quite sure that she never even told him about the baby. She's been emphatic about cutting all her ties with Kingbrook, but that doesn't mean they couldn't run into each other by accident—or that he might not fear the recent events would cause her to put two and two together and point to him as a possible suspect." As she spoke, Miss Worthy twisted the buttons on her cardigan, a habit she had when she was anxious. "You know, in a few days, I'm going to meet with my publishers in New York, and I think I should take Charlotte and the baby with me."

"That sounds like an excellent idea," said Ellie. "Then, with any luck, this business will be resolved by the time you return."

"In the meanwhile, if you would talk to her again—to see if she will tell you anything—I would be very grateful."

"Certainly, I'll come as soon as I can," said Ellie, although she wasn't optimistic about her chances of prying any confidences from Charlotte Worthy.

Once she was back at home, though, Ellie had little desire to go out again. Surely no one was out committing murder on such a cold, rainy day, so talking to Charlotte could wait until tomorrow. The house was quiet, and the blazing sitting room fire had drawn Hector like a magnet; even he did not want to go out.

Isabelle had left early that morning with some friends to go to an end-of-holidays house party in Cornwall; and Graham said he intended to devote the afternoon to *The Times* crossword. Ellie decided she would start reading the new biography of Charlotte Brontë she'd bought at Blackwell's, but she made the mistake of checking her phone messages first.

Morag had called, and there was an urgent note in her voice that was disturbing: "I heard about your accident from Crispin, and I hope you're okay. If at all possible, I need to see you today somewhere private. I've found something I want to show you. Please call me."

Ellie sighed when she heard this and said to Graham, "I guess I'm going to have to go out after all. Morag wants to see me, and she sounds very worried, so I'll meet her and visit Rosie too. I promise not to wreck the red Mini."

"That's fine. The blue one should be back this afternoon," he said, not entirely paying attention. He did the crossword in ink, a challenge Ellie would never even consider attempting. When he had finished putting in his word, he looked up at her, and said, "I will take you out for dinner when you get back. We'll go somewhere we've never been."

Clearly Ellie needed to work on her attitude toward rain if she was going to make it through the winter. She was not at all happy that she got soaked getting from her car to the entrance of The Cat and Mouse in Chipping Martin, where Morag wanted to meet. The tiny tearoom was tucked into one of the few 17th century buildings that remained standing on the square, and it was nearly empty on this dismal Sunday afternoon.

Ellie shook her hair vigorously, before joining Morag at a quiet corner table. The circles under her friend's eyes betrayed her anxiety, and Ellie suddenly worried that something had happened to Seamus. But when they had ordered cream tea, and Morag finally spoke, it was not about her son.

"I don't know if you noticed yesterday, but I'm afraid things may be going sour with Crispin," she said. "Ever since he learned about Seamus playing at detective, he has been distant from both of us."

"I'm so sorry to hear that. I got the impression from what he said to me that he considered himself quite a part of the family. Have you tried talking to him about it?"

She shook her head. "It's too fresh, somehow. Did you know that he was interviewed about the death of that girl, Deborah Woodman?"

"Derek Mullane told me they had interviewed everyone connected to her from the school, and they were all cleared."

"Did he? Derek said that?" She looked a bit brighter at this news. Mullane had gone to school with Morag's ex-husband, and they were old hunting buddies.

They fell silent as the waitress brought their cream teas, and they had to attend to the business of pouring their tea and piling clotted cream and strawberry jam on their scones.

Ellie was hungry and took a big bite of her hot scone, but Morag's moment of relief had passed quickly and now she sat with her chin in her hand, not touching her food.

"The thing is . . . ," she started and then stopped. "Derek wouldn't have said that if it weren't true, would he? I mean they know things that no one else knows, right?"

"I would assume so. They usually do their best to verify what people say. What is it, Morag? It will probably be easier if you just spit it out."

"You're right. It's . . . ," she sighed. "Well, you see, I'm the one who verified Crispin's alibi. Although it seems ridiculous to call it that, and I never thought twice about it at the time."

"What did you tell them?"

"Just that he was there, at my house, on Christmas Eve. Which he was. But the truth is I was late leaving Seamus's gran's, and the snow made the driving bad, so instead of getting home by seven, as we planned, it was after ten when I got back."

"And Crispin was waiting for you?"

"Yes, of course. And he said he'd been there all evening—he has a key—but I don't actually know that, do I?"

"No, I guess you don't. But what's happened to make you question it?"

"I found this yesterday," she said, opening her purse and handing across an unmarked envelope.

Ellie opened it curiously without saying anything. Inside was a photo of a man and a boy in what appeared to be Oxford. The man was wearing a flat cap and glasses, but she recognized him as Crispin right away. The boy was tall and slim, dark-haired, also wearing a cap, jeans, and a rain jacket. Crispin had his arm around him.

"I see it's Crispin, wearing glasses, but I don't see why you found this photo upsetting," said Ellie.

"That's his nephew. The one I met in Blackwell's last August. Do you remember I said I bumped into them there?"

"Yes, but I didn't think anything of it."

"Well, I did. He was very embarrassed when I met them together, and at first he didn't recognize me. He only introduced the boy because he sort of had to, but there was something about them that did not have a familial vibe, if you know what I mean. I also thought he was annoyed that I mentioned this meeting again in front of you the other day, but the fact is I've never forgotten it. And today I found this photo stuck in the book he's reading. Right on the bedside table in my house."

"So what are you saying? You think he was having an affair with that boy?"

"I don't know. I don't know what to think. Why would he use that photo as a bookmark unless it was important to him?"

"He loves his nephew?"

Morag scowled, disbelieving, but she turned pale when Ellie asked, "Are you sure it was a boy? Could it have been a girl dressed to look like a boy to the casual observer?"

She thought a long time and then let out a deep sigh. "Yes. Maybe that was it. Maybe the reason it has bothered me is that, at some level, I knew that even though he introduced Teddy, Teddy was not Teddy."

"Tell me again where found you this?" Ellie asked, being careful to keep her voice as gentle and calm as she could.

Morag twisted her spoon in her hands, looking miserable.

"I never meant to pry, especially after finding Seamus's damn notebook, but I was tidying up in the bedroom yesterday while Crispin was at his place, and the photo fell out when I restacked the books on his side."

"You didn't recognize this 'Teddy', did you?"

Morag flushed, her eyes wide with alarm. "What do you mean?"

"I was wondering if 'he' might have been Anthea Davies."

"That girl who's missing? There was a photo of her in the paper only the other day with an article about how she still hasn't been found. We talked about it, and I asked Crispin if he had known her at Kingbrook. He said he hadn't."

"I could be completely wrong, but I know Anthea liked to dress up as a boy when she was a student at Kingbrook, and she would go into Oxford to meet a man who was also disguised."

Morag went white. "You mean that story Seamus came up with."

Ellie nodded. She set the photo down on the table. "I would try not to get carried away about this yet, but it might be worth showing the photo to Anthea's parents. They can probably tell if it is their daughter."

Morag slapped her hand down over the photo. "You can't take it. I have to put it back right away. He only went back to his place to do whatever he didn't have time to do yesterday."

"I'll just photograph it with my camera. Okay? That should be good enough."

Morag nodded miserably and stabbed at her scone with a fork. "It's incredible how when you find out someone has told you a lie, the door opens to all kinds of thoughts," she said.

"I know," said Ellie, taking out her phone and turning on the camera, "but you know he could have had some kind of long-standing friendship with Anthea that he would be reluctant to mention given the current circumstances. Beyond that, you know nothing and, to be fair, you have to weigh in everything you've learned about him from these past weeks that you've spent together."

Morag seemed to drink up her words, and a little color came back into her skin. She pushed her hair back from both sides of her face and leaned back with her hands behind her head. "You're right. I feel like a fool. What's the matter with me? I spend a month in bed with a man, and now, at the drop of a hat, I switch from thinking he's my next husband to worrying about I don't know what."

Ellie nodded. "Been there." And she had.

The relief Morag felt was palpable, but Ellie also knew from her own experience that one lie could turn the hourglass of a relationship, and that may have happened here.

Morag gulped down her tea and began to eat her crumbled scone hungrily. "Thank you, Ellie," she said, when she was finished. Ellie thought she was ready to leave, but instead she took a deep breath and poured herself more tea.

"There is another thing I haven't told you, and I might as well," she said. "I only remembered it last night when I was lying awake worrying about the photo. There was something that happened at Shepherd's Hill. It was all hushed up very quickly, and it was the end of term, so I never heard what really happened."

"And it involved Crispin?" asked Ellie.

"That was the rumor. It was nothing more," said Morag. "But, you see, he left after that term. That's when he went to teach in China. We all heard he'd got married, and it all sounded very adventurous and, you know, sort of high-minded."

"What was the rumor?"

"That he'd got involved with a student. A girl who also left the school."

"I see," said Ellie.

"I'll tell you one thing, Seamus would be delighted to find out anything untoward about Crispin. He positively hates him, and I'm afraid the feeling is becoming mutual. I've never seen him react like this—and there have been a couple of other men in my life. It's not like he's accustomed to my lavishing one hundred percent of my attention on him, which is what Crispin thinks."

"Seamus is a very bright kid, but I would guess his judgment in this instance is ever so slightly colored by jealousy," said Ellie. "No matter what, I think the next steps are for you to put the photo back where you found it and for me to send the copy to Mr. and Mrs. Davies."

Ellie waited until Morag had left the teashop before sending the photo to Anthea's parents with a message saying she had come across it and wondered if the girl could be Anthea. Much to her surprise, the answer came back from Arthur Davies in less than a minute:

Yes, that's Anthea. Who is that man? Is he the one she ran away with?

Ellie wrote back that she wasn't sure yet and asked him not to share the photo or discuss it with anyone.

She would keep them posted with any new information. Then she texted Morag one word: *Yes*.

She tried to quell her excitement and consider what this actually meant: Crispin did have a relationship with Anthea outside of his role as her teacher at Kingbrook, and, unbeknownst to her parents, she had been in Oxford spending time with him as recently as August, when Morag bumped into them. He had lied to Morag about knowing her, despite the fact that he kept a photo of them together with her in her disguise as a boy. The likelihood of his being the man Gerald Villiers had seen her with three years ago seemed very high, but it was not proven.

She was preparing to call Mullane and suggest that he compare this new, more recent photo with the CCTV footage from the hospital, when the phone rang. Morag.

"It's true then?" she asked.

"Anthea's parents say that it is her in the photo. They did not recognize Crispin."

"But that doesn't mean anything except that he lied about knowing her."

"Correct," said Ellie. "Did you put the photo back?"

"Yes," she said. "I did. And now I'm going to try to forget all about it and cook us a nice meal. I don't want some kind of suspicion creeping into my head. We've been having such a great time. I must be bonkers from lack of sleep to get so wigged out over this." She tried to laugh so Ellie would know why she hadn't been sleeping.

"Well, with two bodies discovered in the past week, everyone is a little freaked out. So I agree. Just put it aside for now. The police could have the whole thing settled soon."

Morag was silent. Ellie could tell she wasn't pleased to have the recent deaths or the police linked in any way to the photo of Crispin, but she felt she had to warn her, even obliquely, that she might be dealing with something more than a man's particular romantic inclinations.

"Right," said Morag, a bit coldly. "Let's hope so," and she hung up.

Ellie made two more quick calls—to Mullane and to Sarah Henning—before leaving the teashop. She explained the gist of her new information in her message to Mullane and felt a little bit less lame than the last time. This was not old news. This was the present—that photo had been taken only a few weeks before Anthea's disappearance.

Sarah had agreed to visit Rosie, so Ellie swung back through Little Beecham to pick her up on the way to Kingbrook Hospital. The girl was silent in the car and grew pale when she saw the police officer guarding Rosie's door. It was as if this were the first time the danger became real to her.

Her eyes filled with tears when she saw the tiny baby in her bare institutional hospital room with its cold light and equipment, but she took Rosie in her arms confidently and sat down with her on her lap. The baby cooed when she petted her, which reminded Ellie that Sarah had three younger siblings, and, unlike her, was very used to babies. She left them alone and went to the cafeteria to get them some tea. By the time she returned, Rosie was sound asleep in Sarah's arms.

"Do you want to put her down?" Ellie asked, and Sarah shook her head.

"I like holding her. I'm pretending I'm Deborah and then I'm pretending I'm her grandpa, so she knows they're here with her. I don't know any prayers, so I said the *Magnificat* for her."

"That's sounds perfect," said Ellie, who sipped her tea and looked out the window at the rain until she thought Sarah might be ready to answer some questions. Then she pulled up the nurse's empty chair and sat down.

"I've been meaning to ask you about something, Sarah, if that's okay. I wonder if you remember the day when Deborah sang the song from Shakespeare at the Drama Club meeting."

"How did you hear about that?" asked Sarah, surprised.

"Mr. Pettibone told me."

"Of course, I remember," she said. "No one expected her to be so good, and she was very proud of that."

"Did she say why she chose that song?"

"I don't think so. Everyone has to do a Shakespeare, and you're supposed to say something about why you picked your speech, but no one says much. I did Puck because it was short. Why Mrs. Kent? Is that important?"

"You told me there were times when she seemed happy and excited, and other times when she didn't. I've been wondering if she believed Rosie's father was going to marry her—and if her anxiety in the last weeks of the term came from the fear that he wouldn't keep his promise."

"Like in the song."

"Exactly."

"I don't know," said Sarah, rearranging Rosie's blanket.

"Did she ever mention Anthea Davies? Do you think she remembered her?"

"No."

Ellie was aware of the decreasing number of syllables in Sarah's answers, but she pressed on. "Did you ever hear any of the girls being called an Oph? As in Ophelia? Referring to a girl with a broken heart?"

A strange look came over Sarah's face. "Why are

you asking me all these questions, Mrs. Kent?"

"I'm trying to understand how certain things fit together: a girl who had rosemary tattooed around her wrist and tucked rosemary into the blanket she wrapped around her baby, a straw woman thrown into the King Brook with a message quoting Ophelia, and a missing girl with a fennel tattoo."

Sarah continued to fiddle with Rosie's blanket. "I don't see why you keep going on about those tattoos. Practically everybody gets them. It's cool, and it gets up people's noses, but it's no big deal. It doesn't have to mean something like you seem to think."

"And was there no meaning to the straw figure you put into the King Brook either?"

"The what?" said Sarah, but her face turned ashen. She stood up and walked with the baby to the window.

When Ellie stayed silent, the girl turned back to her, and there was a shift in her expression. "I don't know how you found out about that, but it was just a joke. I mean the figure wasn't Deborah, it was me. I was just in a mood after Christmas with Dad being drunk and Jackie dead, and then Deborah too. Everything was so horrible. I would have topped myself for real except I knew Mum just couldn't take it and then what would happen to the kids? So I did it pretend-like instead. And it made me feel better, shoving that thing into the icy water."

Ellie was shocked. How could she have spent so much time with this child and not have understood how much she was struggling? But then something in Sarah's bearing reminded her that she was also the wanna-be actress.

It was a risk, but she decided to say: "Sarah, I know you've had a terribly rough time lately, but I think there was another reason why you made that Ophelia figure. You are not Ophelia. Deborah is. I think you heard that she committed suicide, and you wanted to lay the blame at the right door in any way you could. So whose door was it?"

Sarah's face turned stony. She stared at Ellie, as if weighing how to answer, and Ellie held her breath. Finally she said, "I already told Father Kent, I never knew what was really going on with Deborah. She told me the tattoo was for her brother, and I didn't have any reason to question it, even though we talked about that 'rosemary is for remembrance' thing. I only suspected that she was involved with some bloke after she did the Shakespeare. She surprised everyone, the way she threw herself into her performance that day.

"When I heard she killed herself, I was sure it somehow had to be connected. I hoped, I don't know, I was sort of crazy, but I thought if he heard about the woman in the stream, like if it was on the news, he would feel, I don't know what. Guilty. Or maybe worried that Deborah had told someone about them. It was stupid. Useless."

"And when you found out that she'd been murdered? That it wasn't suicide?"

"I knew he must have done it." Sarah set the baby back in her bassinet. "I'm sorry I can't help you more, Mrs. Kent. Deborah and I were close in a way, but I'm one of the ones who failed her. She didn't confide in me, because I didn't want to know. Not really. I was worried about my own problems. Now I need to get home and fix tea for the kids. They'll be hungry. If you can't take me, I'll catch the bus." She picked up her coat and began to put it on.

"Of course I'll take you home, but tell me this. Did she really send you a temporary rosemary tattoo?"

Sarah sighed. "No. She did send me a tattoo, but it wasn't rosemary. It just came yesterday."

"So what was it?"

"A ring of daisies. She told me they stand for innocence. But she also said, 'Someday your prince will come,' as if she thought that's what was about to happen for her. Only when he came, he was no prince, was he?"

Sarah left the car without looking back, when Ellie dropped her off. Watching the lonely figure disappear into her house, where everyone expected her to be the adult she was not, Ellie felt sad, but she had gotten the information she wanted. She could only hope her relationship with Sarah would eventually recover.

A ping from her phone told her she had a new voicemail message. She expected it would be from Mullane, but it wasn't. It was David Pettibone.

"I remembered something last night that might be important to you," he said. "A few years ago, I went skiing over Christmas and broke my leg. I had to be off work for a while, and another teacher was assigned to take the Drama Club meetings. He was new to the school then, a chap named Souter.

"It was a bad season for flu, and a lot of students were ill, so at one meeting he filled in for the boy who'd been rehearsing the 'Get thee to a nunnery' scene from *Hamlet* with one of the girls. Apparently the spontaneous performance they gave was quite something, and it made a big impression on everyone who saw it. A "sizzler" was the term they used. The student was that one we talked about who's missing. Anthea Davies."

Ellie listened to the message over and over, sitting in the dark outside the Hennings' house. This had to be the missing piece: the starting point. She punched in Sybil Bennett's number and was pleased to get her on the first try.

"I need to ask about another event from when you

were at Kingbrook. Do you remember Anthea preparing a scene from *Hamlet* for the Drama Club?"

Sybil was silent for a moment. "You mean when she did the 'Get thee to a nunnery' scene?"

"That's right."

"Yes, I remember that. We practiced it together and, as you might imagine, it was a very strange experience for me. Doing a very conflicted love scene with someone I had such unacknowledged feelings about."

"That must have been very hard."

"I've always thought Anthea sensed how I felt, because we never spoke of it afterwards. I heard from someone else that the scene went very well, even though the kid who was supposed to do Hamlet was sick. I think she did it with the teacher instead."

"So she never talked about that day?"

"No. And the whole thing was like something that came between us. I didn't understand it, but I assumed it was because of me."

"It wasn't. I'm pretty certain that was the moment she first connected with the man she became involved with."

"You mean it was Pettibone all along?"

"No, he wasn't there. He had a broken leg. It was another teacher. Someone new at the time. Crispin Souter."

"Mr. Souter? Are you sure? Because Anthea never missed a chance to say something nasty or dismissive about him in all the time we were in school."

"Well, there you have it. The classic 'I hate him' cover."

"Wow. And you think she could still be with him? Now? After all these years?"

"I learned today that she was seen with him in Oxford in August. So I'm still following breadcrumbs, but the witch's house is in sight."

"You mean that place where all the lost children are turned into gingerbread?"

"Yes, but hopefully, not all the children. I'll keep you posted."

Monday, January 4
Chapter 14

Even before Ellie had a chance to talk to Mullane, to have the satisfaction of telling him she had found the starting point of her mystery, Mr. and Mrs. Davies arrived, pale with agitation, to show them a letter they had just received. The postmark was more than a week old, but the address had been misspelled and the postcode was wrong, so it had been delayed. The envelope was addressed to Anthea in a rather affected, girlish handwriting.

"I almost threw it away," said Mrs. Davies, as she was taking off her coat in Graham's study. They had gathered there, but no one even thought of tea. "I expected it to be just another crank letter—a bad joke because usually they are not addressed to Anthea. Arthur wanted to have a look, though, and this one was so strange, he thought we'd better bring it right to you. Give it to her," she said to her husband with a new more authoritative note to her voice.

Mr. Davies handed over the letter, and Ellie took out the enclosure, a sheet of plain white paper with a message in block letters that said:

"By Gis and by Saint Charity,
Alack and fie for shame,
Young men will do't if they come to't—
By Cock, you are to blame.
Quoth she, "Before he tumbled you,
He promised me to wed.
So would he ha' done, by yonder sun,

And you hadst not come to his bed."

At the bottom, the writer had drawn a broken heart full of arrows.

Ellie paused to take a deep breath. She couldn't believe that the last pieces of her puzzle were falling into place so quickly, one after the other. But that was the way a jigsaw puzzle worked, wasn't it?

The others were watching her silently, and the air crackled with their tension. Before saying anything about the letter, which she was sure she understood, she looked at the postmark again: 28 December in Chipping Martin.

That caused her a moment of doubt so strong she felt sweat break out on her body. Then she remembered where she was. A land of villages with little red Royal Mail postboxes. Village stores that handled mail.

She looked quickly at Graham: "If a letter were dropped in a village postbox on Christmas Eve, where and when would it be postmarked?"

"It would go to Chipping Martin," said Graham, turning to Mr. and Mrs. Davies for confirmation. "There is no service on Christmas or Boxing Day so the earliest it would have been postmarked was last Monday."

"But with the errors in the address and the holiday on Friday, it didn't get to us until a week later," pointed out Mr. Davies.

Ellie felt so relieved she had to sit down.

"So what does it mean, Mrs. Kent? Can you explain it?" asked Mrs. Davies.

"I can," said Ellie. "It's a very important letter."

Mrs. Davies' cheeks turned pink, and her husband clutched at her arm.

"The text is a revised version of a song from *Hamlet*. In the play, it's sung by Ophelia and tells the story of a young woman who is seduced and abandoned by her lover. But in this version, the pronouns are changed so that the cause of her betrayal is attributed to another woman who comes between her and her lover.

"This message was sent to Anthea, and the altered text suggests that Anthea is the sender's rival for the affections of the same man. A man the sender thought would marry her, but he has reneged because he loves Anthea."

"So all that about tumbling. . . that means what it sounds like it means?" said Mr. Davies with a scowl.

"Yes."

"Oh, Arthur, what does that matter? If this letter was written a week ago, the sender must have thought that Anthea was still alive and perhaps not even far away."

"That certainly seems possible," said Ellie.

"So who sent it? Do you know?" asked Mr. Davies.

"I have an idea, and I know how to confirm it," said Ellie. "Then we'll need to turn it over to the police."

"Yes, certainly," said Graham. "But why would. . . the sender. . . send the letter to Anthea at her parents' home when it has been widely publicized that they haven't seen her since October."

Ellie twirled her hair thoughtfully. "It's possible that the sender did not know how else to communicate with Anthea other than through her parents' address, but she desperately wanted to send this message anyway.

"Mrs. Davies, do you remember if you put up your MISSING posters in Chadstone on the twenty-second of December—that is, the same day you put them up in Little Beecham?"

Mrs. Davies didn't even hesitate. "I'm sure I did," she said. "I went to all the villages in the area."

"Of course. I'd better not say anything further until we know that I am right about who sent the letter."

"I want to know who the 'young man' is and what he has to do with my daughter and her disappearance," demanded Mr. Davies.

"You may know that very soon, but not yet. It would be terrible to suggest something that wasn't true."

He looked as if he could barely contain himself, but he managed to say he understood that, and both parents were more agitated when they left than when they arrived, but that was because hope was sending out sparks in all directions.

"I almost gave out Deborah's name by mistake," said Graham, when they were alone again.

"I know, and I'm glad you caught yourself. I didn't want to draw their attention to the idea that the letter was from Deborah, knowing that she was murdered only a few hours after she sent it."

"So where are we exactly?" said Graham.

"I think Crispin claimed he would marry her, but she was uncertain enough, especially in the last few weeks, to worry that he wasn't going to come through. She was acting out those worries when she got the rosemary tattoo and when she sang the St. Valentine song for the Drama Club."

"Do you think she knew about Anthea all along?" asked Graham.

"Something happened at the beginning of October that precipitated Anthea's disappearance—and it didn't clear the field for Deborah."

"I can't believe he was ever seriously considering marriage."

"He had to be convincing enough to persuade her to keep her quiet throughout the school term. Otherwise she might have felt driven to tell someone what was going on or ask someone for help."

He sighed, sat down at his desk, and began sharpening his pencils with a penknife. "We're talking about this like there is actual evidence that Crispin Souter is the man. But there isn't, is there?" he asked.

"No," said Ellie, taking the chair next to the desk. "The evidence linking Crispin to Anthea has gotten solid, but this letter is the first evidence of a triangle with Deborah. Before that, there were only hints of the two girls being involved with the same man—the tattoos and the man in disguise who came looking for Rosie and may have been the same guy who used to meet Anthea in Oxford when she was still at Kingbrook."

"That's it?"

Ellie bridled. "It may not sound like much to you—but it's a lot more than we had a couple of days ago. If Crispin is the lover the letter refers to, it brings his relationship with Anthea forward to the present—even more than the photo Morag found from last summer. It also puts that relationship in direct conflict with whatever plans he may have claimed to make with Deborah."

Graham rubbed his eyes. "It's all pretty flimsy, and there's nothing to indicate he killed Deborah—

or Bill. I hope we haven't got Mr. and Mrs. Davies' hopes up for nothing."

"I don't think we have—if this letter is from Deborah. I am quite sure Sarah has a sample of her handwriting, so the sooner I see her the better."

"I just hope he hasn't already killed Anthea too. He may have, and Deborah may not have realized it," Graham said.

"I know. That worries me too."

"And Bill? Where does he come into this?"

"I think he must have been out searching for Deborah," she said, suddenly imagining her own father's search for her. "If they crossed paths at the wrong moment, Crispin could have felt he had to murder Bill too. I'm guessing he disposed of Deborah in the woods and then pushed the car with Bill's body in it into King Lake, hoping neither would be found until it was very hard to determine the circumstances."

"You realize he would have had to do all this before coming to church with Morag for the eleven o'clock service?"

Ellie nodded. "I know. It gives me the creeps to think of it, and it's a very tight timetable, but not impossible. Morag corroborated his alibi, because he claimed to have spent the whole evening at her house waiting for her—but she didn't get there until after ten o'clock."

"Wasn't that lucky for him," said Graham. "And he was the one who removed the evidence of Deborah's giving birth?"

"I suppose he was frantic to get rid of anything that could potentially prove the link between them." Ellie stood up. "I should go and try to find Sarah."

"Is there anything I can do to help?"

She looked at him thoughtfully. "You know what would really help me? If you could find out when Rosie's grandmother is arriving—and what will happen then. Will the baby be turned over to her just like that? I'd like to be prepared."

"Of course. I'd be glad to work on that."

Ellie found Sarah at home and was quickly able to determine if the handwriting in the letter looked the same as in the message that came with the temporary tattoo. When Ellie told her she would need to give it to the police, Sarah looked subdued, but she agreed without any question.

"You'll get it back," Ellie promised, "but it might take awhile."

"I don't want it back," she said and closed the door.

Mullane came to The Vicarage right away, although he was in a hurry and didn't even want to sit down. Forensic tests on Bill Woodman had confirmed that he had been hit over the head with a heavy metal object and was dead before Deborah's car was driven into the lake. It was hard to pin down the time too closely, but the hypothesis was that he died the same night as his daughter. An intensive search to locate the crime scene was underway, focusing on the area around where Deborah's body was found, but given the amount of time that had passed, Mullane wasn't very hopeful about what they would find.

Ellie was struck with a sudden wave of anxiety. "Wouldn't you say that now there is all the more reason to find out if the same man also killed Anthea Davies?" she asked, handing him the two letters.

"What's this? More Shakespeare?"

"Yes and no. One is a message Deborah sent to a friend. The other is a letter received by Anthea's parents today. The handwriting looks the same to me, and I think it means that the man Deborah was involved with was Crispin Souter—the same man who is in that photo of Anthea from last summer. Deborah's letter implies that Anthea came between them, which I hope means she was still alive just before Christmas and that Crispin must know where she is."

"That's a lot of suppositions," said Mullane. "The photo, while interesting, only proves that he saw the girl last summer; and the hospital's CCTV images are not good enough to make a comparison."

"But couldn't you bring him back in for questioning? Isn't it enough for that? And if you got a DNA sample, you could find out if he is Rosie's father?"

"DNA can be collected as part of a speculative search, but we still have no evidence that he was the man involved with Deborah. It also is not a given that he is the murderer, even if he is the father."

"Really. Seems like you used to think so."

"If you're going to stick your nose into our investigations, Mrs. Kent, you'd better learn the difference between a person of interest, a suspect, and a person who can be charged with a crime."

"You're right. I apologize. I'm just frustrated."

"Aren't we all? But you, at least, are not under the gun to solve these problems."

Despite this rude response, he managed to summon the good grace to thank her as he was leaving and took the two letters away with him.

Ellie was nervous about talking with Charlotte Worthy again. She was never the easiest person, and she expected Charlotte would not welcome Miss Worthy being anxious about her, nor would she choose to confide in Ellie. Nevertheless, she'd promised she would do her best, and that's what she would do.

It was Miss Worthy herself who answered the door this time, and, after saying hello, she pointed down the hall to the kitchen, then tiptoed back upstairs.

Ellie found Charlotte feeding Dolphin creamed spinach. He sat in a high chair and managed to get splotches of green on his face, his hands, and his bib, but he laughed even as he spit out each spoonful Charlotte tried to aim into his mouth—and, oddly enough, she was laughing too. The realization that she would never see Rosie eat caused Ellie a sharp, sudden pang, but she pushed it to the back of her mind and sat down at the kitchen table.

"How can I help you, Mrs. Kent?" said Charlotte, wiping spinach off herself and her son with a damp cloth. When he was more or less green-free, she set him in his playpen. "Aunty said you wanted to talk to me." She still looked cheerful, and Ellie caught a glimpse of the pretty blonde C. Worthy from the Drama Club photo in the yearbook.

"Actually, she asked me to talk to you," said Ellie.

"About what?" Charlotte's smile faded, and she glanced toward her computer, a signal Ellie recognized. She'd used it herself. It meant: hurry up, please leave, I'm busy.

"I'm not sure if she's discussed this with you herself, but she's worried about the recent murders and whether you and Dolphin might be in danger."

"Murders?"

"Yes. Both Deborah Woodman and her father were murdered, and the most likely suspect is the man who fathered Deborah's child."

"What does that have to do with us?" Charlotte looked at Ellie with her best stonewalling expression—and it might have worked if she had not chosen that moment to bend down and pick up her son, who clutched her arms tightly with his chubby little hands.

Ellie knew at that instant that she was on solid ground, no matter how much Charlotte denied it. There was no mistaking those fingers. She had been looking at them, admiring their tapered shape, every day since Christmas Eve.

"I expect you have figured out the answer to that, even if it is the last thing you want anyone else to know."

"I don't understand what you mean," said Charlotte.

"You probably could have fobbed me off again, the way you did last time I was here, but that was before I noticed that Dolphin and Deborah's baby have exactly the same hands."

"The same hands? That's ridiculous. All babies' hands are alike," said Charlotte angrily.

"No they aren't. And if their hands are alike, and it's not because they have the same mother, it must be because they have the same father—in this case, a man who has already committed murder twice to keep his identity a secret. So, I think Miss Worthy has good reason to be worried about you."

Charlotte did a good job of looking outraged and surprised, which she may well have been. "And who is this murderer that you imagine to be my son's father?"

"Crispin Souter."

"Mr. Souter? From Kingbrook? You're mad! I met Dolphin's father in a pub in Brighton, and we spent the weekend together, but that was all there was to it."

Ellie gave her such a long look that Charlotte got up and began pulling food out of the refrigerator to make Miss Worthy's tea.

"You know you really shouldn't go around speculating about things like that," she continued. "It's not right. You're the vicar's wife. You should be above gossip. If that theory got around, it would end Mr.

Souter's career, and he's one of the only good teachers Kingbrook has.

"And if you think I'll ever say that Mr. Souter is Dolphin's father, you're dreaming. What would that accomplish other than to ruin my baby's life?" She began slicing bread with a long serrated knife.

"It might help us find out what happened to Anthea Davies."

"That's the police's job, not yours. Not mine."

"Charlotte," said Ellie, trying one last gambit. "You seem to enjoy being a mother, and you're clearly doing a good job of it, but how old were you when you became pregnant? Sixteen?"

"Yes, and, in this country, that is the age of consent."

"Not if the other person is your teacher."

"Mr. Souter was never my teacher."

"But he was a teacher at your school, and the evidence is piling up that he has had inappropriate relationships with students there. In fact, he seems to have preyed on a number of girls."

Charlotte laughed, but it was an angry sound. "No one has ever preyed on me, Mrs. Kent, and those laws are totally arbitrary. Girls have married and started families as soon as they reached puberty for centuries and in every culture. What really ought to be illegal is the criminalization of love.

"I choose not to be in touch with Dolphin's father, but our baby was conceived with love, and, as far as I'm concerned, that's all my son ever needs to know."

"I understand your wanting to keep the identity of Dolphin's father a secret, and you have succeeded so far, but it won't work any more," said Ellie. "Things have gone too far."

Charlotte turned to her with the knife in her hand, and the look of an enraged bear ready to defend her cub.

"I don't agree," she said. "You are on the wrong track. As I said at the beginning, this mess has nothing to do with me or my child."

"Okay! I get it! I'm leaving! But please, be careful!" said Ellie, holding up her hands. She grabbed her coat and made for the door before Charlotte decided to commit murder herself. Maybe the police could require her to talk, but she certainly couldn't.

Ellie hurried down Chapel Lane, bent against a brisk cold wind. At the high street, she decided to go to The Chestnut Tree, rather than back to The Vicarage. Michael-John would find more humor in Charlotte threatening her with a bread knife than Graham would, and she needed that.

She found him taking down his Christmas decorations, and she was happy to be able to lend him a hand. When all of the greens had been cleaned up, and the ornaments stored away, he made tea and they sat down in his office to drink it. Not until then did either of them mention the investigation.

"I think I need to retire as a detective," said Ellie. "When you have to live in the same place as all of the people affected by the crime and the investigation, it makes one hell of a mess. I seem to have alienated all the people in Little Beecham who didn't already find me alien as an incoming foreigner."

"Now, now," said Michael-John. "I hope you're not including me in either category, even if I did develop chilblains from standing in that brook."

Ellie smiled. "Not if you don't want to be," she said.

"Of course, I don't. Now tell me what you've done to create so much wreckage."

"Mainly I've been trying to persuade people to give me facts in exchange for my guesses. For example, I just tried to make Charlotte Worthy admit that her baby is Rosie's brother. Needless to say, she wouldn't, since I also said that their father is the murderer. In fact, she seemed to seriously consider slicing me up with a breadknife."

"Hmm," said Michael-John. "Well, maybe you do need one of those correspondence courses on interrogation."

Ellie dropped her chin into her hands. "I know. It's critical to be patient and indirect, and sometimes I'm not. I'm sure I'm right about this, though. Those babies have identical fingers."

"I see. I guess you know who the murderer is then, and, in that regard, you seem to be a bit ahead of the police. Have you found your missing girl?"

"No, but it appears she was still alive and probably right in this area just before Christmas."

"That's good news, isn't it?"

"Yes, but where is she? I mean, if you wanted to go missing, where would you go?"

"Somewhere warm and pleasant with lovely food."

"Definitely not here, in other words," said Ellie, sipping her tea thoughtfully. "That's the problem."

On the way home, Ellie stopped at the village shop for a supply of red licorice sticks, something she considered essential for the hard thinking and writing that she planned to do. Ever since college, all her best work had been fueled by licorice. She was sure, by now, her brain must be red.

Mrs. Wiggins, the shopkeeper, reluctantly set aside the latest *Hello* magazine to ring up her purchase. She was a plump, middle-aged woman who was always reading or gossiping when Ellie came in, yet she singlehandedly kept her small shop neat, clean, and stocked to the rafters with everything from fresh bread and produce to toys and office supplies.

"Did you have a pleasant Christmas, Mrs. Kent?" she asked.

"Yes, it was very nice," Ellie replied. "And you?"

"Oh yes," she said. "It was brilliant. This has been an especially good year for the shop. It's terrible to say but murders are good for business. So many strangers come to the village—and those journalists! They kept asking for lattes. I'm thinking of getting one of those espresso machines."

Mrs. Wiggins had always been nice to her, so Ellie put a smile on her face that felt like wax lips. "Well, I hope this will be a good year too," she said. She wanted to add "but preferably without any murders." That would be rude though, so she tucked her licorice into her bag and went home.

Her plan was to write down everything that she had learned since she first saw the posters about Anthea's disappearance. When she was settled in her study with a mug of tea, she opened her computer and created a fresh document. Then she began to write, hoping to see what she had been unable to see:

• Crispin read a scene from *Hamlet* with Anthea that, according to those who saw it, "sizzled." After that time, her closest friend Sybil observed a change in her and began to think she was having a secret relationship.

• Gerald Villiers followed Anthea into Oxford and saw her disguise herself as a boy so she could spend the day with a tall, older man who also appeared to be disguised. Although that man was never identified for certain, she repeated this trick during the previous summer, and a photograph existed in which both she and Crispin had been identified. The photo was in Crispin's possession.

• David Pettibone called Anthea a Juliet (AKA a girl who knew how to get what she wanted) and she and Sybil nicknamed girls who dramatized their broken hearts as "Ophelias" or "Ophs" (AKA girls who didn't know how to get what they wanted) yet Anthea complained about "false flattery" and got the fennel tattoo shortly before she left Kingbrook.

• No information had come out about Anthea's relationships, new or old, at Oxford. There was also no information about any girls who may have been involved with Crispin during Anthea's first year at Oxford. Was this significant?

• In the following year (Anthea's second year at Oxford), Charlotte became pregnant in October, left school in December, and cut off her ties with everyone at Kingbrook. She denied that the man she was involved with was Crispin. Her son Dolphin was born in July.

• A few months after Charlotte left the school, Deborah became pregnant. She may not have realized this right away.

• In May, Anthea had sex with Richard Crowley that he said seemed like revenge against an absent lover. In June she left Oxford to spend the summer working in London. Morag saw her with Crispin in August at Blackwell's. She was disguised as a boy.

• In September, Deborah went back to school. No one seems to have been aware that she was pregnant because she had regained the weight she'd lost the previous year.

• At the beginning of October, Anthea was photographed looking happy in Oxford, but she never showed up for Michelmas term and had had no contact with family/friends since then.

• Crispin became involved with Morag in November, spending a lot of time with her up until the present. Was this to provide cover for his complicated relationships with Deborah and Anthea?

• Some time late in the school term, Deborah may have been expressing her anxiety about Crispin's intentions when she sang Ophelia's Valentine song about betrayal at the Drama Club. She also got the rosemary tattoo, probably in late November.

• Right before Christmas, Deborah wrote a letter addressed to Anthea that accused her of coming between her and the man she would marry. Rosie was born; Deborah and her father were murdered.

• A man in a disguise similar to the one worn by the man who used to meet Anthea in Oxford years before tried to get in to see Rosie at the hospital.

• Dolphin has the same hands as Rosie.

Ellie read this all over twice and decided it sounded so improbable that she deleted the file.

The only definite outcome was that her supply of red licorice was all gone.

Tuesday, January 5
Twelfth Night
Chapter 15

A dark morning with a sharp wind that blew icy rain against the windows made a dreary start to the official end of the holidays. Graham had to spend the day at a meeting in Oxford, though he would be back to get ready for Twelfth Night. This, he explained, was a traditional event where they would sing and dance and bless the apple trees to ensure a good harvest.

"Seriously? You worry about the apple harvest in January?" asked Ellie, as they ate breakfast in the kitchen. Usually she loved any and all British folk customs, but this morning she had a pang of longing for the new-year rituals of her own homeland: big bowls of hot, buttered popcorn, ice cold beer, and a seemingly endless number of football games on television. That is, what she considered "real" football. Not the soccer that went by the same name in other parts of the world.

"Buck up," said Graham, smearing Marmite on toast. "You're just feeling down because we've been through so much unpleasantness, but it may soon be behind us."

"How do you know that?" she asked, spreading peanut butter on a rice cake.

"Mullane called earlier, while you were out walking Hector. He wanted to know if we had any idea where Crispin Souter might be found, since he was not at home."

"And you told him?"

"Certainly. I thought your whole case had come to revolve around him and you'd be glad Mullane was looking closer at him."

"I am, but I hate the thought of Morag being dragged into this," Ellie said.

She also felt miffed to find out that Mullane and Graham had been discussing the investigation without her. After all she had done. Or tried to do.

"This is no time to be having qualms about the price of solving the case. You were the one who was hell bent on finding answers."

"Hell bent is right," said Ellie, "since I haven't accomplished much except to create wreckage trying to find them. I don't know if Morag will ever forgive me."

"Of course she will," said Graham. "Why wouldn't she?"

"I think she really hoped this would be a lasting relationship."

"Along with several others in the queue. What is it about that bloke?"

"He is very handsome—and can be charming, when he wants to be."

Graham shook his head as if that were no explanation at all. "Well, Morag will eventually find out that she's had a lucky escape—and you'll feel better after the wassail. If you're here at three o'clock, we can go out to the orchard early together. Otherwise, come along with Isabelle. She'll be back home today in time for the procession."

But Ellie wasn't so sure how reparable her friendship with Morag was going to be when she showed up at The Vicarage shortly after Graham left.

"The police came to my house looking for Crispin this morning," she said, waving away Ellie's offer of tea. "They told him they wanted to interview him again about Deborah Woodman. He was livid, understandably, and they made him go to the police station in Chipping Martin with them. I couldn't believe it. I mean, how would they know to come looking for him at my house?" She glared accusingly at Ellie.

"I didn't tell them," she said and didn't mention that Mullane had spoken to Graham.

"So was it Seamus?"

"I'm not aware of Seamus ever talking to the police––are you? But Morag, they are the police. It's their job to find out things."

"I can't imagine who else would even know that we know each other."

"You were seen at church together, but that's not the point, is it? The point is there must be something they want to ask him about."

Morag's chest heaved. "Did you give them that photo? The one I showed you?"

"Yes, I did."

She shook her head, anger and fear in her face. "I should never have showed it to you. They're going to use that to fit him up for I don't know what—and he's bound to know that I'm the reason they have it."

At that, Ellie felt a sudden wave of fear herself and wondered if Mullane would put his sources at risk in questioning someone. She sincerely hoped not and tried to deflect Morag's own anxiety.

"They are not going to fit him up. And anyway, the photo only shows he knew Anthea after she left Kingbrook. Nothing more.

"Remember when Mullane had me as his top murder suspect? You kept reminding me that I had done nothing and eventually the police would realize it. This is the same situation. They're collecting information, and, if Crispin is not involved in the crimes they're investigating, he has nothing to worry about. It's annoying, humiliating, even frightening, but that's all.

"You also have to keep remembering that asking him to help with their inquiries is not arresting him, and even being arrested does not make you guilty, if you're not."

Morag gave her a long, searching look. She tried to control her expression, but her hands were shaking, so she crossed her arms over her chest to hide them. "I don't believe you really think this situation is parallel to yours," she said.

Ellie turned to the window overlooking the churchyard where soon Bill Woodman and his daughter would be buried, unable to meet her friend's gaze.

"If you knew something," said Morag, "something definite, you'd warn us—Seamus and me—wouldn't you?"

Ellie turned back to her. She could tell in that moment that Morag had crossed over from flatly denying Crispin's involvement to considering the possibility. "Of course I would," she said.

"Then this is the time to do it."

"I'm being perfectly frank when I say that I don't know anything about the murders or how Anthea Davies disappeared or where she is. But I have seen evidence like that photo, which implies Crispin had ongoing relationships with both Anthea and Deborah."

"You mean at the same time as he's been seeing me?"

Ellie nodded.

"What kind of evidence?" Morag asked, angrily, but then she pushed back from the table and stood up. "No. Don't tell me. I don't want to know. I'm taking Seamus to his grandmother's right now. Please don't communicate with him." And with that, she stormed out the door.

Alone in the house, Ellie made herself tea and went up to her study. She tried to imagine what the police might be asking Crispin and what he would say in reply. Did they have evidence that she didn't know about? Of course, they must. She searched the internet in hopes of seeing breaking news of an arrest in the murders of Bill and Deborah Woodman, but there was nothing.

She was tempted to call Mullane, but she couldn't think of any reasonable pretext. She was not about to tell him her new theory that Dolphin and Rosie were related because their fingers had the same shape. At the very least, Charlotte had persuaded her to leave her out of what she called "the mess" unless it was necessary to solve the more serious crimes.

Morag was right to go away with Seamus. He had to be her top priority, and Crispin would be angry if he found out that photo had ended up in the hands of the police. Even if she wanted to stand by him and support him, he may feel she had already let him down. Betrayed him with Ellie's help.

She took her cold tea down to the kitchen and poured it out. The rain was heavier now and slid down the glass, blurring the outside world. Hector looked at her hopefully, but they had already had one walk and that was enough for her. Instead she said, "Sorry, pal," and let him out the back door on his own. He returned in two minutes flat, shaking himself off indignantly.

Unable to settle down, she decided to spend the afternoon with Rosie. Once her grandmother arrived, she would begin another life in which Ellie had no part. At the hospital, she held the baby for a long time, feeling the soft, warm weight of her little body in her arms. She sang to her and read her the Peter Rabbit story and told her what a wonderful life she was going to have in America with her grandma.

Rosie was her sweetest self that day, gazing at Ellie with dark eyes that seemed to understand everything that had happened and would happen with complete acceptance. Before she left, Ellie fed and changed her—quite expertly, if she did say so herself—and tucked her into her bassinet with her little teddy bear beside her.

She was reluctant to return to the empty Vicarage and headed down to the hospital cafeteria instead, trying not to dwell on all of the milestones ahead for Rosie that she would miss. She was looking out the window at the sodden, darkening landscape, debating whether she was really hungry enough to eat the stale scone on her plate, when her phone pinged, and she saw that she had a text from Michael-John: *Very important. Call me.*

She punched the call button with no expectations, but when Michael-John answered right away, his excitement was contagious.

"I've figured out the whole thing," he said.

"What do you mean? What whole thing?"

"You asked me where I would go if I wanted to go missing—and I told you. But my answer was based on my wanting to go missing, and I have never heard you say a single thing that supports the idea that your Anthea wanted to do that. She wanted to go to Oxford. That's all she's ever wanted, right?"

"Yes. So you're saying she must be dead. Someone must have killed her," Ellie replied in a flat voice, as she pulled on her coat to go home. She hated that what he said made so much sense.

"No, that's not my point at all. At least, that's not the only option. The alternative is that someone made her go missing. In which case the question to ask is where would you, could you, completely hide someone and keep them incommunicado for three months."

Ellie stood stock still in the hospital corridor with her phone at her ear. Doctors, nurses, orderlies with trolleys, patients dragging IV poles, and visitors with bags of grapes all hurried past, and she barely saw them. What she was seeing was something else altogether and every word Michael-John said made the picture clearer.

"It would have to be somewhere you could come and go without being noticed—but, at the same time, nearby. Convenient. The logistics of hiding someone are not very romantic, if you think about it. Access to the hidden person and plumbing are essential, among other niceties like heat, electricity, and food. If you see what I mean. Someone's been shopping for two."

"I do see," said Ellie, and she meant it literally.

"Of course, there must be a motive," Michael-John went on. "Otherwise why go to all that trouble?"

"Perhaps," said Ellie, "you've realized that you can't live without someone, but that someone doesn't want to live with you. So you make them."

"Exactly. But, of course, it's an absolutely rotten solution. No good can ever come of it. Is your hidee going to decide to love you after that? Can the hider ever resume a normal life? It's definitely one of those lose-lose arrangements."

"And when the hider is about to be caught, what does he do with the hidee then? That is the question," said Ellie, starting to run for the door.

She drove as fast as she dared, focusing her mind on remembering the Google map that showed the location of Crispin's cottage, rather than on whether what she was doing made sense. She was relieved when she suddenly spotted the narrow, unmarked lane that led to Alder Cottage, but from the road she couldn't tell if

Crispin was there, so she had to take the chance of driving in without knowing.

Fortunately, his car was not in the drive. Unfortunately, there was no place to hide her car, so she could only hope that the police had a lot of questions for him—and that he was not too upset with Morag to go to her house when they were finished. No matter what, she would have to make her visit a quick one.

The front door was locked, as she expected, but Ellie was in luck. A kitchen window at the back of the cottage was open a crack and, when she shoved at it, the frame moved upward a few inches. She looked around for something to stand on and found a small garbage can that she could climb onto and push the window open farther.

Slithering in was not easy, but, by hauling her weight up and squirming, she managed to get through and only knock over some cookbooks that were on the counter inside. Her arms ached and her chest and knees felt scraped, but she was in.

The cottage was completely quiet, so every noise she made sounded as if it were being telegraphed to Crispin, urging him to come home. She took a few deep breaths, while she surveyed the one large room that served as living room, kitchen, study, and dining area. It was a pleasant, airy space, and nothing looked out of the ordinary, so, for a moment, she wondered if she had made a huge mistake to come here.

But then she thought of Rosie's sweet face, of Deborah's frozen body hanging in that tree, of the father who searched and failed to rescue his daughter, and of Anthea's mother, ashen-faced, clutching the hanky embroidered with the word "Mum."

All we want for Christmas is our Anthea. Please help.

The words came back to her like a mantra, and, without further hesitation, she began to search for any sign that Anthea Davies was living there—or had been. She went through the bedroom, the closets and drawers, the bathroom, the desk, the kitchen, and even scanned the bookcases, CDs, and DVDs. Aside from the fact that the refrigerator had more fresh food in it than she would have expected, considering Crispin spent so much time with Morag, she found no sign that someone else had been living in this quiet, isolated cottage.

She sat down at the desk and tried to gather her anxious thoughts. What had she learned: first, obviously, that Anthea was not there; and second, that it did not appear that she had been there recently either.

Was there anything she had missed? Any stone left unturned?

As she glanced around the room, she noticed a wastepaper basket pushed under the desk, and it was not empty. How could she have forgotten that? A good detective always checks the trash for evidence.

And there she found it.

Not what she was looking for, but something even more important: a crumpled copy of Form M10 Application to Marry in Scotland. The instructions at the top of the page stated that both applicants must be at least 16 years old, and the form had to be submitted 10–12 weeks before the marriage.

A familiar girlish hand had filled in the names and addresses of the applicants and signed the form on September 25th, but the other applicant had never signed it. In the corner, there was a red smear that looked like blood.

This was it. The motivation and the evidence. With shaking hands, she whipped out her phone and photographed the document to send to Mullane, but there was no reception. Then she tapped the keyboard on Crispin's computer to send the news by email and discovered that there was no wifi in the cottage either.

Incommunicado. Wasn't that the word Michael-John used? Crispin had certainly set up his hideaway well for that.

Carefully, Ellie folded the marriage application, tucked it into her parka's inside pocket, and zipped it shut. A sharp volley of raindrops against the window reminded her that she had been there too long. She glanced through the glass panel in the front door, fearing that any minute she would see the lights of Crispin's car coming down the lane.

Then she remembered the other night when she wanted to find out what was taking Crispin so long and had peered through that window from the outside. She had seen him descending a folding staircase that came down from the space above this room. Ostensibly, he had gone up there to find his Monopoly set. But what if that were not the only reason?

She looked up at the hatch in the ceiling high above her head and tried to remember how those things worked. She thought there should be a pole with a hook that you used to open the hatch and pull down the stairs, but a quick search produced no such tool, and besides there was what appeared to be an expensive new lock on the hatch. That seemed surprising for a man who went away and left his kitchen window cracked open.

She took a deep breath, listened for any sounds coming from above, and heard nothing. But that didn't mean no one was up there, and she couldn't leave until she had done everything she could to find out without delay. If the police were closing in on Crispin as a suspect, Anthea's chances of staying alive surely would diminish proportionately.

In the kitchen, she found a broom and tried to tap the ceiling, but it wasn't quite long enough. Quickly she pulled a chair under the hatch, climbed up on it, and tapped.

"Anthea? Are you there?" she called, tapping the ceiling. There was no response, but Anthea might also be bound and gagged when Crispin was not there to supervise her.

"Anthea, my name is Ellie Kent, and I've been helping your parents search for you. Crispin is not home, so it is safe for you to let me know if you are there."

This time she heard a soft thump, as if someone in stocking feet were trying to make a noise. Ellie was so excited that she almost fell off the chair.

"Listen, Anthea, I can't get the hatch open, but I'm going for help right now, and I'll be back as soon as possible!"

More thumps.

"I'm so happy to know you're there. Help will be here soon to get you out!" she shouted. Then she leapt down from the chair, ran to the kitchen, scrambled through the window, and dropped to the ground outside.

It was only four o'clock, but already quite dark and the temperature had dropped. The ground was slippery under her feet as she ran to her car, but it wasn't until Ellie turned on her windshield wipers that she realized the rain had begun to turn to sleet. The car stuttered for what felt like hours before the engine caught; then she lurched into first gear and took off.

She was about to turn onto the B road, when she saw a car coming toward her that had slowed down as if preparing to enter the lane leading to Alder Cottage. She pulled out and sped off, but not before she saw in her rearview mirror that the other car had stopped and turned around to follow her.

It could only be Crispin.

Driving as fast as she dared with one hand, she took out her phone and punched redial to try to reach Mullane. Of course she got his voicemail, but she blurted out, "Anthea Davies is locked in the attic at Crispin Souter's house. Please get her out immediately. Crispin is following me."

Then she stepped on the gas to try to escape the lights of the following car, which bounced off her mirror and blinded her. No matter which way she went, he stayed right behind her, and the road was becoming slick with ice.

Ellie quickly lost track of where she was and drove toward what looked like lights ahead. If she could only reach a village or town, she could dash into a pub and wait there for Mullane. No matter how angry Crispin was, he couldn't kill her in front of a room full of people.

But as she drew closer to the lights, she realized this was not a town ahead. It was an apple orchard, its bare trees hung with lanterns. Then she caught the faint sound of drums, music, and singing. She was speeding down a lane with Crispin right behind her, when she saw a procession of people with lanterns in the road ahead. She even thought she glimpsed the waving white handkerchiefs of the Beecham Morris dancers.

Graham, she thought, and she hit her horn and held it down for all she was worth. The blaring horn and oncoming cars caused the procession to break up as people scrambled out of the road into the ditches and onto the verges. Ellie braked and turned quickly onto a narrow road running off to the left, still going as fast as she could to stay ahead of Crispin.

He turned as well, right on her tail, then, suddenly, he went into a skid, and slid broadside into a stone wall. There was a terrible crunching sound as the car went up and over the wall, landed upside down in a field, and burst into flames. Ellie pulled up and jumped out of the Mini without even shutting it off. The burning car transfixed her, and, even before she could form the idea of moving out of the way, she saw Graham running toward her, with Isabelle close behind.

Later, Ellie had only blurry memories of lanterns bobbing in the dark, the burning car, people rushing to help but driven back by the flames, and the sing-song sound of police sirens. Someone wrapped her in a blanket, and Graham hurried her away, while John Tiddington drove home with Isabelle. There was no need to ask if Crispin had survived.

When they were all safely back at The Vicarage, Graham made hot toddies, and they sat together on the sofa, Ellie and Isabelle on either side of him. He lit a single candle that glowed in the dimly lit sitting room, while sleet beat against the windows, glazing them over and shutting out the world beyond their small circle of light and warmth.

None of them had ever witnessed anything like the accident that ended Crispin's life so dramatically, and they all felt shaken. No one said it, but Ellie knew she could have been killed too. Just like that.

"I hope he died in the crash. Before the fire," she said, after they had sat silently watching the candle flicker for a long time.

"I hope so too," said Graham.

"It seems strange to feel pity for someone who killed two innocent people, but I do. Sort of."

"Dad, can we please say a psalm for him?" asked Isabelle, who still looked very pale.

"Of course," said Graham. "One-hundred-and twenty one?"

She nodded, and together they recited the beautiful words about the constancy of the Lord's help. Ellie listened with her head bowed. She understood the power of the psalm's message, and she was deeply grateful to have survived this night, but how was it decided that she would live and Crispin would not? And, if the Lord could and would preserve you from all evil, where had he been on Christmas Eve?

It was only about eight o'clock, but felt much later, when Mullane called to let them know that Anthea had been rescued and reunited with her parents. Ellie put him on speakerphone so Graham and Isabelle could also hear what he said.

Crispin's attic turned out to have been quite well equipped to house a captive, and Anthea appeared to be physically unharmed, but in shock. Her statements about what happened were very contradictory, and, when Mullane told her that Crispin was dead, she had burst into tears. He couldn't tell whether this was from relief or grief. He had personally taken the girl to the hospital to be checked out, despite her resistance, and had stayed with her until her parents arrived. Their gratitude was overwhelming, and he said he had felt embarrassed, knowing that it was really Ellie who had found their daughter.

"So that ties up your little project, Mrs. Kent," he said. "We've begun searching Souter's house, and we'll search his property when it's light, but, unfortunately, we still have no solid evidence tying him to the murders. I'm sure he only chased you because he was furious you were snooping around. After the long day with us, that was the last straw."

"Evidence?" said Ellie, feeling her face flush. "But I have it. At least, I think I might. With everything that's happened, I forgot all about it."

There was a silence on the other end of the phone. Then Mullane said, "What do you mean?"

"When I was in the house, I found an application for marriage in Scotland filled out and signed by Deborah, but not Crispin, and, obviously, never submitted."

"Where was it?"

"In the wastebasket under his desk. It has blood on it."

"I'll be right over," said Mullane, all weariness leaving his voice.

Ellie unzipped the inside pocket of her parka and took out the marriage application with gloves on. It seemed like lifetimes had past since she'd searched Crispin's cottage. Now it was empty, and he wouldn't be back.

She waited for Mullane in the front hall, looking out at the glistening ice-coated night. When the police car slid to a stop in front of The Vicarage with its blue lights flashing, he jumped out and hurried to the door that Ellie held open for him. His hat and coat were streaming wet, and he had dark circles under his eyes.

"Here it is," she said, handing him the paper. "I'm afraid I handled it before I knew what it was."

"You should never have removed it from the scene, you know," he said irritably, and she felt rebuked. "Your whole search was highly illegal, but, lucky for you, it doesn't matter now." He took the document with his gloved hands and dropped it into an evidence bag. "I'll let you know what we find out," he said, and then he was gone again.

"Was Mullane pleased to get what you found?" asked Graham, when she returned to the sitting room and took up her place, leaning against him.

"In his usual gracious way," she said. "He told me I was lucky that they aren't going to charge me with theft."

Wednesday, January 6
Epiphany
Chapter 16

Despite everything that had happened, Ellie slept soundly for 12 hours and woke to a sunny day. This was the 40th and final day of Christmas, and they already had one minute and 36 seconds more daylight than they had had on the shortest day. She used this extra time to stare at a spot of sunshine on the wall, while she debated whether to get up or not.

When she finally came downstairs, Graham and Isabelle were taking the ornaments off the Christmas tree and packing them into the same old cardboard boxes from which they had emerged two weeks ago. In the background, the boy carolers were cheerfully singing "I Saw Three Ships Come Sailing In" as if it were still Christmas morning.

"Hello, love," said Graham, smiling. "Feeling better?"

Ellie said yes, but the truth was she was still riding a seesaw of relief and sadness. Too much had happened, both good and bad. She couldn't make sense of it yet, so she turned her attention to helping with the tree.

Mrs. Finch had been deputized to screen calls and visitors, but several people came by whom they were glad to see. The first was Seamus MacDonald, who arrived with a bouquet of red and black licorice sticks from the village shop. "There's not much to celebrate, but you did a great job, Guv," he said. "We tried to help, and we did."

"You did a great job too," she said, giving him a hug, which made him blush. Then he mumbled he'd better go, because his mother was completely gutted and didn't know he'd left the house. They were driving up to stay at his grandmother's for a while, even though the danger had passed.

Michael-John Parker turned up with a box of Belgian chocolates, saying he had heard the news on television and was glad to have helped, but even gladder to know that Ellie was all right.

"My New Year's resolution is to focus my talent for detection on finding valuable antiques," he told them.

"And I will limit mine to searching for lost sheep," volunteered Graham.

Isabelle looked curiously at Ellie to see what she would contribute, but all she said was, "I've never met a New Year's resolution that wasn't broken, so I'll just wait and see how you two get on."

Detective Inspector Derek Mullane arrived soon after, freshly showered and shaved, but he tucked into the shortbread that Mrs. Finch had just taken out of the oven as if he hadn't eaten for days. Which, perhaps, he hadn't.

"It's good to see you all getting back to normal," he said, nodding toward the nearly bare tree. Isabelle and Ellie had begun to unwind the strings of lights, releasing a shower of dry needles that filled the air with their fragrance for the last time. "I thought you'd want to know some of the details that we've learned since last night."

Of course they did, and they all sat down immediately, passed around cups of tea, and prepared to give him their full attention.

"First off, you were right, Mrs. Kent," Mullane said. "The baby you found in the manger is the daughter of Crispin Souter and Deborah Woodman. The hospital has agreed to keep her until her grandmother arrives from the States tomorrow to take custody of her.

"Secondly, that document you found does tie up the murder case. In addition to your fingerprints, we found clear prints from Deborah, her father, and Souter; and the bloodstain is a match for Bill Woodman.

"Our theory now is that Woodman arrived home from work on Christmas Eve and found his daughter had left the house while in the middle of making their tea. When she didn't return, he must have tried to figure out where she was, come across that marriage application, and gone to Souter's home in search of her. That led to a confrontation, in which Souter killed him and recovered the document. We're very lucky he didn't destroy it. A careless move on his part, but he must have been so accustomed to the privacy of his cottage that he forgot the risk it represented."

Graham sighed. "Very sad, but it all fits," he said.

"And that's really all you have to show how their lives intersected? A piece of paper with invisible fingerprints?" asked Ellie.

"So far," said Mullane. "Hopefully there will be more forensic evidence when we identify where Woodman was killed or find the murder weapon. We were looking in Stevens Wood where Deborah's body was left, but today we launched a new search of the grounds surrounding Souter's cottage.

"Not that there is any question about who killed them both. Souter must have used Deborah's car to dispose of the two bodies on Christmas Eve and later parked Woodman's car in Oxford in an attempt to implicate him in his daughter's murder and suggest that he had left the area."

"So was it Crispin who tried to see Rosie at the hospital?" asked Ellie.

"There don't seem to be any other candidates. Also a tall man, similarly dressed, appears on the CCTV footage in the Oxford Station car park at the time Woodman's car was left there."

"That sounds all wrapped up," said Isabelle, looking pleased.

"Needless to say, we're glad to have a conclusive result," said Mullane. "But it is my duty to re-emphasize that what you did, Mrs. Kent, was both illegal and extremely dangerous—not at all the kind of help the police want from the public. We would have found that document ourselves when we searched the cottage, as we were preparing to do."

Ellie was tired of being scolded, instead of thanked, so she couldn't resist saying, "Unless you were planning to get there before Crispin did, I doubt that. I'm sure he left your police station with only one thought in mind—to be certain that you would find no evidence of any of them, including Anthea, in that cottage."

Mullane cleared his throat, as if a piece of shortbread had caught on its way down. "Speaking of Anthea Davies, I tried to talk with her at her parents' home today, but they were very reluctant to let me in. They said that there would be no charges brought and no court case related to the kidnapping now that Souter was dead, and they would prefer that no one ever knew Anthea had been in that cottage."

"Wow," said Ellie. "Talk about denial. What did Anthea say?"

"Not much," said Mullane. "In front of her parents, she didn't want to talk about what happened and seemed most concerned about whether she could still register for the Hilary term at Oxford starting next week."

"I can understand that," said Graham. "They all desperately want to put this terrible time behind them."

"But it doesn't work like that!" said Ellie, thinking of her own experience.

"I agree," said Mullane, "but that is something they will have to find out for themselves. Anyway, when I was leaving, Anthea followed me out to the car and told me not to mind her parents. She wants to help, if there's anything she can do, and she was glad to know that the baby is all right."

"She didn't know?" asked Ellie, surprised.

"No, she didn't know anything, but she still feels somewhat responsible for what happened. Apparently Deborah came to the cottage when Anthea was there, and she immediately realized that the girl was pregnant. Afterward, she confronted Souter, and they had a huge row. She had taken up with him again because he persuaded her that he'd always loved her and had only broken off with her so she could focus on her studies. She suddenly saw their past relationship and everything about him in a new light; and he seemed to suddenly recognize the hopeless bind he'd put himself in. His reaction was not pretty."

"So instead of letting her go with this newfound knowledge, he locked in her his attic. Very symbolic," said Ellie.

"Yes. She knew from that moment there would be no happy ending."

"But she couldn't escape?" asked Isabelle, who had been following every word closely.

"No," said Mullane. "He was very careful about that. But he did bring her books. He told her to imagine she was on that radio program "Desert Island Discs" and gave her a copy of *The Complete Works of William Shakespeare*. She said it helped."

After Mullane had gone, Isabelle asked Ellie and Graham if Anthea was going to be all right. Ellie thought Graham would answer, but he turned to her instead with an equally expectant expression.

She looked at the open, honest faces of her husband and stepdaughter, and said: “It won’t be easy. She’ll never forget what happened. But she seems resilient, so, yes, I think she will be all right.”

By late afternoon, the Christmas tree was out by the garden shed, the decorations were back in the attic, and the sitting room had been restored to its everyday aspect. Mrs. Finch had left for the day, so when the doorbell rang again, Ellie went to answer it.

There on the front step stood Mr. and Mrs. Davies, with the girl who reminded Ellie so much of herself between them. Her dark wavy hair framed a pretty face that was too thin and pale, but her dark eyes shone with a spirit that was clearly unbroken. Her mother couldn’t even look away long enough to say hello, and her father kept one arm heavily around her shoulders, as if he hoped to restrain her from ever leaving his side again.

“This is our Anthea,” he said to Ellie. “We’ve come to thank you for giving her back to us.”

Epilogue

Rosie's christening was held at the end of January on a sunny day with a gentle breeze that Ellie was sure hinted of the spring to come. She had decorated the font at St. Michael's with posies of snowdrops and decided to shed her tweeds and wear a wool knit dress that was not at all warm enough. Thankfully, Graham had turned on the heat in the church early in the day.

Daphne Woodman, now Morrissey, and her American husband George had proved to be a very pleasant, easy-going couple in their 40s, who had quickly fallen in love with their new granddaughter. Before they took her to America, they wanted Rosie to be christened in the church where her mother had left her for safekeeping, and they asked Ellie to be her godmother.

"We would like her to have a happy link to this place," Daphne told Ellie, "and when she is older, perhaps you and Graham can help us decide what she needs to know about her English family."

For the christening, the baby wore a white silk and lace christening dress and was well wrapped in a white wool blanket. Ellie held her proudly, amazed at how much she had already grown in little more than a month. She looked beautiful and healthy and was universally admired by the people who gathered at the church, which included all of the hospital staff who had taken care of her.

Ellie had suggested that, as Deborah's good friend, Sarah Henning should be Rosie's co-godmother, while

Mr. Morrissey stood up as godfather. Graham performed the sacrament, and they all took their vows with great seriousness, so the abandoned baby, once wishfully wrapped with rosemary, was well fortified for the future through this new ritual.

Afterward they drank a toast at The Vicarage, and Ellie presented her "little you" with a gold chain on which hung a golden sprig of rosemary. "For remembrance," she said, as she put it around her neck and gave her a final kiss.

The End

Acknowledgements

Many thanks to Jim Mullins for our life and adventures in England and elsewhere around the world, as well as our decades-long discussion of mysteries, old and new, real and imagined.

This book also owes much to my well-loved and inspiring mentors who introduced me to the English folk traditions celebrating the Winter Solstice: John Langstaff (1920–2005) and Lisby Mayer (1947–2005). To echo Susan Cooper's poem, "The Shortest Day," through all the frosty ages, I will hear them reveling.

Every writer has people who believe in them and their books when they can't. For me, these invaluable friends are Kathryn Chetkovich, Martha Conway, Michelle Dionetti, Marianne Faithfull, Marion Gibbons, Victoria Schultz, and Marty Wingate. Special thanks also go to my editorial advisors: Ann Mansbridge, Rev. Carol Sanford, Seamus O'Connor, and Janet Basu. Any errors are my own.

I am also very grateful to the readers who loved *Under an English Heaven* and who kept asking me "Where's the next book?" and to Patricia Rockwell of Cozy Cat Press for her ongoing support of the Ellie Kent mysteries.

Sources

The title of this book comes from the English carol "What Child Is this?" It is traditionally sung to the 17th century tune, "Greensleeves."

Other quotations and references come from the following:

A Christmas Mumming: The Play of Saint [Prince] George in *Medieval and Tudor Drama.* New York: Bantam Books, 1963.

William Shakespeare. *Hamlet: Prince of Denmark,* Act III, Scene 1; Act IV, Scene 5; and Act V, Scene 2
William Shakespeare, "Sonnet 116"

The Gospel According to St. Luke 1:46–55 and 2:11 KJV

Christmas carols: "In the Bleak Mid-Winter," text by Christina Rossetti, 1872; "Break Forth, O Beauteous Heavenly Light," text by Johann Rist, 1641; "O Little Town of Bethlehem," text by Phillips Brooks, 1867; and "Lo, How a Rose E'er Blooming," Anonymous German, 17th century.

ABOUT THE AUTHOR

Alice K. Boatwright is the author of the Ellie Kent mysteries, which debuted with *Under an English Heaven* and continue with the sequel, *What Child Is This? Under an English Heaven* was awarded the 2016 Mystery and Mayhem Grand Prize for Best Mystery from the Chanticleer International Book Awards. Boatwright is also the author of *Collateral Damage*, an award-winning collection of novellas about the long-term impact of the Vietnam War. She lived in Oxfordshire and Paris for 10 years before returning to the U.S., where she now lives in the Pacific Northwest.

For the latest news about the Ellie Kent mysteries, visit http://alicekboatwright.com and sign up for a newsletter at http://eepurl.com/cER4Cj

Photo: Maria Aragon

Made in the USA
Middletown, DE
24 July 2021